Frederick Pollock

The Etchingham letters

Frederick Pollock

The Etchingham letters

ISBN/EAN: 9783337108984

Printed in Europe, USA, Canada, Australia, Japan

Cover: Foto ©Andreas Hilbeck / pixelio.de

More available books at **www.hansebooks.com**

THE
ETCHINGHAM LETTERS

BY

ELLA FULLER MAITLAND

Author of "Pages from the Day-book of Bethia Hardacre," etc.

AND

SIR FREDERICK POLLOCK, BART.

London
MACMILLAN AND CO., LIMITED

No. 377. 1899

CHIEF PERSONS OF THE LETTERS.

SIR RICHARD ETCHINGHAM, lately retired from Indian service (political department), widower.

HARRY ETCHINGHAM, Major R.A.; CHARLES ETCHINGHAM, of the Equity Bar, Sir Richard's brothers.

JAMES ETCHINGHAM, assistant tutor of Silvertoe College, Oxbridge, Sir Richard's cousin.

The REV. EDWARD FOLLETT, Vicar of Much Buckland.

The REV. SEPTIMUS WEEKES, his curate.

STEPHEN LEAGRAVE, of the Education Office.

WILLIAM SHIPLEY, of the Record Office.

ELIZABETH, Sir Richard's sister.

MARGARET, Sir Richard's daughter.

LAURA, LADY ETCHINGHAM, second wife and now widow of the late Sir Nicholas Etchingham.

MRS. VIVIAN, mother-in-law of Charles Etchingham.

MINNIE, wife of Charles Etchingham.

MRS. FOLLETT, wife of the Rev. Edward Follett.

CYNTHIA LEAGRAVE, sister to Stephen.

ALICE, wife of Col. Newton, sister to Shipley.

THE
ETCHINGHAM LETTERS.

—•◦•—

I.

*From Miss Elizabeth Etchingham, 83 Hans Place,
London, S.W., to Sir Richard Etchingham,
Bart., Tolcarne, Much Buckland, Wessex.*

MOST EXCELLENT RICHARD,

As much of your sister's mind as remains when painters, carpenters, bellhangers, electric-lighters, sanitary engineers, chimneysweeps, and "men about the kitchen range" have done their worst and their work—or rather done their worst and left their work undone—now proposes to address you.

Harry very kindly met his stepmother, his sister, and a pyramid of luggage, which included a bicycle and a bath-chair, at Paddington. (Cynthia only joined us yesterday, after three days spent at Oxbridge with the Gainsworthys.) Trelawney, Tracy, and the bullfinches were more *en évidence* than conventionality permits certainly, and perhaps

I   B

the sight upon a platform of a flustered cat and dog and a cage of fluttering singing-birds proved too much for my brother—greatly as he appreciates the creatures in private—for he vanished from among us as instantaneously as if he were a conjuring trick, and, though I heard his foot upon the still uncarpeted stair at midnight, we saw him no more till the next morning. ("I *was* surprised, M'm, and so was Grace and Mrs. Baker, that Trelawney did not catch the Major's eye at the station ; set off so, as he was too, by his blue riband, and the cat looking for notice," was Blake's comment on the platform episode—the espisode not of defective vision, but of cutting dead.)

Please, Richard, learn one lesson that no man ever learnt yet—learn that a woman does not of necessity enjoy all that she endures with patience, nor welcome every ill she tolerates. The hammering and the hugger-mugger, the upset and upsidedown condition of everything that I have striven to suffer, if not gladly, heroically, Harry evidently believes to be welcome as the flowers of May to his sister. " Elizabeth likes a disturbance—all women do," he says with a touch of irritation, as he seeks, poor dear, among the chaos for his hat (upon which the furniture-removing people yesterday had thoughtfully placed the refrigerator). But was not this conclusion of Harry's a tribute to his sister's powers of self-control ?

I hope our joint *ménage* may prosper.

Between you and me and the doorpost, I think we were mistaken as to the fragmentary condition of Harry's heart. He looks extremely well, and this Intelligence Department appointment is just what he likes. I am thankful that Ada Llanelly did not marry him. She is such a worldly little thing, and he is so perfectly simple-minded, really, that the marriage must have come to grief. Between the worldly and the unworldly there is a greater gulf fixed than even love and affection can cross.

By the way, if you are writing to Charles, do give him a hint of the desirability of sending Minnie to see us speedily. I do not wish to worry Minnie ; she and I have never particularly cottoned ; but, as you have good reason to know, our step-mother holds to her lbs. of domestic and social flesh, and she begins to be a little prickly on the subject of the delayed visit. She has shown herself on the defensive indeed ever since Minnie indirectly refused to provide her relations-in-law with " orders to view " unfurnished houses in the Lower Berkeley Street region, and despatched sheaf after sheaf from Sloane Street and Cadogan Place agents. (There Minnie was right. The Park is an excellent buffer between kinsfolk, and we are best where we are.) But, alas, for all of us, if we begin our London existence with a clearly defined " unpleasantness ; " and Charles having in the past always rather failed—failed even more than the rest of us—to give satisfaction, much do I fear that the appre-hended " unpleasantness " will soon be an accepted fact. Our stepmother is making ready to feel slighted, and has already taken the huffed tone. (Are we armoured with pride or humility, you and I, to whom it never occurs that any one should wish to slight us ?) What with his work and with this notion of getting into Parliament (Minnie, I gather, is very keen for the carrying into effect of the Parliament scheme), Charles, likely enough, is too busy to come himself immediately, but he would do well to send his wife. " Charles owes it to the memory of his father to call at once, whatever may be his engagements ; and the walk across the Park from Lower Berkeley Street to Hans Place is nothing for an active man in the prime of life," is what I hear, my good Richard, very, very often ; and, as you may remember, Laura's appetite for a grievance has always grown with the talking.

Do you know, I feel sure that your sister is on the high-road to becoming a shocking gossip—a *mauvaise langue* of the worst description. I find that there are predicaments in which the good-natured thing is to be ill-natured, the charitable thing to be malicious.

You see, our poor stepmother is held in such durance vile by rheumatism as to be at present unable to drive or walk, and she therefore requires a good deal of within-doors amusement. And, though this evident law of nature is sometimes forgotten,. people can only be amused by what amuses them. "Who did you see?" and "What did they say?" is asked of me after every outing. When I have seen next to nobody, and next to nobody has said next to nothing, rather than disappoint her news-hunger I am almost induced to draw upon my imagination, or to take away one woman's character for the sake of diverting another.

Now that I come to think of it, sharp-tongued, fault-seeing women are, surely, oftener than not the stay and support of invalid mothers or stepmothers. Poor wretches, I have no doubt their power of apparently malevolent criticism or ruthless backbiting is the outcome of good hearts and filial piety. Invalids, for their health's good, must be entertained and diverted, and old ladies are not to be interested by political crises. I doubt if the being in attendance upon an old man would foster evil-speaking, lying, and slandering. The old man probably would prefer the dullest newspaper leader or most unfathomable stock-market quotations to the turning inside out for his benefit of his neighbours' characters and conditions.

I am impatient for news of Tolcarne, and I must be told quickly what you think of everybody, and how things generally prosper. Is Margaret ordering the house as wisely as if the child were her own grandmother? and is she mothering the garden? The almonds and the mezereon must be now ablow, and soon there should be white violets everywhere. You will, I fancy, come to like the Vicar and Mrs. Follett, and you will, I know, terrify poor Mr. Weekes, the very meekest of meek curates. Let me hear, too, if the dear old dogs, "Tray, Blanch, and Sweetheart," are taking kindly to the change of masters. I hope so. Mr. Weekes said to me once, in his painful conversation-manufactory efforts, "I like your dogs, Miss Etchingham; they don't bite curates." Our Tracy walks abroad in Cynthia's company—Tracy wearing a coat cut with a *Medici* collar.

(Tell Margaret that Blake, when reproached for the inordinate length of time spent in the running up of a coat for his spaniel dogship, brought forward the plea, " I'm making Tracy's coat, Miss Cynthia, with a *Medici* collar.")

Poor Tracy, he looks pathetically bewildered by the uproar of the traffic and the perplexing avenues of bricks and mortar. Cynthia must write and ask Mr. Follett whether spaniel history is repeating itself, and if Herrick brought his " Spaniell Tracie " to his " beloved Westminster " from " dull Devonshire." If so, the poet's Tracy had little to trace, poor fellow, but his master; though London precincts were not as birdless then as now. As to Margaret's friend, Trelawney, we are congratulating ourselves that his cedar-wood-hued fur is a " good wearing " colour, and comes through a fog less discreditably than could the white coats of his still-in-the-country Persian relatives. Looking just now at his green eyes that shine like emeralds, it occurred to me that, besides flame, there is yet another thing—eyes—that London smoke cannot tarnish.

Later.—My letter-writing this afternoon was interrupted by the welcome arrival of Charles and Minnie. Minnie was pleasanter perhaps before she wrote her novel. (You really must read "Only a Woman's Heart"—or, at least, try to read it. It is "expected of you," to quote an habitual phrase of our stepmother's.) Minnie is thoroughly literary now, and is surrounding herself with the ragtag and bobtail of poets and story-tellers. I had no opportunity of *tête-à-tête* speech with Charles. Various people appeared, and had to be dealt with : Sir Augustus Pampesford, among others, very solemn on the wrongs of "our honourable order," and confiding his woes to Admiral Tidenham, who, notwithstanding his ear-trumpet, believed himself called upon to sympathize with the plague of barrel-organs, not the provocation of baronets. Then old Mrs. Carstairs came and discoursed upon the iniquities of the young girl of the present day, quoting as text to her sermon one of Mrs. Baxter's daughters, who always dines in her own room because her parents bore her, and Lady Clementine Mure's child, who insists that her mother should winter at Pau, so that she herself may follow her studio avocations without the hindrance of Lady Clementine's requirements. Stephen Leagrave, too, walked in. He and Minnie seem to fuse as they never did before she wrote her novel, and they have much to say to each other of authors of whom I, in my ignorance, have never heard. Stephen's work at the Education Office does not wear him to a thread-paper seemingly, and he has taken, in a moderate degree, to journalism. Cynthia's pleasure in her brother's company is pleasant to witness; and he is proud, as he should be, of his sister. She really is a very pretty creature. She is also a singularly relationless creature, lacking as she does—with the exception of our stepmother—all female kith and kin. I do hope she will be happy with us until Colonel Leagrave comes home and takes possession of his very attractive property: unless, which does not seem unlikely, some one else has succeeded in doing so meanwhile.

The door closed upon Charles and Minnie, Harry, who had maintained an ominous silence during Charles's visit, and during Charles's references to a possible Parliamentary career, kicked, to Trelawney's intense disgust, the fireguard on to the hearthrug, and in quite ferocious tones begged me to inform him how a man with any pretension to the character of a rational being *could* be a Gladstonian, a Home-Ruler, and out-and-out Radical. "Charles I *believe* to be an honest man. I wish to *believe* Charles to be an honest man. But just tell me—how can an honest man go in for plunder, for downright swindling, for betraying his country, for pandering to the worst instincts of the dregs of humanity? How do you reconcile the two, Elizabeth? *Are* they reconcilable? I hold the Radicals responsible for everything that has gone wrong during the last——" (I forget Harry's figures). I tried to disown responsibility for opinions that I do not share; but Harry's wrath was really kindled, and he continued to heckle me till the dressing-bell rang my release.

Why are the electric-light folk, of all workmen, the most troublesome and dilatory? Is it because with electric-lighters evolution has not yet had time to play its part, and so not only the fittest electric-lighters survive?

Yours ever and alway,
ELIZABETH.

P.S.—Write soon and tell me of things interesting, and of a book or two beyond my comprehension—to read what I don't understand makes me feel on the high-road to scholarship. A correspondence with you was always a solace in your Indian days; and now, as then, your learning and wisdom are sufficient for the two of us, and I need not strain myself by pretending to either.

At present (11 p.m., Saturday night) I am not wholly reconciled to London, though, all things considered (how much lack of consideration this convenient phrase can cover), I think the coming here was the best move possible. It was a choice of evils—as everything in life is—I, to-night, am inclined to think, tired to the quick as I am by my efforts to cope with this "settling-in" process. But, take notice, when I am old—really quite old (Cynthia considers I have passed the allotted span of life already, and sees little to choose between my years and those of Methuselah)—I shall drag myself back to Tolcarne, to "the dull confines of the drooping west." Old age does not strike me as pretty in cities. You must lend me a hovel somewhere, and I will be no trouble, nor expect any vegetables. Remember, remember the vegetable grievance, and, please, let old Enticknap, for peace's preservation, despatch a hamper sometimes, if only filled with his beloved cabbages. I will keep bees, and sow annuals— the annuals that used to grow in "the children's garden" when we were children. And I will sit and sun myself on a seat, wind-sheltered, and cut in a wall betrained with apricots.

It will be very comfortable.

Good night, good brother.

P.P.S.—Do not forget the vegetables. Do not forget "Only a Woman's Heart."

II.

*From Sir Richard Etchingham to Miss Elizabeth
Etchingham.*

My dear Elizabeth,

I congratulate you on having effected
the concentration of your miscellaneous forces in
town without having any casualty to report.   As
to good order, perhaps I had better say nothing.
Your description of the scene on the platform is
rather like the too famous retreat of Colonel
Monson : *Ghore par haudah, háthi par zín*—in
English, adapted to the circumstances, " Dogs in
cages, and dicky-birds in muzzles."   However,
there you are, and still the best of correspondents,
though I no longer have to rely on you for home
news.   We used to dream of being together when
India had no more use for me ; instead of which
we find ourselves comparing notes on settling
down in different places.

It is good to be here in English country, among
bright English faces, hearing the rich Western talk.
And yet there is a kind of Asiatic home-sickness
with it.   One does miss the cheerful brown babies
(clear, lustrous bronze, not the muddy tint that
comes of mixing negro and white), and the cop-
persmith with prehensile toes who sits hammering in his open shop-front, while a small boy next
door is making his first copy of bold square

Nagari letters in an equally open manner, and quite unmoved by the noise. And I am sorry to think that I may not expect to see my old friend Ram Singh again. I have told you of him—a poor gentleman with nothing in the world but his bit of land and his grandfather's tulwar, which he carries tucked under his arm, according to the privilege of Native States. And he will look any one, from the Viceroy downwards, straight in the eyes, and talk to him with the most perfect manners, knowing what he owes to himself as a Rajput of ancient family, and assuming that the Englishman knows it—as, if he is worth his salt, he does. Walter Scott would have understood Ram Singh down to the ground. (I hope to live to see the public understand ; that is the only final security against the formulizing creatures of pens and ink who infest all governments, even the most God-granted.) There must have been such people in the Highlands, almost within living memory.

I have broken off for a hunt in my battered copy of Colonel Tod's "Rajasthan," one of the most fascinating and worst arranged books in the world. At length I find the story of the young Rajput sepoy, who, being alone in charge of an elephant, was set upon by about fifty robbers, fired on them, and was cut down and left desperately wounded. Having been brought into camp, "he was firm, collected, and even cheerful ; and, to a kind reproach for his rashness, he said, ' What would you have said, Captain Sahib, had I surrendered the Company's musket without fighting?'" All this packed away in a casual footnote. *Compani ká bandúq* is dead and buried, and John Company too; but the Rajput breed is there still, and, moreover, can shoot straight as well as fight, now that there is something better than the musket of our ancestors to shoot with.

But this is Tolcarne, and I am no longer a Political, but a squire, or squireling, of Wessex; and you ask me for the news.

Vegetables you shall have as soon as it pleases the elements and Enticknap. Talk not to me of terrifying curates, but teach me how I may be delivered from grovelling before Enticknap. A certain dignity is "expected of me" by the traditions of the service; but what is a poor man to do who knows nothing of English gardening? I have corresponded with official superiors, interviewed holy men of several religions, clean and dirty, clothed and unclothed, in their right minds and otherwise, and all unshakeable in argument (Harry knows the other end of one of those stories. I mentioned, by the way, to the Mullah at parting, as a piece of family news, the impending arrival of Harry's battery in camp, and we heard no more of the tribal saint growing half a cubit a week in his grave); and I have wholly failed to make any impression on a globe-trotting anti-opiumist; but your gardener is the only true infallible. Enticknap says the almonds are blighted like. Do I know what he means? No. Why don't I ask him? What? Would you have me tamper with the foundations of belief? Perhaps you may know, though. Enticknap admits no difference of opinion in matters of gardening, but I believe him to admit that you are capable of understanding his reasons. Anyhow, there is no almond blossom yet.

As to our people—animals first, of course. Merlin the ancient, who was young and frisky when I last went out, is confirmed in his opinion that I am really the same person. Songstress, apparently so called from being of a rather silent habit, and of even more melancholy looks than a basset-hound has any right to be, has taken a sort of quiet fancy to Margaret. Curates' legs do not interest them, naturally. Why should they? Bishops' legs, now—nice tight gaiters all over, buttons to take hold of—are quite different. Dear old Bishop Abraham was irresistible to the college beagles at Eton. It was against etiquette for him to notice their existence—and he didn't. Mr. Weekes must either be nervous about dogs, or generally anxious about his own person, or—as indeed you most plausibly conjecture—at a pass for something to say. He is but a *kutcha* sort of young padre, or it might be juster perhaps to say, in literal English, half-baked, for he may make a man yet. Just now he is distracted between shyness and zeal to improve in cycling (it will be so useful to him for visiting his flock in a scattered parish). Margaret is the only person here, for the moment, who knows much about it, and she conducts us on easy rides fit for beginners. She says she won't answer for the consequences if either of us is turned loose on these roads before she certifies us quite safe. If I am a good old man, she holds out hopes that in a few weeks more I may ride all the way down the hill to Little Buckland. You know the curve and the steepness thereof—no, you don't; looking down a hill from a bicycle is quite unlike looking down it in any other position. At present, that caution-board is more formidable to me than any Ghazi's green turban to any soldier. Our cousin Jem of Silvertoe is said to be a mighty man of wheels; I am writing to him for some general advice, as Mr. Weekes, having an inordinate respect for every kind of authority, and having heard of Jem in that capacity from some Oxbridge friend, would not rest till I did. That youth would rather be stuck on the devil's pitchfork — being the real proper devil — than wafted to heaven on the wings of an unlicensed seraph. However, Jem ceases from his lectures in a week or two now, so there is no harm in asking him. Weekes is, so far, less able on his machine than I am; but he has got up the slang elaborately, and indited a list of questions for Jem which I don't more than half understand. . . . Margaret sends me packing to dress for dinner. What a treasure is a methodical daughter! . . . I came home to enjoy a spell of being governed.

Monday night.—Also not to have a mail-day to think of. This Aryan brother is going to say *abby-nay* when he likes, now he is mustered out. Yes, we like the Folletts already. The little old gentleman is quiet, seems dry at first; I thought we should never get much forwarder. But never make formulas about people till you know them (did not you teach me that principle?), and best not then. Towards the end of his return visit, Margaret mentioned that the eminent restoring architect, Mr. Newpoyntz, had been seen at the station. "Not to do anything to the church, Mr. Vicar?" says I. "Saving my cloth," says he, "I would sooner curse him with the curse of Ernulphus than have him touch a stone of it." "Is it so?" cried I, and took down the little "Tristram Shandy" that used to go my rides with me in one pocket, to balance the Penal Code in the other. "Indeed, Sir Richard," said he, just a little taken aback, with the book in his hand, and a queer little pucker about his lips, "by the virtue of this book, I am bold to profess myself a humble admirer of the late Mr. Sterne—as a man of letters." So thereupon we are friends: not yet so far as the friend-of-your-friends-and-enemy-of-your-enemies footing. We shall see. Nobody can tell me to what school of theology Mr. Follett belongs, and that I like well, too.

For one fruit of our acquaintance, the Vicar is to show me in Selden's " Titles of Honour," when I am next at the parsonage, some profitable matter for Sir Augustus and the Honourable Order.

I note your family news,. and perceive that my training in the political department is not to lie rusty. Meanwhile, I guess many things will answer themselves. There is surely something I forgot—yes, we call the new cart-horse " Job," because there is nobody else he looks like. From your loving brother, these—nay, we have royal names, and it pleases me to sign as a sovereign.

Sur ce, Madame et sœur, que Dieu vous ayt dans sa tressainte garde.

RICHARD ETCHINGHAM.

P.S.—I have read " Only a Woman's Heart." You can tell Minnie I think it excellent. What I mean is the title. Not that I believe it was her own invention.

III.

*From Miss Elizabeth Etchingham, 83 Hans Place,
to Sir Richard Etchingham, Tolcarne.*

DEAR, oh dear, oh dear—the vegetables have never come. Elements and Enticknap permitting or not permitting, send, best of brothers, a mildewed beetroot or frost-bitten cabbage at once. Remember that our immortal feelings, not our mortal appetites, are at stake, and in such a case a very turnip's top may prove ambrosia.

"Lady Clementine Mure never buys a cabbage." The cabbage-tide flows in fast from Mure Hall. "Mrs. Carstairs never——" As you love me, Richard, send a leaf or root.

I was very glad to have your letter. To see your handwriting on any but the transparent envelope, stamped with the far-away-looking, light-green stamp, gives me a shock of pleasure, and somehow I am not wholly sorry that you in Wessex do in a manner regret the Land of Regrets. The Land of Regrets does not get its share of sentiment. Our countrymen and country-women pass years and years of life there, and—unless there is a child's grave to leave for ever also—they can say an eternal farewell to India with not the slightest pulling-up of themselves by the roots.

Yes, I seem to know your friend Ram Singh, his nice honour, his gentle manners, and high courage, and I wonder if he is the Rajput Colonel Newcome—Colonel Newcome with a prouder ancestry behind him.

I wish you would make a book of Indian heroes for the children's reading by-and-by. (It goes without saying nowadays that by "the children" we mean Charles's and Minnie's boys.) These recent Frontier campaigns have brought forth deeds of heroism sufficient for the filling of many chapters. I wish you would tell, with other stories of valour, of the Sikhs who last June, by that garden wall in the Tochi Valley, lost their lives to cover the retreat of their wounded comrades. I wish you would put into print the names of Subadars Sundar Singh, 1st Bengal Infantry, of Narain Singh and Sundar Singh, 1st Sikhs, who, seeing all the British officers wounded, got together a party of their men, making a most determined stand, and covering the withdrawal whilst themselves under heavy fire. The wording of the despatch concerning that Tochi Valley garden-wall site, which I read first in the copy of *The Madras Weekly Mail* sent by Colonel Leagrave to Cynthia, stuck in my memory like a burr. "The conduct of Subadar Sundar Singh, 1st Punjab Infantry, at the place where he died was most heroic. At this place many other men also behaved with great heroism. All those who fell there gave their lives to cover the withdrawal of their comrades."

You will like the boys. Your namesake is an attractive creature, and little Harry a Puck-like spirit. Their Uncle Harry, who from the first found great favour in their sight, proved in levee harness a ravishingly splendid spectacle. "I speak gwuff and wear a sward like Uncle Hawey," Harry now declares; and since the levee day he and his brother try with more assiduity than success "to speak gwuff."

I don't know if "everything is spoilt by use," but the faculty of seeing likes and unlikes seems to be, and seems to fade with childhood. "Are they the petals of my feet?" Dicky asked, looking at his pink toes after his first botany lesson. (The transcribing of babies' babble no longer needs an apology, since wise men and learned have turned their scientific attention that way.)

The children will prove, I hope, a source of interest to our stepmother; but as character fixes the point of view of every situation, woe be it to each one implicated should the perambulators stand oftener at the maternal grandmother's door than at the door of the step-paternal ancestress. And please bear in mind, lest the gravity of the situation escape you, that the dwelling of Mrs. Vivian, measured by a blue silk inch-measure on the map of London, is, if anything, further removed from

Lower Berkeley Street than is that of Laura, Lady Etchingham ; so the doctrine of propinquity cannot excuse the too frequent progress thitherwards of the nursery people.

I thought that you and Mr. Follett would discover each other. The neighbours generally— not the cottage folk ; they swear by " Parson Follett "—are inclined to look askance upon him, and to call his orthodoxy in question. Every one in the country does not go with you in preferring charity to the Creeds.

Tell me if the " Titles of Honour " supplies intelligence meet for Sir Augustus, who, for some reason best known to himself, has developed a tendency to visit us incessantly. He seems keen, also, that we should go to have tea at the Heralds' Office with some one known to him. (What a pity it is that he is not a pursuivant himself. He would idolize his tabard.) If, as I expect, Mr. Follett unlocks for your benefit both his heart and his book-cases, Tolcarne will blossom out in books like the rose. I hold in affectionate remembrance the shelf of old folio editions of the English classics. It was from that shelf, one afternoon in spring, when the birds sang and the sunlight came slanting through the network of mulberry branches, that Mr. Follett took and laid upon the study table the great brown volume in which I first made the acquaintance of " The Faerie Queene." The rightful adjuncts to "The Faerie Queene" still seem to me to be the song of a thrush, gold sunlight slanting through the branches of the old mulberry tree that adorns the parsonage lawn, and the scent of Mrs. Follett's pale-blue hyacinths.

I was called yesterday from my writing to the drawing-room, there to find Mrs. Vivian—between whom and Laura, by the way, there is no love lost. Mrs. Vivian shocks Laura; Laura bores Mrs. Vivian. Is it better to be bored or shocked? "To be bored," would say the holy; "To be shocked," would think the profane. (There is one thing about it: no one likes to be bored, and many like to be shocked.) However, I trust that on this occasion neither Laura nor Mrs. Vivian was, thanks to the other, *in extremis*, for fate, in the person of Harry and Sir Augustus, provided Mrs. Vivian with her panacea for all ills—an audience, and dowered Laura with a dock to her nettles in the guise of a sympathizer—old Mrs. Carstairs.

Mr. Vivian's taciturnity was the subject of Mrs. Vivian's flow of words. (She looks as pretty as ever, and grows younger with the years; she is ten years younger than her daughters already.) "My husband," she said, "never speaks, unless it is to ask if any one has seen his umbrella, or knows where 'Bradshaw' is. When I tell him he really *must* talk, he says he can't—he has nothing to say. I dare say he hasn't. Still, it

would be a relief if he would even groan, or
strike the hours, like the clock." A solemn "Very
true", here, from Sir Augustus, who is too self-
occupied to catch the gist of words that have
no bearing upon one of his own hobbies, and
a significant cough from Mrs. Carstairs, whose
collection of present-day criminals now includes
Mrs. Vivian.

By Laura, of course, these utterances were taken
seriously, and, fortified by Mrs. Carstairs' sympathy,
she was prepared, had a pause in Mrs. Vivian's
oration allowed of more than an ejaculatory reply,
to argue that "a groan from the lips of a dumb
animal, even, must be excessively painful to right-
minded hearers. How much more so from the lips
of a human creature whom we love and honour."
Mrs. Vivian, speaking in the direction of Harry
and Sir Augustus, went on to say that she did
not know how it might be with *right-minded*
people, she seldom came across them, but she
would often be glad to hear her husband groan,
just to prove that she was not sitting alone with
the tables and chairs.

At this point we were invaded by Mr. Biggleswade (once Jem's Oxbridge acquaintance, now
the Vivian's Dampshire vicar). Having pretty
well ignored our stepmother, whose politeness to
clergymen of every persuasion is unfailing, he
produced from his pocket a very slim volume, and
presented it to Cynthia—"As I promised."

" Are those your pagan love-poems, or the verses in which you generously patronize Christianity, Mr. Biggleswade ? " inquired Mrs. Vivian. " It is so kind of Mr. Biggleswade to believe— most thoughtful and considerate, is it not ?" Thereupon Harry's "gwuff" laugh was heard, and a repetition of Sir Augustus's impressive "Very true." Mr. Biggleswade, however, lost none of his jaunty airiness of demeanour. He fixed his Oxbridge smile for a moment upon Mrs. Vivian, and admitted, as he seated himself upon the sofa by Cynthia's side, that he "did not pretend to be one of the old school of clerics." What, he then went on to say to Cynthia, "not knowing, can't say," to quote old nurse ; but evident was it that his discourse embarrassed the child. As the colour which had flickered in her cheek since Mrs. Vivian announced, in quite audible tones, " Miss Leagrave is just like a Romney," heightened, Mr. Biggleswade's bantering laugh grew more frequent. Will Harry go to the rescue, I wondered, or shall I ? But as I wondered, lo and behold, suddenly the Oxbridge smile petrified, Mr. Biggleswade's cheek blanched, and terror wrote itself in his eyes. Had influenza marked him for its own ? Had he just developed a conscience, or a heart disease ? No. Dropping my gaze from his face to his feet, there saw I our Trelawney suspiciously snuffing the Biggleswade boots ; and having sniffed and not approved what did our Trelawney but proceed to sharpen his claws upon the leg of Mr. Biggleswade's chair, as if preparing weapons of attack. Poor pseudo-pagan love-poet. Poor patron of Christianity. Poor disconcerter of shy Cynthias. With an incoherent reference to train-catching, the Thing was gone.

"Does your cat like cream, Elizabeth?" then asked honest Harry. To murmur "Not enough to go round" was to waste breath. Out ran the contents of the cream-jug into the saucer of Harry's teacup, down to the very last drop. Lowlily bent Harry, and with a very fair imitation of the air of self-conscious condescension with which Mr. Biggleswade serves the Church, did Trelawney deign to lap the cream held conveniently by a major in Her Majesty's army to the level of his Persian lips. There, now you know all about it.

As to that bicycling business, well can I picture your wicked child entertaining herself with Mr. Weekes's timidities ; but should Jem unbend in his reply to the cycling questions, the poor "half-baked" man will, I trust, be supplied with an expurgated edition of Jem's wit.

And now, Richard, put kind inquiry concerning his rheumatism to Enticknap, pat the ancient Merlin and the mute Songstress for me, and beg Margaret, as cats do not always care for caresses to make Luna's pat from me a—pat of butter.

Yours to command,
ELIZABETH.

P.S.—Here, as a postscript, is a pretty old sad song for you :—

> " Qu'il pleue, qu'il vente, qu'il neige
>   Orage ou autre temps,
>   On voit toujour sans cesse
>   Le laboureur aux champs.
>
> " Le pauvre laboureur
>   N'ayant que deux enfants
>   Les a mis à la charrue
>   A l'âge de dix ans."

<h2 align="center">IV.</h2>

From Sir Richard Etchingham to Miss Elizabeth Etchingham.

MY DEAR ELIZABETH,

How like you this return of winter out of season? There is no talk now of almond blossom or any other; lucky is the plant that has not been over-hasty. Luckily for Enticknap's temper, too, he is not idle, for there is a good day or two's work in clearing the snow off every piece of exposed roof. The drift is two feet deep in the Little Buckland lane, moulded by the wind in places into crests running almost to a knife-edge.

For my part, I am glad to be away from town, as I prefer clean snow to dirty mud ; and that you are swimming in mud I make no doubt. And so yesterday being, as Pepys would say, a very foul, snowing, windy day, I trudged across to the Vicarage, and had a good time with Parson Follett among his books. I have fancied now and again that I was really meant for a book-worm. On the other hand, the professional scholars I know have mostly given me to understand that they envy those to whom scholarship is a recreation; and I suspect that a man who gives himself to books before he has seen anything of the world is but penny-wise in his own craft, for it may be doubted if he will ever more than half understand his books. The Vicar, at any rate, thinks that pure ignorance of men and affairs is answerable for many astonishing conjectures and futile controversies of learned persons.

We had out Selden's " Titles of Honor "—not Honour with a *u*, so much for the new-fangledness of " American spelling "—which seems to be an inexhaustible mine of elaborate frivolities. He sets forth the authentic documents about the origin of Baronets at large, and nothing can be less romantic. We date from 1611. King James I. founded us in the most undisguised manner to raise money for the settlement of Ulster. It must be allowed that he did, or endeavoured to do, the business in a decent fashion, not by way

of selling the dignity to the highest bidders. The
transaction was for a fixed price, with ready
money for part, and good references for the rest.
There were Commissioners "for treating with
such as desired to be created upon the terms in
the preamble of the Patent," and they were
instructed to inform applicants "that those who
desire to be admitted into the dignity of Baronets
must maintain the number of thirty foot-Souldiers
in Ireland for three years, after the rate of eight
pence sterling Money of England by the day;
And the wages of one whole year to be paid into
Our Receipt, upon passing of the Patent." Mr.
Follett bade me observe the Scottish prudence
of the king as to the sterling money of England;
Irish money was worth much less (like Scotch,
with which—or the lack of it—he was of course
well acquainted). The applicants had to show
both a personal and a property qualification
besides their money: the Commissioners are to
"proceed with none, except it shall appear unto
you upon good proof, that they are men of quality,
state of living, and good reputation worthy of
the same; and that they are at the least descended
of a Grandfather by the Fathers side that bare
Armes, And have also of certain yearly revenue
in Lands of inheritance in possession, One
Thousand pounds *per Annum de claro*," or an
equivalent. Knights were not necessarily to be
preferred to esquires, knighthood being "such a

mark as is but temporary." There was sense in this, too, said Mr. Follett, as in James I.'s time several of the best and most ancient families in England had never been anything but esquires from father to son, as indeed some of them are to this day. Mr. Follett himself has stayed with a western squire who still punctually receives a rent of a pound of black pepper reserved by a deed of the thirteenth century, and he has seen a writ of William Rufus in the Record Office containing the identical Christian names and surnames still used by the same family at the same place. The secret of these fortunate stocks must have consisted in being just big enough people to hold their own, and not so great as to be tempted into high treasons and other dangerous adventures. I don't think James I. caught many of them to be made baronets. I am glad they went on, and still go on, as plain gentlemen ; it is one of the things that make an English gentleman's position unique.

James I. (to return to his new creation) was even careful to provide against corruption and extortion ; every newly created baronet was to take his oath that he had not directly or indirectly given more for the dignity than the regulation price as laid down, and "the charges of passing his patent." Also there is a strict injunction that all money paid in is to be kept as a separate fund. Selden does not tell us how far these excellent intentions were carried out in fact, and perhaps he did not choose to inquire. Within a year "a certain controversie touching Place and Precedence between the younger sons of Viscounts and Barons and the Baronets" arose "out of some dark words contained in the Letters Patents of the said Baronets." It was solemnly heard by James I. in person with the aid of his Council, and decided in favour of the younger sons of viscounts and barons by a long and pompous decree. This decree contains the king's promise to the baronets not to create any new title or dignity beneath that of a Lord of Parliament and superior or equal to a baronet's, which has ever since been repeated in the patents issued to new baronets. And now you are at least as well qualified to discuss the Honourable Order and its privileges as Sir Augustus Pampesford. Mr. Follett explains to me (for I really knew nothing about it) that the grievance of our Order consists in the Crown having declared that the sons of Lords of Appeal (who are barons only for life) are to go before us. I suppose the Crown took good advice, and Mr. Follett as much as said he could see nothing in the point; the question seems to be whether a Lord of Appeal is a real baron, or, if you please, whether, if James I. had made Lords of Appeal, he would have considered them real barons. It might have been a pretty question for Jacobean heralds to argue. But I hope Sir Augustus will not meet our good brother Charles in Hans Place or elsewhere while his head is full of this, as Charles would certainly deliver a discourse of half an hour, proving to Sir Augustus, on the most infallible Liberal principles, that he has no business to exist. Perhaps I should have swallowed formulas too if I had stayed at home.

Margaret and I have performed our dinner at the Squares. The dullness was just what you told me to expect, with the addition of their long dining-room being horribly cold; you know they are people who live by the calendar; so they have taken down their curtains and reduced their fires because the equinox is past. Well, " I have seen colder," as an early saint said when they asked him how he could bear standing in ice-cold water; and perhaps I have seen duller at Indian official entertainments. But formal dinner-parties are a necessary evil to me at best. Margaret is anxious to keep me up to my social duties, and tells me we really owe it to the neighbours. No doubt she is right, especially as you do not contradict her.

Jem has written to me from S.T.C., and it won't do to show to Mr. Weekes at all—in fact, I can think of nothing better than sending it on to you to be out of harm's way. Not that Laura would be pleased with it either, so treat it with the discretion due to a demi-official communication. By the way, you know Laura's little habit of questioning people about their letters and wanting to see them. She can very seldom—perhaps never —be gratified so far as mine are concerned. As to Weekes, I must tell him that Jem is still too busy to answer in detail, which is true so far as it goes.

How shall I have my Tod's " Rajasthan " bound ? He is barely holding together. You need not tell me to ask the Vicar. I want the benefit of your taste as well as his wisdom.

Your affectionate brother,
RICHD. ETCHINGHAM.

[ENCLOSURE.]

From James Etchingham, Assistant Tutor of Silvertoe College, Oxbridge, to Sir Richard Etchingham, Tolcarne.

MY DEAR SIR RICHARD,

It is the end of term, true enough, but with that end comes a business called Collections, not conducive to leisure for tutors. Anyhow, I don't see how I could answer a string of questions from a man I have never seen which range over the whole art of cycling, and every part and fitting of a machine, from lamp to backstays. The short answer to about three-quarters of them is that it is a matter of taste, and he had better find out what suits him, and stick to it. Otherwise the Rev. Septimus may take in a penny cycling paper and become a valued correspondent. He can get as many answers as he likes that way, and I should think it would just do for him. If you wanted to know anything I could tell you for yourself, that would be quite different. But I guess I may be riding about your country in the vacation, and it will be simpler to call in person one day and see how you are getting on.

However, our scholar Blunham was in my rooms when I got Mr. Weekes's requisitions. He is an odd fish : I think I pointed him out to you when you were here. He is said to have dropped his eyeglass one Sunday when he was reading the first lesson in chapel (it was a chapter of the Proverbs), and to have found it less trouble to invent the rest of the chapter than to pick up the glass. He has taken to the wheel as the most independent pastime, and rather taken to me because I don't mind what he says, don't expect him to say anything, and am indulgent to his experiments in scholarship, even when I have to point out to him that he should reserve originality till he is through the schools. We were going out for a ride. I showed him Mr. Weekes, and he twinkled silently. During the ride he seemed meditative, and latish in the evening he came in and asked me abruptly if I had heard of the Professor of Aramaic's last discovery of some new fragments apparently belonging to an apocryphal wisdom-book. Now, Aramaic is not a Greats subject, and so I gave him my thirteenth variation this week on the theme that a fourth-year scholar who aims at a first should not be too much interested in too many things at once. He remarked that he had no intention of reading the original, but had obtained a private copy of the Professor's translation in the first draft, and thought I might like to see it. This is what he offered me.

As a pair of wheels that run truly with a pleasant murmuring, so is the talk of man and wife in an house which is well ruled.

As the noise of a cheap crock which rattleth, so is dissension in the house of a niggard and a sloven.

The inches of our gear are three score and ten; and though there be some so strong that they ride four score, yet is their speed but labour and sorrow at the day's end, when they fetch their wind short upon an hill.

Blessed is the damsel whose cruse of oil faileth not, and who looketh to her own tires; and behold, he that taketh her to wife shall prosper.

Three things are plagues to a wheelman—yea, and a fourth is abominable: a boy which leadeth an unruly horse, and a swine which strayeth in the road, and a rash woman among traffic which regardeth not the right hand or the left; but the most grievous is a County Council which scattereth heaps of stones in the highway and saith, It is well mended.

My son, beware of inventors which promise marvellous things with their mouth, lest when thou puttest thy trust in their many inventions thou be overthrown in stony places.

Take heed unto thy riding in strange boroughs, and fall not into transgression of their by-laws, lest thou be worsted in striving with them that swear valiantly before the judgment-seat.

Of two manner of people thou shalt have a care, and flee from the third as an host of the heathen : a deaf man which walketh in the darkness, and children which run violently out of school at noon-tide, and a constable with girded loins who lurketh after sunsetting.

Perhaps even Mr. Weekes need not be warned against the current advertisement of this type :—

Genuine Offer.

SELVEDGE & TRIMMINGS

Have taken up the Cycle Trade as a branch of their world-wide Drapery Stores.

Selvedge & Trimmings will *present* Every Lady Customer who sends in *One Hundred* of their Five-Shilling Coupons within the half-year with one of their *dainty and deliciously running*

Roly Poly Cycles.

Voters roll to Early Polls
　On ROLY POLY CYCLES ;
Bustling bakers bring your rolls
　On ROLY POLY CYCLES ;
Holy Missioners mind your souls
　On ROLY POLY CYCLES.

DEAR MADAM,—*Have you passed your youth?*　You will pass

him easily if you are riding a ROLY POLY CYCLE and he is riding anything else.

A fair customer writes :—After being unable for many years to take any kind of exercise, I have been for a fifty-mile ride on a ROLY POLY CYCLE. My doctor agrees with me that I shall never want to ride any other.

You will never want to repair your ROLY POLY CYCLE after its first season.

Chainless cycles are largely advertised at fancy prices. Your ROLY POLY CYCLE will be chainless after the first hundred miles.

Madame Sarah Bernhardt writes :—I never fully realized the joys of decadence before I coasted down the Eiffel Tower on a ROLY POLY CYCLE.

Ask for SELVEDGE & TRIMMINGS's Illuminated Cycle Catalogue.

Here comes a man with an essay on the Platonic Number. I know it will be about everything except the text.

Yours most truly, rigidly, and rotarily,

JAMES ETCHINGHAM.

V.

From Miss Elizabeth Etchingham, 83 Hans Place, to Sir Richard Etchingham, Bart., Tolcarne.

DEAR, DEAREST RICHARD,

Thank you very much for the vegetables ; but, oh, the irony of life. The vegetables waited to come till a time when my spirit refused to feed upon Wessex beetroot or to find solace and refreshment in a Tolcarne Brussels-sprout.

I am about to issue a writ to inquire into the state of Sir Augustus Pampesford's mind. You will say that the proceeding is not premature when I tell you that since Monday my time has been fully occupied in refusing the hand and heart of the honest man who condones mental inferiority for the sake of respectable birth. And there seems no end to the business. What am I to do ? I have been driven to hint that I would rather— so low are my tastes—tramp the country selling baskets than live or die as Lady Pampesford of Pampesford-Royal ; but nothing penetrates, and notes still come on the thickest, glossiest paper, emblazoned with the Pampesford crest and motto (crest—a crowned peacock ; motto—" I lead "), in the when-you-have-duly-considered-the-matter strain. "An alliance between two ancient and honourable families," "The houses of Etchingham and Pampesford "—no, " Pampesford and Etching-ham." It is more than I can cope with, and I beg and implore you to write to him yourself and tell him—tell him that I am a Katherine Shrew sort of person ; that I am a certified lunatic, and only at large for the Easter vacation and to help my family settle themselves in London (the very task for a lunatic) ; that we are not the real Etchinghams, after all, of Tolcarne, Wessex, and Heddingley, East Anglia, with a forbear who represented his county in Edward II.'s Parliament, but mere mushrooms, who took the name and arms of the original stock. Tell him, too, that though I accepted a copy of "The Armorial Families of the Universe," and wrote and thanked him for the book before I cut the pages (a plan I learnt from you, when doubtful as to the matter to be found therein), I did not look upon the acceptation of the volume as a preamble to marriage with the man. Tell him that I am married already : so I am—to a memory.

You see, I have no one here to whom to speak of this absurd affair. Good Harry's fidelity of nature extends to his jokes ; and did this subject for ridicule reach him, he would not have done with chaffing till Doomsday. Experience, in fact, teaches that the longer he has a joke about him the more valuable and serviceable it becomes. And did I confide in Laura, not only would she weep over me as I broke the news, but for days after I should see tears gathering in her eyes whenever she looked in my direction. Laura has always held tears to be the fit environment of marriage engagements, and even tidings of a Pampesford proposal would unnerve her at once.

Later.—Your letter has just come. Would it be judicious or not, under the circumstances, to make over the baronite-lore to Sir Augustus ? Were my heart as bad as my temper, I should be inclined to wish that he would take to a " Roly Poly Cycle " himself. Doctors no longer required, only grave-diggers. I never saw a man who looked to me as if he would, if he could, so thoroughly enjoy the importance of his own funeral as does Sir Augustus. I am not really brutal enough to desire his removal by death, but he is making my life a burden to me at present, and I think Jem's ingenious friend might be less usefully employed than in producing an apocryphal Book of Job for my recitation.

How these days that have something of spring about them make me wish to shake the dust of London off my feet and take tickets to Much Buckland for poor, country-loving Tracy and myself. I long to see the blowing of the daffodils, the Wessex "Lent-roses," in Little Buckland meadow, and the flitting to and fro of the long-tailed tits, to whom the alders by the river serve as withdrawing-rooms. (Birds are conservative, I think, in their vocabulary.) The first breath of spring, when it reaches one in a town, is depressing. It is at least to me, and gives me, with its suggestion of the unattainable, a doleful, Amiel-melancholy. But stay here I must, for Laura cannot be left. If you ever see in your sister any sign of this inconvenient inability, please crush it out at once. People who cannot be left, and who, therefore, must be provided with constant companionship, levy a rather hard tax upon their relations. But Laura is made so, and I do not feel it my duty to discipline her out of her faults, as would some one cast in the special constable mould. It is impossible to persuade her to leave home herself during the rheumatism régime. She is starved in her friends' houses for want of proper food, poisoned by the strength of their tea, roasted by their fires or blown out of window by their draughts. (Other people's draughts are draughts; our own are ventilation all the world over, you may have noticed.) So here I am, and here must I remain.

Laura now breakfasts in her own room—the habit is one to be encouraged—and when letters come by the first post I am not bombarded with questions; so write, write, write, write, Richard. Do not fail me in this ridiculous Pampesford affair.

Your loving Sister,
ELIZABETH.

P.S.—I have the blues. Be very amiable when you write.

VI.

Sir Richard Etchingham to Miss Elizabeth Etchingham.

MY DEAR ELIZABETH,

This is the most extraordinary joke: don't think me unfeeling, but read on and understand

why you can afford to take Sir Augustus with
levity. Have I ever seen him ? I rather think not.
Certainly I have not seen "The Armorial Families
of the Universe," but I suspect you will find in
that great work a certain vagueness about the
circumstances attending the succession of the great
Pampesford family in its present branch. For now
I know what I know, and what you shall know
in a few lines more. In short—but I think the
method of all female gossips and most male
pleaders, namely, to begin from the beginning in
strict order of time, will be best in this case. You
know old Mrs. Tallis who lives by herself at Little
Buckland—at least you know about her—and how
she has wanted for years to negotiate an exchange
of two little odd-shaped corners of our respective
properties to round off our boundaries, and how in
my father's time Laura, for no reason she would
assign except that she thought Mrs. Tallis's cap
not suitable to her years, would not let him hear
of it, whereby such slender relations as Tolcarne
ever had with Fuchsia Dene were suspended ; or
rather all this is better known to you than to me.
Now you may be guessing (with swift feminine
skipping of all the intermediate diplomatic events
and matters of inducement) that Mrs. Tallis has a
niece with prior claims on Sir Augustus, or is even
entitled by precontract, and prepared with all the
terrors of a breach of promise action, to lead him
to the altar herself ; and, indeed, it would be no

more than proper dramatic justice—but it is not that. A shame to keep you in suspense, you say? Pray, how often have you told me that men always spoil a story by leaving out all the beginning and letting out the end in the middle? So please attend to the real story, which is coming.

It seemed to me that Mrs. Tallis had been rather badly treated; but, as an old Political, I was afraid of starting an official correspondence without knowing the ground a little; you see the old lady might have fired off her accumulated store of temper in some form that would have made further approaches hopeless. So I betook myself to our excellent Parson Follett, with whom I have now an understanding as good as an alliance in most things that concern the two Bucklands, and authorized him to convey my expressions of personal regret, and assure Mrs. Tallis that, without discussing past unpleasantness in which I had no share, and which I had no means of preventing, I should be happy to reconsider the affair in a neighbourly spirit. At the date of my last letter the parson had seen Mrs. Tallis, and she said very little, so I did not mention it to you then, not knowing whether anything would come of it. However, two days later I get a very polite note wishing me joy of being at home for good, hoping to be out and about and call at Tolcarne when weather is warmer, though the Buckland hill is hard work for a small pony-carriage; finally asking me if I will not call at Fuchsia Dene next Sunday and take a dish of tea without ceremony. Not a word of business, or boundaries, or Laura. Mrs. Tallis has not lived sixty—or is it seventy?—odd years for nothing. So that looked promising, and I went.

Mrs. Tallis was as gracious as might be in a pretty old-fashioned way, and gave me the best of tea—you know my weakness that way. She wanted to know all about the Indian Empire, including a second cousin once removed who had been on railway work in Travancore about ten years ago; whereby I had humbly to point out to her that Travancore is a good deal farther from Rajputana than Little Buckland from Thursborough, and yet we don't know everybody in Thursborough; as also, one house and one division at Eton are far enough from one another to disable Arthur from giving Mrs. Ginx full information about her nephew in the fourth form who has just come to Poole's, a house of which, as it happens, they don't think much at Lytewell's. Luckily Mrs. Tallis took no offence, and we maffled and talked on. Did you not once tell me, long ago, family history was Mrs. Tallis's strong point? Anyhow —and most luckily—it is. We came somehow to the grievances of the baronets, and I mentioned Sir Augustus Pampesford as among those who were making, in my opinion, an absurd fuss. "Pampesford, indeed!" cried Mrs. Tallis, "he is as much Pampesford as you and I are De Coucy:

not that you or I, Sir Richard, have any call to want anybody else's name." And out comes the whole story, I little thinking how useful it was to be to us, but taking it in most attentively, both because it was part of my business to appear amused, and because it really amused me. You shall understand, then, in brief, that Isaac Pfanders-furth of Bremen, merchant, transferred his principal seat of business to England some little time before the French Revolution, and prospered. This Isaac had a son, Solomon, who increased the paternal wealth, and became acceptable, doubtless for solid reasons, to H.R.H. the Prince Regent. Now at that time the Pampesford estates were encumbered, the family on the point of extinction ; and one fine day the world learnt that Solomon Pfandersfurth, Esq., had become the owner of Pampesford Hall (it was not "Royal" then). Then it was put about that a younger branch of the Pampesfords had gone crusading against the heathen Prussians in the fourteenth century, perhaps in company with Chaucer's knight, and had left representatives in Germany whose name had been Germanized for convenience. Presently it became known that Solomon Pampesford, Esq., formerly Pfanders-furth, had, with all proper licences, assumed the name and arms of Pampesford ; and lastly, after a decent interval, his Majesty King George IV. was pleased to create Sir Solomon Pampesford, of Pampesford-Royal, a baronet of the United

Kingdom. Sir Solomon, Mrs. Tallis added, per-
petuated the testimony of his Englishry and
orthodoxy by building a church in the most
approved style of early nineteenth-century sham
Gothic just outside the park gates, and becoming
a strict game-preserver and an indifferent shot—an
example which, it is said, has been piously followed
by his descendants. We have all read these things.
in our classical novelists, and it seems they sometimes happen.

Well, thereupon I enclose you a letter for Sir
Augustus, which you may close and forward, if
approved, making sure that the address, of which I
am a little doubtful, is quite correct. If you think
it too risky, I will alter it ; but I suppose you are
not over-anxious to keep up the acquaintance.
May I trust that the blues are dispersed ?

As I was taking leave of Mrs. Tallis after this
long talk, of which she had done most, I asked her
in a by-the-way manner if she remembered that
odd three-cornered piece of our east hams that runs
into her land, and said it had occurred to me in
walking round that it might be for our mutual convenience to have a little adjustment of boundaries
on that side. Mrs. Tallis answered that she had
talked enough for one afternoon, and had no wits
left for business, but she would be pleased to think
it over and let me know. Then she caught sight
of Margaret on her bicycle, who had been round
on errands, and came back to convoy me. We

had meant Mrs. Tallis not to see it the first time ; in fact, Margaret was quite sure it would be shocking to her. But she was only pleased and amused, and we rode off with a blessing waved after us from the porch. If you have any interest left for my small affairs, know that I had actually ridden, with exceeding caution, down the Little Buckland hill. Margaret says I begin to do her credit. Jem may be here any day now, and will perhaps condescend to put some touches to our education. There is a shade of something amiss about Margaret these last days ; she looks worried at times, and I don't think it is the housekeeping or anxiety for her or my improvement in cycling. No doubt she will tell me in good time if it is really anything.

The Folletts are expecting one Shipley, a very learned medievalist from the Record Office, to spend a few days at the Vicararge, and examine some documents in the neighbourhood, or in the Thursborough archives, I am not sure which. They have hardly met Mr. Shipley, though Mr. Follett knows his work well. Margaret and I are to help to entertain him. We are all rather in fear of the learned man, and try to comfort one another with the hope that he may not turn out altogether too weighty, or otherwise very formidable.

Your affectionate Brother,
RICHARD ETCHINGHAM.

[ENCLOSURE IN No. VI.]

*Sir Richard Etchingham to Sir Augustus
Pampesford.*

DEAR SIR AUGUSTUS PAMPESFORD,

My sister has communicated to me, as head of the family, the substance of the very flattering proposal you have been pleased to make to her, as well as of her own views already expressed to you. She is, as I need not point out, fully competent in age and otherwise to form her own judgment, and I must add, having known her from our childhood, that nothing I could say would be likely to affect her judgment in such a matter. It is not for me to indulge my own feelings by confirming your estimate of her qualities, and still less to cast doubt on your discernment by pretending to dispute it. However, as your ancestor, Sir Solomon, the first baronet, is reported to have said to some one who presumed to censure his full and final adoption of English customs, shekels are silver, but sovereigns are golden. I cannot bring myself to think that it will be long before your golden talents and advantages find in some other quarter metal as attractive and more congenial.

Believe me, dear Sir Augustus,

Yours very faithfully,

RICHARD ETCHINGHAM.

Sir Augustus Pampesford, Bart., etc. etc.
Pampesford-Royal.

VII.

*From Miss Elizabeth Etchingham, 83 Hans Place,
to Sir Richard Etchingham, Tolcarne.*

DEAR DICKORY,

Why are not postmen who drop letters into wrong letter-boxes decapitated on the spot, to prevent like wrong-doing in future? Why, if postmen drop letters into wrong letter-boxes, is it always the wrong letters that are thus consigned? Why was it not the black-edged appeal from a clergyman for funds to repair a north-country church, of which I had never heard, or the splendidly gilded and blazoned offer from a money-lender to Harry of the mines of Golconda, or the bill for Laura's Sunday bonnet, or the invitation to Cynthia to dance at Vivian-End in Easter week, that the folly of the postman delayed in transmission rather than your Pampesford epistle? I will tell you—because man, and woman also, is born to trouble as the sparks fly upward, and because desperately wicked is the heart of postmen.

You see, thanks to this postman folly and wickedness, I never had the letter, which should have come at breakfast-time, till the moment when Turnbull brought it into the drawing-room ostentatiously laid upon the tea-tray and all unsheltered from Laura's eyes. Never trust short-sighted eyes not to see, nor deaf ears not to hear. Blind eyes and deaf ears are freakish things, and will play you false if you put your trust in them. Laura saw in a moment from whom the document stamped with the Tolcarne postmark came, and before I could forge a reason for letting it lie unopened, Turnbull ushered in no other than Sir Augustus himself. Really, Laura's policy of the open door has much to answer for. (As is known to you, we are never allowed the protection of a "Not at home," unless we are down with an infectious disease, in bed, or in the street, but sit at the receipt of custom the day through at the mercy of all the unemployed in Christendom.) To fill up the cup of my woes, our stepmother frustrated my attempts to leave the room, and, alas, I can't take flight through these French windows into the harbour of the shrubbery, as, in such a predicament, would have been my course at Tolcarne. "Pour out the tea, dear Elizabeth," was my order ; "if it stands too long the tannin will ruin our digestions." Better be tanned to shoe-leather, I thought, than retain one's digestion in Sir Augustus's company ; but this reflection I had to keep to myself. "And now let us hear the Tolcarne news," Laura persisted ; "I am sure Sir Augustus will forgive my impatience when he knows that it is a fortnight since we heard a word from our old home." (I have, you will observe, treated your communications as private.) Alas, alack, from first to last the luck was against me, for, when forced to open the letter I proceeded to break the seal, up leapt Trelawney with a robust purr to my knee, and, jerking my elbow as he leapt, jerked out the enclosure, address upwards, to Sir Augustus's feet. Alack, alas, the envelope I saw was open, and probably meant for my perusal before delivery. Means of escape, however, if not of victory, were at hand, and sweeter than the song of nightingale was the sound at that moment of Harry's hoarse shout of " Elizabeth ! " echoing through the house. And never was man's call more quickly responded to.

Harry, poor fellow, has a cold in his head, and, in passing, I may mention that far less to-do would he make were a gun-shot wound his complaint. " I could not go to the drawing-room after you," he explained, "as Turnbull told me that ass Pampesford is there again ; and I want to know if the time hasn't come round to inhale this beastly eucalyptus stuff." So your letter was read whilst the bath-towel that enveloped brother and inhalation shrouded Harry's proud head : and read to the accompaniment of the sufferer's sighs and piteous appeals to be told if " it isn't long enough." And yet Harry without a qualm would have stormed Dargai's heights, and anything else really formidable that you like.

As to the Pampesford antecedents, I am not surprised by what you tell me. The glitter points to an origin of the sort. I do wonder what the enclosed missive said. It is pretty sure to be effectual, for you are rightly held to be an effectual person with a pen.

Later.—And what do you think? When—Sir Augustus safely out of the house—I went back to the drawing-room, there I found Laura bathed in tears and declaring herself to be most deeply hurt by our secrecy, our duplicity, our all things imaginable that are bad, in concealing from her matters that concerned our very heart's blood. Sir Augustus had evidently let her know that he has spent his time during the last fortnight in offering what I have not the sense to accept. I fear that poor Laura's feelings are really injured, and, of course, *à la mode* of Laura, she turns her injuries into an instance of disrespect to our father's memory, who put her "in the place of his wife." Her sympathies, I need not tell you, are entirely with Sir Augustus, who is, she says, " a very good-hearted man." I dare say he is good-hearted, but it is useless to argue with her that the absence of brutality in his nature does not establish his right to marry any unwilling woman he may fix upon as a desirable wife.

Thursday.—Laura still wears a stone-wall face, and treats me with a sort of offended-governess air, as if I were a child in disgrace. "I am not in your confidence, Elizabeth, and therefore am not surprised to see you wearing your grey gown instead of your black, or buying new shoe-laces without consulting me." As an olive branch, I have written to beg Mrs. Carstairs to come to tea this afternoon, and I shall retire to my room early in the entertainment, so as to give the aggrieved one a good opportunity of complaining of me. What more to please can woman do?

Harry's cold, I am happy to tell you, is better, and he is not to die of it. It is an acknowledged thing, indeed, that his sneezes will not land him this time in Hades, and he talks of going north for a week at Easter, a-fishing. The Vivians have invited Cynthia, also Stephen, to stay with them at Vivian-End, for a hunt-ball next week. Vivian-End, you know, is Mr. Biggleswade's cure, and I am thinking of packing up Trelawney with Cynthia's dancing-frock as Biggleswade defence. I must not again forget what I have intended to tell you before, which is that Stephen would very much like an invitation to Tolcarne. He is writing the life of some west-country mariner for the "Naval Notabilities" series, and thinks that you or Mr. Follett can afford him some valuable information on Wessex sailor-lore. Mrs. Vivian affronted him by inquiring if Noah was to be included in the "Naval Notabilities" series.

It is not for the first time, perhaps, that Jem's expected arrival has given Margaret a worried look; but if there is anything to be told to you, she will tell it herself.

I think I know the Folletts' expected guest, Mr. Shipley. Is he not brother to my dear Alice Newton? I think so. The Newtons have taken a house in Sloane Street for three months, and I shall see something of her, I hope. Her sister-in-law, Mrs. Ware, came to see us the other day, a woman devoid of understanding, who thinks it is time that Alice, whose child died a year ago, "roused herself." Prolonged grief bores the on-lookers :—

> "They bid bereavèd Priam smile,
> And Niobe, the childless, dance."

We are all allowed to be unhappy for a little while, you know; but, then, we have to "begin to get over it." Poor Alice, I think she found in her child consolation for her marriage. (It was Mrs. Ware who, in Indian days, finding that some one she considered a black sheep was not tabooed by Bombay, pleased Harry by the inquiry, "What is the use of being respectable if such people are to be asked to Government House?")

Don't forget that it is "expected of you" to invite Charles and Minnie in the course of time to Tolcarne. I am really sorry for Minnie, *à propos* of the treatment she receives from her mother in the matter of "Only a Woman's Heart;" and I feel that we must all be very good-natured

about it, and make the most of our liking—
or, rather, the least of our disliking—of the book,
to make up. When I went to see Mrs. Vivian the
other day, I was followed into the house by Minnie,
who came in quite excited and breathless over a
most polite newspaper notice of the novel. "My
dear Minnie, these ridiculous reviews are either
written by people who have not read the book, or
who know me," was Mrs. Vivian's comment. "And
now I come to think of it, Hugo Ennismore writes
in the *Minerva*, and there is nothing foolish that
he would not say or do to please me," etc., etc.
This was hard on Minnie, and she was all tears
and tremors in a moment. Blanche, the pretty
younger sister, is much happier in her relations
with her mother. She laughs when attacked, and
Mrs. Vivian receives the laughter as a tribute to
her humour, and is appeased. From Mrs. Vivian,
on the same occasion, I got the latest intelligence
in printers' blunders. The printer of a report of
some philanthropic work in which she is interested
turned " L'Union Internationale des Amies de la
Jeune Fille " into "L'Union Internationale des
Arries de la Jeune Fille." What do you think of
that ?

Thursday evening.—Whilst Laura was confessing
my sins to Mrs. Carstairs this afternoon, I read
some chapters of Earle's " Microcosmography "—
the new reprint. Perhaps I am right, perhaps

I am wrong; but, wrong or right, I prefer the portrait gallery of Theophrastus to that of Earle, and that of old Fuller in his "Holy and Profane State" to either. For your guidance, as an elder brother, I might make over to you an extract from the character of "The Elder Brother" in "The Holy State:"

"He relieveth his distressed kinred, yet so, as he continues them in their calling. Otherwise, they will all make his house their hospitall, his kinred their calling. When one being as Husbandman challenged kinred of Robert Grosthead Bishop of Lincoln and thereupon requested favour of him to bestow an office on him, 'Cousen' (quoth the Bishop) 'if your cart be broken I'le mend it; if your plough be old, I'le give you a new one, and seed to sow your land, but an Husbandman I found you and an Husbandman I'le leave you.' It is better to ease poore kinred in their Profession than to ease them from their Profession." Very, very true.

Wars and rumours of wars: what will come of it all? I pity those who sit in kings' and presidents' and prime ministers' places—

> "One would have lingering wars with little cost;
> Another would fly swift, but wanteth wings;
> A third man thinks, without expense at all,
> By guileful fair words peace may be obtained."

So it was, so it is, and so, I suppose, it will always be.

Do not dock me when you write of the Tolcarne news, of the Tolcarne sayings and doings. They throw up the window and freshen the air of the room (ventilation, not draught). Is Enticknap, as usual, grudging growing-room to everything but a cabbage, and hungering—I trust futilely—to dig the borders? Don't let him. If he had his way he would destroy every vestige of blossoming vegetation. The good creature confuses a Sahara and a flower-garden, and all that he does not cut down he holds it his privilege to dig up. I wonder if Merlin, poor old dog, still, every fine morning, takes a sun-bath on the terrace? I liked to see him throw himself down before the big myrtle with a sigh of reposeful content. And tell me if the cocks and hens flourish, and if you now are called upon to find names for the infants of the poultry-yard. Great was Enticknap's embarrassment when Margaret gave her own name and Cynthia's to two of the chickens. With " Miss Cynthie the cock" and " Miss Margrot the pullet," he finally solved the etiquette difficulty.

My *salutations empressées* to you and to everything at Tolcarne, and those of Trelawney to the birds—robin, linnet, thrush. Much does he wish, horrid fellow, that it were for him to devastate the nests this spring. Much do I rejoice that it is not. Good-bye, good-bye.

ELIZABETH.

VIII.

*Sir Richard Etchingham to Miss Elizabeth
Etchingham.*

My dear Elizabeth,

Laura may go to Dúzakh, which is in
the Persian the opposite of Bihisht ; and if you
don't know what those two places are, you may
guess. Seriously, can you go on living with her
much longer ? There is a point where self-respect,
after a fair trial, sets limits to every social duty.
However, Sir Augustus's exit is assured, and I
shall not break my heart because it was a little
more abrupt than we meant.

For once your penetration was at fault about
Margaret. Her little worry had nothing to do
with Jem : we have had a refusal here too, but of
a very different person. Mr. Weekes, the curate,
who began his relations to me with a rather
exaggerated version of the civility due from a
younger man to a considerably older one, has
become more and more obsequious the last week
or two, till at last it was positively oppressive.
Margaret, regarding him as an inoffensive person
to whom it would be a sin to refuse charity,
continued to instruct him in cycling along with
me. Last Thursday morning he came round when
I happened to be well occupied with letters and

Enticknap (I do remember that Friday is outward mail-day, for the sake of keeping up with some old colleagues), and I said that if Mr. Weekes and Margaret would start on our usual run—the one approximately flat piece of the Thursborough road near us which you once complained of as our one dull walk—I would come after them presently and overtake or meet them. "Huzur," said Margaret (she will call me Huzur, though I have explained to her that it is quite pointless), "can't you really come with us?" But I really could not very well, and saw no need for it. In about half an hour I stepped out to fetch my hired machine from the portion of the stable which Margaret has converted into a cycle- . house, when Margaret came riding in at the gate, faster than usual, and almost ran against me, with Mr. Weekes panting and wobbling after her. They dismounted and took their bicycles in (Mr. Weekes's lives here till he can find storage elsewhere— there is no place at all in his lodging in the village, and as his and mine were hired from the same shop in Thursborough at the same time, it seemed the natural thing), and as I was moving in the same direction there came out in Margaret's most practical housekeeper's voice—the one she uses when something stupid aggravates her— "Do stop talking nonsense, Mr. Weekes, and don't upset my machine." Then a limp black figure, dusty as to the knees, came scrambling

past me with a hasty salute most unlike Mr.
Weekes's usual ceremony ; and when he was well
out of the gate, Margaret emerged and half drew,
half drove me into the study. "What," said I ;
"you don't mean to tell me he has——? " She
looked as if she did not quite know whether to
laugh or to cry—you know I become imbecile
when people cry—but happily the laugh turned the
scale, and, after giving a little choke or two, she
collapsed on a stool in a violent fit of laughter.
" Yes, indeed," she said, when she could find
words, "and he's been proposing all the time."
Apparently Mr. Weekes accepted the chance as
a providential omen, and as soon as they were
fairly started he began to blurt out incoherent
compliments, in which the virtues of Margaret,
Much Buckland, and myself were hopelessly
tangled, and then reeled off what he intended
to be a proposal in due form, with a full exposition
of the secular and spiritual advantages that would
accrue to both parties, and to the people of the
Bucklands, from Margaret becoming Mrs. Septimus
Weekes. As he is barely capable of riding and
talking at the same time, his discourse was adorned
by narrowly averted collisions with the Squares'
family coach, a farmer's cart, a donkey, a wheel-
barrow, and Margaret herself. All these events
gave Margaret plenty to do in looking out for
herself and ejaculating imperative cautions, so
she could only get out a few words of dissent.

When he followed her into the stable he essayed to go down on one knee, but, the space being limited, he only achieved stumbling over Margaret's machine and barking his shin against the mud-guard. Net result—Mr. Weekes must find quarters for his bicycle somewhere else without loss of time. By good luck there was Jem's coming— now come, in fact—and I wrote a little note explaining to poor Septimus that Jem was very particular about having plenty of room. So there is another exit, and I have escaped, I trust, a solemn letter or a solemn interview, or both. And Margaret, I think, now feels more intimate with her half-known parent from the Indies. She had been suspecting the catastrophe for some days, but looked, as I should have looked, for something much more formal and dignified. She is not exactly angry with the man, but vexed at his folly. Such persons do seem a blot on the reasonableness of things.

Now concerning the arrival of Jem and Mr. Shipley, which also has had unexpected elements. Arthur's movements are known to you, as he did his duty by calling on you before he came on here for the holidays, and you have verified for yourself his healthy state of indifference to the problems of the universe. I don't think he will turn out the sort of young man who considers that his own opinions must be of serious importance to God Almighty. Well, Jem telegraphed to us on Tuesday to expect him by the Thursborough road, and the three of us set off wheeling after lunch on the chance of a meeting. About four miles out we perceived, as the old-fashioned first chapter used to say, two riders approaching at a swift and steady pace from the cathedral town. Meanwhile we had been discussing the unknown Mr. Shipley. My guess was a dry, precise little man. Margaret's was a tall, thin, anæmic man, with a stoop and blinking eyes. "Oh! no," said Arthur, "that's not the sort. I know those awfully clever history chaps; we had one to give a lecture to the School Society this half. He was red and smooth, and just like a Rugby football, and looked as if he couldn't stand up by himself. He talked of nothing but common fields and grass-farming and mangold-wurzels; that's what they make us learn for history now." "Look," said Margaret; "isn't that Jem?" "Somebody with him, then," said Arthur. A few minutes showed that it certainly was Jem, and with him a proper enough man of no remarkable dimensions any way in excess or defect, and of decidedly cheerful aspect, old enough to wear a full beard in defiance of the modern fashion of youth—that is, enormously old to Arthur's eyes, and in the novelist's "prime of life" to mine. "Let me introduce Mr. Shipley," said Jem; "we met at Oxbridge some time since, and we have fallen in on the road." Not a bit like any of our guesses. Things very seldom are, so far as I know, and people never. So we rode back to the Vicarage quite an imposing procession; and if Jem thought the pace funereal, he did not say so.

To the Vicarage, because Mr. Shipley did not know the way; and Mr. Follett, who was walking in the garden, had us all in to tea. We took the back way by reason of our machines, and thereby were surprised. For who should be sitting with Mrs. Follett but poor Weekes! She is a motherly, comfortable person (all the more so to the world from having no children of her own), and he doubtless had come for consolation. Margaret made herself a rampart of Jem and me. Mrs. Follett asked if there was any more talk of war in London, but Jem, not having been in London for some days, disclaimed knowledge, and Mr. Shipley said there was nothing certain. "Is it not shocking, Mrs. Follett," said Mr. Weekes, "that war should still be possible? My friend Dr. Woggles, of the Universal Arbitration League, writes to me in a truly painful state of anxiety." "I am not sure that the Vicar agrees with you," said Mrs. Follett. "But on all Christian principles——" he replied, and, catching sight of Margaret, gasped and came to a dead stop. "But," said Mr. Follett, who, of course, knew nothing of our late episode, "a clerk in orders is hardly free to deny that Christian men may sometimes lawfully bear arms. Dr. Woggles is probably not bound by the Articles.

And there are some other archaic writings which we are bound at least not to dismiss without consideration. Sir Richard, will you kindly take down that Vulgate which is just behind your head on the shelf? Thank you. And you, Miss Margaret, will you read this verse? You learnt Latin at your High School, doubtless with the true Italian vowels—one thing at least that girls are taught better than boys." "Please, Mr. Vicar, I don't know Latin," said Margaret. "Enough to read a text in the Vulgate," said Mr. Follett, "and our barbarous English Latin is not what the Vulgate deserves." "A good judgment," said Mr. Shipley. "It will save you talking," I whispered to Margaret. So she took the book from the Vicar, and with a ring in her voice quite different from the housekeeper tone, and (it seemed to my ears, which have heard a good few tongues between Gibraltar and Bombay) a mighty pretty Italian accent, she read out :—

"*Accingere gladio tuo super femur tuum, potentissime. Specie tua et pulchritudine tua intende, prospere procede et regna, propter veritatem et mansuetudinem et iustitiam: et deducet te mirabiliter dextera tua.*"

"I suppose," said Mr. Shipley, "those last words are wrongly translated; but in themselves I like them better than the 'terrible things' of the English version." "That was why I chose the Latin," said Mr. Follett. Mr. Weekes had vanished.

"Well," said I, not having attended much to Western public affairs for some years, and having no clear or decided notions about the Cuban question, "and who is your mighty man that is to gird himself with his sword upon his thigh?" "The President of the United States," said Mr. Follett. "*Et deducat ipsum mirabiliter dextera sua,*" added Mr. Shipley. "He's all right," said Jem.

So there you have incidentally the answer to your question about rumours of war. We are to dine at the Vicarage to-morrow. Merlin, who you remember came from Jem's old home, is quite spry at seeing him again. Arthur, who patronizes us all except Jem in cycling, took out the family and Mr. Shipley for a ride to-day, and on the return was cautioning us about the incline down to the house, when the learned man, remarking that the slight breeze against us was an excellent substitute for the brake, put up his feet, and, drawing ahead of Arthur by the advantage of a man's weight over a boy's, sailed in neatly through the one open leaf of the gate with just enough way on to dismount easily. Whereupon Arthur has confided to Margaret and me that he considers Shipley an old brick, and doesn't believe he can be an historian at all.

I am asking Charles and Minnie to come here for the short Whitsuntide vacation. You have never told me your opinion about the binding of Tod's

" Rajasthan "—and lots of other things. I must contrive to see you soon, though they have given me an infinite deal of nothing to do as Chairman of the Parish Council, and Wessex farmers are less manageable than Rajput princes, and trains at Buckland Road Station are few and evil. The only fast thing one sees there is the Midland express running through to the north, which is obviously not of much use to a man who wants to go to London. It is said that it once slipped a coach for a director, which made a nine days' wonder for all Buckland folk. Think of a time to suit you, and I will make it out somehow. No more at present from

Your loving Brother,
RICHARD ETCHINGHAM.

IX.

From Miss Elizabeth Etchingham, 83 Hans Place, to Sir Richard Etchingham, Tolcarne.

DEAR, DEAREST CREATURE,

Poor Margaret—poorer Mr. Weekes. But what a goose the poorer man must be to have supposed himself capable of converting Margaret into Mrs. Septimus Weekes. There is a certain ingenuousness about him that I always rather liked, and a meekness not in keeping with the hardihood of his last move. Do you know, I wonder, the tale of his first appearance in the Tolcarne pulpit one Sunday afternoon, as told by Blake?—" Mr. Weekes, M'm, up he went, and he looked round and round all in a flutter, and then says he, 'My thoughts have gone from me. Will you excuse me?' and down he ran, scared as a hen by a hawk." I don't feel sure that valour was absent from this explanation, though terror certainly takes people differently—making some speak when conscious that thought has left them.

You will be welcome wherever you appear ; and as to the time, the sooner the better. "Ask the Rajah if he isn't coming up for the May Meetings or the Empire Ballet," was Harry's last injunction before departing this life on his way north, armed with much fishing-tackle. *Votre couvert est mis,* and we all consider you to be due.

I really fear that my memory is failing me, and senile decay is setting in, when I think how often I have meant but failed to answer your question as to the binding of Tod's " Rajasthan." Were the book mine, and did I love it, I would give it brown calf—good, solid, sober, russet calf. For all but butterfly books, I think I prefer brown calf to other bindings. It has the demure look, the durable look, and, if fittingly treated, the look of quality.

About what you ask as to living on with Laura,

well, yes ; without a violent asserting of myself, I
don't see any way out of it at present. She means
well, as tiresome people according to your doctrine
are apt to do, and in her tiresomeness we see the
defects of her good qualities. She is keen for
affection, and she has always meant to "do her
duty," and I really believe that it would distress
and astonish her beyond measure to find that I
wish to cut myself free. And then the opinion
of her neighbours assumes mammoth dimensions
in her eyes. "What people would think"; "What
people would say," if I went my own way—we
should see her with straws in her smooth hair.
(Laura is precisely like a picture by Sant that I
came across the other day.) I am capable, I need
not tell you, of being odiously disagreeable
momentarily when my temper is touched, but I
am not capable of sustained effort in the direction
of my own benefit. I must therefore, I suppose,
suffer for my ineptitude, which, by the way, rather
reminds me of the Burmese proverb: "The ass,
though fatigued, carries his burden."

I am glad that Margaret's reading from the
Vulgate pleased you. Her voice is a valuable
possession. Had I been present I would possibly
have asked that the reading might be continued
over the page—"Deus noster refugium et virtus."
"Auferens bella usque ad finem terræ."

Do you remember the "antique song" that our
mother used to sing?

" O, if I were Queen of France, or still better, Pope of Rome,
  I would have no fighting men abroad, no weeping maids at
    home ;
  All the world should be at peace, or if kings must show their
    might,
  Then let those who make the quarrels be the only ones to fight."

But you need not brand me as a Wogglesite, for the way to peace, I admit, is often through war.

I regret to inform you that Sir Augustus Pampesford, after a week's absence, has again appeared upon the scene. He, however, now asks pointedly for Laura, and pretty well ignores me. Laura, who always had a great respect for anything in the shape of a man, thinks he is "a very pineapple of politeness," and I dare say that he is an agreeable contrast to her crowd of ancient women. Aunt Jane comes to visit us rather often, and she and Laura have struck up an intimacy. She sits for a long while and puts many family questions. "And what news have you of Richard ?" "Do you hear often from Margaret ?" "Is Charles quite well ?" "How is Harry ?" "What news has Richard of Arthur ?" and so on, and so on ; and this just suits Laura. There is no fatigue nor mental exertion about it, and while it lasts they both look sleepy but comfortable. Laura is really kind to Aunt Jane, and Aunt Jane says truly enough that Laura has nothing in common with the objectionable women —if one can call them women—who unsex themselves, and who, she hears, are really, really——

You know Aunt Jane. But I like to hear Aunt Jane tell of the long past days at Tolcarne—of our grandparents and their punctilious ceremony, and of the formal politeness, which ruffled temper but increased. When the *entente* was not perfectly cordial, the Eliza and Nicholas became "Your Ladyship" and "Sir Nicholas." Our grandfather was something of a martinet, and our grandmother did not forget her beauty and heiressdom, and so the ceremonious mode of address was from time to time in requisition.

Later.—A letter "to hand" from Harry. He seems happy. The river—oh, unique river—is in good condition, and he has killed and is sending south a fish. He begs to inform me that his "waders, when hung upon a hedge to dry, were the subject of much perplexed discussion by some French tourists t'other day. Mystery finally solved to the satisfaction of all parties. Waders were undoubtedly worn ' for the ascent of Ben Nevis.'"

So effectually mended is Harry's heart—if by Ada Llanelly ever broken—that I should not be surprised if—can you guess? No? Well, answer me this : Is it all in the day's work that our good brother should spend hours in the attic box-room sweeping the leads and roofs through a field-glass, when Trelawney, worshipped by Cynthia, has wandered far? I, too, worship Trelawney; but would Harry throw over anybody, everybody, anything, everything, rather than Trelawney should vanish into space, were his sister's heart alone lacerated by the thought of Trelawney's disappearance? And why, please, did he nearly put out his sister's eye with the rib of her best umbrella, snatching the umbrella from her without so much as a " by your leave " lest Cynthia's feathers should suffer? Are not my eyes of more value than many feathers, except in the opinion of one under the spell of the wearer of the feathers? And does it not require some passion equal to that of love to banish, when rain falls, all regard for the welfare of his own hat from a man's remembrance—of his own *new* hat, not of the hat that had been sat upon by the refrigerator? Dear Harry. His hat was new, and he ruined it yesterday, which surprised me almost more than did the careless grace with which he nearly put out my eye. But even if Cynthia is disposed to like him, I do hope that he will be content to " mark time " for a while. For Cynthia is very young, and I would not have Colonel Leagrave written to just yet to say that his child is engaged to our brother. He might consider that an unfair advantage had been taken of the living-together circumstances. But this would never occur to simple-minded Harry. What do you think ?

Cynthia is an attractive thing. Pretty as a Cosway miniature, and pretty to live with : which beauty is not always. And she seems to be an affectionate, lovable little soul ; not possessed, perhaps, of Margaret's strength, but the strength may be there, dormant, for all I know. And then she has that invaluable old-fashioned possession— a conscience. The Fates would be kind to Harry did they give him Cynthia as his wife, nor would they, in my humble opinion, do Cynthia the while an ill turn, for men as kind, as upright, as crystally honest as Harry are not plentiful as blackberries on hedges.

Laura begins to think that it would suit her to be braced, and the last notion is that she and I should go somewhere for bracing benefit in June. Mrs. Carstairs tells her that the air of Scotland would serve the purpose, and she intends to consult Harry on this point when he returns. I cannot quite imagine Laura upon the hill—can you ? It would be from inn to inn we should go, as, if our friends were disposed to entertain us, their tea would be too strong for our digestions, or their climates too enervating for our constitutions, I suppose.

It is, alas, Laura's intention to give a lamentably large dinner-party in your honour when you come to London. Poor, poor Dickory ; try and bear the trial well. This is just a case of Laura's compassing the very thing detested, with the idea of pleasing. I repeatedly implore her never to do to others as she would be done by, but my prayers are unheeded. She welcomed a dinner invitation, even when at Tolcarne, and drove with alacrity, whenever the neighbours gave her the chance, through darkness to depression.

Thank Margaret for her nosegays. The great boughs of pear-blossom and the forget-me-nots have dressed us out elegantly in white and blue ; and the violets, if the Jinnestan romance tells truly, should ward off the cruel and evil spirits "whose malignant nature is intolerant of perfume." How is the flower-perfumed world at Tolcarne ? To-day, Good Friday, potato planting, according to Devon tradition and superstition, is the rule in every cottage garden ; and in yours too, probably, for Enticknap is a stickler for old custom and luck-lore. Bid him transplant some parsley, and see if your will or his superstition prevails. He said to me once, with a note of interrogation in his voice, that he had "heard say" the whooping cough was never taken by a child who had ridden upon a bear. In reference to this, Mr. Follett, I remember, told me that when bear-baiting was in fashion, the bear-owner's profits were largely augmented by money received from parents whose children, for their health's good, had ridden the bear.

Now good-bye. Take care of yourself, and don't forget to outlive me. I enclose a letter from Cynthia, and rest

Your loving sister,
ELIZABETH.

[ENCLOSURE.]

Vivian-End.

MY DEAR MISS ETCHINGHAM,

Thank you very much for sending my satin shoes. I do not know how I would have danced to-night without them.

You would like the woods here; they are so full of oxlips and wild hyacinths and wood-anemones. There was a dinner-party on Monday evening. Mr. Biggleswade and another clergyman and his wife and some other neighbours came. Mr. Biggleswade asked me, if I had the opportunity, to explain to Mrs. Vivian that he was perfectly willing to meet London people; that he would prefer it to being invited to dine with the aborigines, with whom, he says, he has absolutely nothing in common ; but that Mrs. Vivian did not seem to understand that it is so. But I think that Mrs. Vivian understands it quite well. Stephen thinks that she does, and Stephen thinks she makes a point of introducing Mr. Biggleswade to people as "our vicar" because it amuses her to irritate him. Stephen thinks, too, that she speaks to Mr. Biggleswade about the *Guardian* for the sake of hearing him say stiffly that he does not see the paper. He has not talked to me much since Lady Honora and Lady Wilfrida Home-Lennox came. I do not think they like him, but they say his poems are supposed to be very clever and Elizabethan, and he is now going to write a play. I hope my darling Trelawney is well, and that he has not been brought back in disgrace from anybody's dust-bin again. (If he strays away, does Turnbull look for him now that Major Etchingham is not there?) I hope also that Blare and Atholl are well, and that Blake is not turning them black with two much hemp-seed. Mr. Biggleswade lets his gardener shoot bullfinches, Blanche Vivian says, because he thinks they eat his orchard buds. I think this is very horrid. I shall not care for his pretty verses about Glycera's bullfinch any more. I hope that Major Etchingham is having fine weather in Scotland. He sent a great salmon, that arrived last night. I will bring you some oxlips ; and please tell Aunt Laura I do not want the goloshes. The ground is quite dry.

With best love, your very affectionate

CYNTHIA.

X.

Sir Richard Etchingham to Miss Elizabeth Etchingham.

MY DEAR ELIZABETH,

Harry's attentions to Trelawney, which you report with so much interest, afford a curious example of what the modern naturalist calls " throwing back." Pursuit of strayed animals was amongst

74

the earliest functions of Intelligence Departments. In fact, there is a stage of society, still possible to observe in parts of India, where the chief occupation is lifting your neighbours' cattle, diversified by expeditions for tracking, and if possible recovering, the cattle which he has lifted from you. When the cattle-lifter comes, by the progress of other industries, to be in a distinct minority, people begin to call him a thief, and to make rules for the game of hunting him, as to which he is not consulted. Mr. Shipley tells me this is one of the few topics on which Anglo-Saxon law was copious. And, substituting the comparatively modern horse for the archaic herds of kine, we may find similar developments in the history of California and of the Australian colonies. Now it is the law of all forms of hunting that ultimately they are carried on with regard to the sport as an end in itself, and the original purpose of acquiring food, destroying dangerous or noxious animals, recovering valuable property, or whatever else it may have been, falls into the background, and, after serving for a while as an excuse, finally disappears. This may be well seen in Somerville's poem on the Chase, where fox-hunting is just beginning to take rank as a sport for gentlemen, and the hunters are still represented as the farmer's allies and protectors, who deliver his hen-roosts from Reynard's depredations. Such was the transition towards the middle of the eighteenth century. Now the sport of tracking stolen oxen is not easily practised in modern England, least of all in cities; but by the legitimate substitution of the cat, a smaller and swifter animal, and following the trail across house-tops, where the signs of passage are less obvious than on a road, the material conditions are reconciled with modern civilization, and the discipline of intelligence, with the concomitant satisfaction of the sporting instinct, is not only preserved but improved. There is a piece of evolutionary argument for you. I have heard young civilians just come out with their heads full of Herbert Spencer deliver themselves of less plausible ones in all seriousness—and seen them do right good men's work a few years later, when they had found out that the gods of Asia don't rule their world according to Western books. But a quite different alternative hypothesis occurs to me about Harry's conduct: perhaps our War Office wants to go one better than the Germans, and train cats to act as orderlies. In any case, it is evident that he is carrying out some kind of experiment under secret instructions; so be careful how you talk of it. As for the sunshade and feathers incident, I give it up, having never had anything like it in my official experience. My good old friend Colonel Leagrave is too far off to consult on the point. Cynthia is a pretty name, but Cynthia Etchingham would make a rather awkward hiatus. Has she no second name that would go between?

You may remember that in one of the less dull pages of Eckermann Goethe is reported to have said to some one who urgently asked for his advice, "I shall be happy to give you as much as you please on one condition." "And what is that?" said the young man, eager to pay any price for Goethe's wisdom. "That you do not take it." And so it falls out as to the binding of Tod's "Rajasthan," and your advice to put it in brown calf. In Elizabethan and Jacobean bookland, my dear sister, I do homage to only one Queen Elizabeth, and she is alive. Brown calf is good for your Fullers and Burtons, and all the better if it is the old binding; indeed, modern calf binding, when it is not the very best, has a kind of shiny smugness about it which I detest. Do you remember those old school prize-books, the remaining stock of travels and antiquities bought cheap and dressed out in tawdry gilt calf with a greasy surface, and the hideous so-called ecclesiastical binding with thick ribs on the back? However, I cannot see Colonel Tod in any sort of calf at all. Those dare-devil Rajputs, as splendid and as impracticable as any heroes of European chivalry, who, when all was lost, would put on saffron garments and perish in a last desperate sortie, will not be constrained to your sober Anglican livery. The Five Colours of Rajasthan, on the other hand (you have never ridden on an elephant with his trunk painted in them!), are both too many and too gaudy to put on the outside of a book. On the whole, since we live in a clean air here, I think I shall fall back on white vellum, with a sparing use of some little Oriental or quasi-Oriental decoration. Jem has a pet binder at Oxbridge whom he swears by, and is sure I could get it well done there.

We had a pleasant little dinner-party at the Vicarage last week : just our two housefuls, and, if you please, Mrs. Tallis, and a niece who is staying with her, to redress the balance of the sexes. The old lady is really more active than she will admit to most people ; she is cunning in getting off duty visits. I wish I could learn the trick of her. After dinner I told Mr. Shipley how the Vicar and I began to fraternize over the curse of Ernulphus. But Shipley spoke of that immortal document with some levity, saying that, though it contains passages of great merit, it is a late and diffuse formula not of the best period ; so that Mr. Follett and I began to doubt if such sentiments were compatible with a sound Shandean faith ; which, as we had already made up our minds that the suspected heretic was a good fellow, would have been an occasion of sadness. But he proceeded to clear himself. "Don't suppose," he said, "that I would in any way detract from Sterne's merit in finding and using the curse. He was a royal thief, and stole the best thing he could find, and no man of letters, with the best intentions, can steal more. It was no fault of Sterne's that nearly a century was to pass before we had the 'Codex Diplomaticus' in print." (I had not the least notion at the moment what the "Codex Diplomaticus" might be, and, indeed, I had rather assumed that the curse of Ernulphus itself was largely improved, if not wholly invented, by Mr. Sterne. I am beginning to know a little more now.) "I have had to look at Anglo-Saxon charters, though not often," answered Mr. Follett, "and I have noticed those clauses, which I suppose you refer to, denouncing various penalties in the world to come upon any one who may attempt to interfere with the pious king's gift; but they seemed to me fragmentary and fantastic work." "Only you should consider the variety," said Mr. Shipley. "You may have your portion with the traitor Judas, which is perhaps the commonest form; you may be swallowed up with Dathan and Abiram; your soul may be hooked out of your body with devils' claws to be boiled in Satan's cauldron world without end; you may be devoured by the Salamander; you may be smitten in sunder with the falchion of Erebus; or, contrariwise, you may be delivered over to the malice of the Pennine demons, that they may plague you with the iciest blasts of the Alps." Here it seemed to me, though knowing nothing of ancient European charters, that I had one card useful for this game, so I mentioned that Colonel Tod had translated a Rajput grant, though not a very old one, containing a clause of this nature which might possibly compete with most Western productions. "I have heard," said Shipley, "that the Eastern vernaculars are unsurpassed in terms of vituperation." "Certainly," said I, "and the most elementary of them will not bear translation in respectable company; but that is not exactly my point." "Yes," said he, "I suppose you mean some precise form of spiritual condemnation." "Well," I continued, "what do you say to being a caterpillar in hell for sixty thousand years?" After a moment's reflection, Shipley admitted that for compendiousness and comprehensiveness he could not beat that out of the whole of Kemble's "Codex Diplomaticus," or any other European collection. Then he began questioning me about the Rajputs' charters, and wanted to know many more things than I could tell him without book; so we settled that he should come over and inspect them in Tod for himself. Meanwhile he had found, as he says one always does find, that the Thursborough documents wanted much more looking into than he had been told, and he was somewhat easily persuaded by Mr. Follett to stay on a few days more instead of rushing back before Easter Day. Mrs. Tallis was in a most festive mood, and we made an appointment for a view of those boundary pieces of land.

Somehow we were all a good deal occupied the next few days, the parson with his Good Friday and Easter duties, Shipley with his copies and notes of documents, so that he could only join the young people in short rides or potter with this ancient squire, and the said ancient squire in the still continuing process of putting things to rights, or what the father of didactic poetry called "Works" (not *Weeks*, as I have seen it mis-printed) "and Days." Talking of the garden, I cannot get any good word for the bullfinches from Enticknap. He sticks to it that they are a down-right mischievous lot, and he has seen a "proper rendyvoo" of them eating the buds zo vast as they could. As to sparrows, I am inexorable myself: they behave like land pirates of the worst kind, as I remember from old days at home. Turning the martins out of their nests is a favourite sparrows' trick.

On Monday, however, being a welcome fine day, parson and antiquary came in together and called for a sight of Tod; I desired Mr. Follett's mind about the outside of him too. We adjourned to the garden, book and all, for the Vicar is a great lover of sun, and calls himself an old wall-fruit. "Mr. Shipley," said Arthur, after due salutation, "I suppose it comes quite easy to you to make out history from all those parchments written in dog-Latin?" "That depends on what you call easy," said Shipley. "Construing medieval Latin is easy

enough mostly, when you know the common words
that are not classical—not that I allow it to be
dog-Latin. Reading medieval manuscript is only
an affair of practice if it is fairly well written and
you have some notion what it is about. But as
for knowing what tenth-century or even thirteenth-
century people really had in their heads, and how
things looked to them at the time, that's another
story, and the more I learn about these things the
less easy I find it to think I understand them.
About as easy, I should say, as "—here he seemed
to cast about for a simile—"getting a goal from a
shy in Bad Calx." " Why, sir," exclaimed Arthur
with a sort of explosion, and struggling with his
company manners, "can you be *the* Shipley who
was Keeper of the Wall and got that goal at the
tree?" "Do they still keep up the memory of
that old fluke of mine?" said Shipley, and beamed
all over like a schoolboy; and Tod lay on the
bench, Mr. Follett carefully putting it in a shaded
corner, while we discussed the question of binding,
and Shipley and Arthur were deep in mysteries of
Eton football and other shop, which sounded to
me like the far-off bells of one's native village
church—they would be about as intelligible to an
outsider as the difference between a zamindar
and a taluqdar to the globe-trotter who knows
all about India when he comes home. And the
study of the Rajput charters didn't come off that
morning.

Just as I am closing this I get a note from Charles accepting for Whitsuntide, with some obscure remarks about fitting in with probable engagements in Dampshire. Pillarton, the member for the Clayshott division, who is a furious old-fashioned Tory, and cannot abide the modern social legislation of his party, is said to be on the point of resigning in a huff. I wonder if that seat is what Charles is after? He won't take much by it in my opinion: but if so be, let it be. As I cannot in decency be expected to oppose my own brother, it will be a good excuse for me to keep out of party politics for a season.

There will be lots of things to talk about. I begin to count the days till I am to see you again, and I will gladly endure Laura's dinner-party.

Your loving brother,
RICHARD ETCHINGHAM.

XI.

From Miss Elizabeth Etchingham, 83 Hans Place, to Sir Richard Etchingham, Tolcarne.

MY DEAR DICKORY,

Thank you very much for the vegetables that have just come, and thank you very much for your letter containing the curses, &c. Cauliflowers and curses thankfully received, dear. And as you

83

are all so learned in such matters, tell me now the words of Hecate's ban, " With Hecate's ban thrice blasted, thrice infected," or perhaps Merlin or Songstress, though not ban-dogs, would gratify my curiosity. When I begged Tracy to do so he said the thing had slipped his memory. The dog seems preoccupied. He detests the town.

For your banning I will return blessing, or rather for your curses a charm. Do you know the old West-Country charm for the prick of a thorn ?

> " Happy man that Christ was born,
> He was crownèd with a thorn,
> He was piercèd through the skin
> For to let the poison in ;
> But His five wounds so they say,
> Closed before He passed away.
> In with healing, out with thorn,
> Happy man that Christ was born."

Ask Margaret to recite the charm if ever, in my absence, the thorn of a rose-brier dares to prick you.

, Harry, the hunter, instigated by a primal instinct, sweeping the chimney-pots through a field-glass for Trelawney, the prey, is a picture pleasant and profitable to contemplate. That the job pertains to the work of the Intelligence Department is an equally pleasing suggestion, and as Imperial interests may be bound up in the business, I will take your advice and not divulge the fact to any but an Anglo-Saxon when Harry and field-glass are again so engaged. Cats are full of contrivance

and resource, and with Trelawney as his orderly—
or perhaps rather as his colleague, for the race is
intolerant of authority—my brother might go
further and fare worse. Talking of throwing back
and kindred subjects, is Harry the hue of the
primal man ? According to the author of a book
I lately read, Trelawney's cedar-coloured coat is
not far removed from the colour of the primal
cat—sandy.

I really do feel mentally obliterated by what you
say of brown calf ; reduced, in fact, to the point of
thinking that I might possibly better my condition
by changing places with the caterpillar your letter
mentions. Yes, yes, yes, I remember, when you
refer to them, those horrible bindings, your school
prizes, and, later, Laura's devotional works. But
my memory, when left to itself, seems to select, as
does the eye of the artist, and seems to leave out
of the picture everything not in keeping with the
time "which now shines with so much splendour
before our eyes in chronicle." I was thinking when
I wrote of the dear old Tolcarne books, attired
in their comfortable russet livery — pleasantest
of all linings, to my thinking, for a room—and I
was for the moment quite oblivious of the modern
binder's work. Ask Colonel Tod's " Rajasthan " to
forgive me for venturing to suggest that the heroes
should go clad in a garment that it disgusts you,
their admirer, to touch or to contemplate ; and let
me make amends for the worthlessness of my

advice by the gift of a book for your birthday—
any procurable book that you will—and bound by
Jem's Oxbridge binder in vellum ; unless, by any
chance, you would not despise silk, embroidered by
my needle ? One of the few things your sister can
do decently is stitchery. (Were I not ground to
dust by your rejoinder I should attempt now, at
once, I think, something gorgeous and slightly
barbaric for your dare-devil Rajputs. The five
colours could be sufficiently subdued by intrench-
ment in dead-gold and white.)

Or would you prefer for your birthday present a
coppice of pot-nectarine trees? I ask this because
Alice Newton and I (your Mr. Shipley *is* her
brother) went this morning to the Botanical
Gardens flower and fruit show. The flowers were
a lovely sight—a paradise of Crimson-Rambler
roses and silver-white spiræa—but it was the little
nectarine trees, thickly hung with fruit, that I
think I liked best. Fruit trees are not sufficiently
used for decorative purposes in gardens of pleasure.
First the flower and then the fruit, and though
" the flower that once has blown for ever dies," the
melancholy is lessened when the falling of the
petals means the forming of the fruit. Say, then,
if little nectarine trees shall go to you, or a book?
And if a book, please, Sir Richard, what book?
The arrival of the nectarine trees would, I fear,
throw Enticknap into the dolefullest dumps.
Everything green that grows he looks upon as an

addition to the long list of his grievances ; and I never could see why he objected to the bull-finches : if they really do devour the fruit buds they by so doing save him the trouble of gathering in the fruit.

I see that a Tolcarne volume that is rightfully yours is here with our possessions : " A calendar made at Stratton in Norfolk in 1755." The authorities quoted are calmingly remote, " Pliny says that bees do not come out of their hives before May 11th, and seems to blame Aristotle for saying that they come out in the beginning of spring." " According to Ptolemy, swallows return to Ægypt about the latter end of January." (How much Ægypt loses in appearance by the loss of the diphthong.) " Pliny says the chief time for bees to make honey is about the solstice, when the vine and thyme are in blow. According to his account, then, these plants are as forward in England as in Italy." " Aristotle says this bird " —the ringdove—" does not coo in the winter." The calendar ends abruptly October 26. " Here ends the calendar, being interrupted by my going to London."

The Vivians are in Prince's Gardens again, and Mrs. Vivian visited us yesterday. Azore, the coffee-coloured poodle, whose top-knot is tied up twice daily with new blue riband, and Mr. Vivian, looking benevolent and saying nothing, were in attendance. Mrs. Vivian is not too well pleased with Charles's decision to stand for the Clayshott division of Dampshire. His agent, she says, will, she supposes, prevent his doing anything extraordinarily foolish ; but she asked every one present to explain to her why a radical son-in-law should be her deplorable fate. A Radical is always mannerless, she says, and when any one takes her into dinner and immediately begins to talk across her to her other neighbour, she decides at once that "the man is a Radical," and she is never wrong. I wished that you could have been present to see the expression of Laura's face whilst Mrs. Vivian proclaimed Azore's merits and the sentiments that the merits inspire. " The dog is a perfect saint, and I would far rather lose my husband than lose him ; and the worst of it is that he is infinitely more likely to be lost or run over than John is." Laura, of course, talked as if we could not have heard aright, and tried, as though with the object of sparing Mr. Vivian's feelings, to twist the meaning of his wife's words. Her well-intended efforts, however, I need not say, were needless, for the office of a peacemaker between Mr. and Mrs. Vivian is a sinecure. Poor Alice Newton's listless rejoinder of " Certainly, if you wish it," to Colonel Newton's endless demands is really significant, though Laura cannot see it, of an unhappier state of things than Mrs. Vivian's flow of words and Mr. Vivian's admiring silence. He thinks her the loveliest, cleverest, wittiest woman in the world, and she finds him invaluable as a background.

I am distressed about Alice Newton. She is killing herself with her good works and her societies, and if one expostulates she only answers that it is not as easy to kill oneself as people suppose. And do you remember what a lively creature she used to be? How was she induced to marry Colonel Newton I wonder? He boasts and he fidgets and he is rude to her, and to it all she says " Certainly, if you wish it," and he evidently takes the compliance as a tribute to his superior worth.

I hear through Alice that her brother is very happy at the Parsonage and is in no hurry to come away. You and Mrs. Tallis seem to be growing very thick. Don't make her an offer of marriage, there is a dear. It's not " expected of you."

Laura is still bent upon spending June in Scotland, and this house will be at the disposal of you and yours whilst we are away. Selfishly, I am glad that Cynthia wishes to come with us, for to travel *tête-à-tête* with our stepmother would only, if amusing at all, be amusing in retrospect. But Harry looks sad when Cynthia speaks as if the prospect were delightful to her, for he, with or without his orderly, Trelawney, will be tied to London and the Intelligence Department during June. In answer to your question, Cynthia's second name is Rose—Cynthia Rose—I like the name Rose for love of the Rose Aylmer lines. What over and above the bracing, which is a passive, not an active process, Laura will find in Scotland of a satisfactory nature, I cannot imagine. She has never crossed Tweed yet, and she seems to think that to do so " is expected of her," and, being Laura, she will in the future have a certain satisfaction in feeling that she has "done" Scotland. (Mrs. Carstairs' small grandchild told me the other day that she had done astronomy.) But to Laura I believe the Highlands will be savage and horrid as mountainous country was to an ancient, or, at any rate, no more attractive than the Swiss Alps, as scenery, are to me. Then, except as dinner-table decoration, she does not care for flowers. So what does she expect to find congenial in Scotland during June ?

I dreamt of you last night—an absurd dream. I dreamt that you told me that it was your practice, before falling asleep, to set a row of lighted candles beside your bed "to attract Fate's attention." Fortunately for my dreaming peace, the dream did not go on to tell that Fate returned the compliment by setting you on fire. And then I turned to dreaming of Alice Newton kneeling before a white-draped altar as Calantha, and for candles there was a torch reversed. " Our orisons are heard, the gods are merciful," she said, and went on to tell me, as if it were good news, that at last she was to be allowed to die. " My child is dead you know, Elizabeth."

The scholarship now assembled at Tolcarne can no doubt give us the right reading of " The Broken Heart" dirge. Alice, in a volume of lyrics, has it in one version and I, in my head, have it in another. Is this right or is this wrong, your worships :—

" Sirs, the song."

Glories, pleasures, pomps, delights and ease
Can but please
Outward senses when the mind
Is untroubled or by peace refined.
Crowns may flourish and decay,
Beauties shine, but fade away ;
Youth may revel, yet it must
Lie down in a bed of dust ;
Earthly honours flow and waste,
Time alone doth change and last ;
Sorrows mingled with contents prepare
Rest for care ;
Love only reigns in death ; though art
Can find no comfort for a " Broken Heart."

Farewell, Dickory, for now, " Multa habui tibi scribere : sed nolui per atramentum et calamum scribere tibi. Spero autem protinus te videre, et os ad os loquemur. Pax tibi."

ELIZABETH.

XII.

*A.—From Sir Richard Etchingham's Note-book :
left with Miss Elizabeth Etchingham in London.*

*Friday in Easter Week, in the garden at Tolcarne.
Enter to* SIR RICHARD, MR. FOLLETT *and*
SHIPLEY, *bringing back Tod's "Rajasthan"
and Sir A. Lyall's "Asiatic Studies."*

Mr. Follett. Sir Richard, I hope you will keep
these books well now that you have them again.
It is not good for Shipley to see too much of them,
and not good for your parson to be tempted to
envy and jealousy. You have made me live in fear
that you will entice Shipley away from our Middle
Ages to these heathen Asiatics.

Shipley. The Vicar may well say he is jealous ;
this is the very censoriousness of jealousy. No
such thing as deserting the Middle Ages is in my
mind. What pleases me about these Rajputs,
their manners, and their documents, is that they
have continued early medieval institutions into
the nineteenth century. It is like seeing a piece of
what we call the Dark Ages come to life.

Sir Richard. There is much talk of feudalism
in Tod ; but to me who know nothing of European
feudal history, his analogies darken more than
they enlighten ; they need a fresh commentary of
their own.

Mr. Follett. Learned authors in all ages have been drawn by a fatal attraction to the method of explanation which we call *obscurum per obscurius,* or, in English, trying to throw light on something you partly understand from something else which you understand much less or not at all.

Sir Richard. In this case the correction is supplied by Sir Alfred Lyall in his essay on the Rajput States ; I mean so far as he has shown the true nature and connexion of the Indian facts on their own ground. But the result seems to be to cut off the Rajput clans from any distinct European analogy, unless your modern scholars have got some new theory of feudalism that you can fit them into. I understand there is a new one about every ten years. Only just now, as Arthur said the other day, history seems to be all running to mangold-wurzels. Perhaps Shipley can give us some light, as he seemed to be hunting.

Shipley. No light of mine, but the clan system of the Rajputs does fit in beautifully with what has been worked out as to the origins of feudalism in France. These good people are, or in Tod's time were, in a quite regular Carolingian stage— only they never had a Charlemagne, and never developed real feudal tenure out of their tribal allegiance. And what is very curious and pleasing to a student of charters is that the Rajput charters are good for much else besides the caterpillar in hell which any one who resumed the grant was to be turned into. Lyall does not mention them, but they confirm his view exactly. The forms are wonderfully like those of Carolingian documents in the West nearly a thousand years earlier. Why, it is lucky that the gulfs of time, place, and language are wide enough to cut off all suspicion of forgery or imitation. And one understands how your Colonel Tod jumped at full-blown feudalism as the nearest thing he could think of. He could know nothing of the times just before the birth of feudalism in Europe—times which are dark to us, as somebody has said, in respect to our ignorance at least as much as theirs.

Sir Richard. Good for Lyall; not that I should have believed you without compulsion if you had found anything against his work ; and I am glad you have a good word for Tod.

Mr. Follett. Even the cursing clause appears to be quite in its proper place by analogy to the corresponding European period.

Shipley. Yes, those curses disappear from English documents when true feudalism comes in. The Norman clerks were too business-like to indulge in such fancies, and devised better methods of assurance for worldly purposes. But the history of solemn documents and their various set forms is a great matter, and one might talk of it, on English materials alone, from now to midsummer.

Sir Richard. You scholars whose talk is of charters ought to know about seals. Where is the resemblance to a seal in the flower called Solomon's seal that grows in the border here ?

Mr. Follett. Wait till it is out, and you will mark how the blossoms hang under the leaf all in a row ; when a charter has many seals, they hang along the foot of it in the same way. Medieval gardeners who had heard of Solomon's seal would certainly think of it as appended to Solomon's charters in the fashion they were accustomed to see.

Shipley. Just as fifteenth-century illuminators put Joshua and his knights into plate armour.

Mr. Follett. While the armourer himself was minutely copying in steel the latest Court fashion in pointed shoes.

Sir Richard. But would the gardener be much in the way of seeing charters ?

Mr. Follett. He would in many cases—those of monastery and collegiate gardens—be a brother or clerk told off for gardening duty, and so learned enough to know at least what the outside of a charter looked like.

Enter MARGARET *and* JAMES ETCHINGHAM.

James. Are you still on your medieval swear-words ?

Mr. Follett. Curses on the breakers of charters are a commodity you should have need of at Oxbridge, Mr. Etchingham, if all I hear of your reforms be true.

James.   I wish you could spare us a few for the makers of our college statutes.   We are always having verbal wrangles over some clause or other.

Margaret.   Why are learned men so fond of bad language?   To be sure, artists are worse.

Mr. Follett.   I think it is an affair of nation more than of profession.   Fantastic imprecations and devilries in general are mostly Teutonic, or at any rate of Northern stock.   Our grandfathers' favourite adjective *Gothick* is in its place when one talks of grotesques.

Shipley.   I always see that *Gothick* with a *k*.   It suggests a special note of contempt to the nine-teenth-century reader, though I suppose it was not intended.   As the Vicar says, the Germans are easily masters in that branch of art.

Sir Richard.   But what about French gro-tesques?

Shipley.   I count them as Frankish, not pure Gallic, and therefore as Germanic in the larger sense.   Your Italian is nowhere when he competes with the Northerner in devilments.   He can be terrible, but not terrible and ludicrous at the same time.   Fra Angelico could make nothing of devils.

Margaret.   Why should he, Mr. Shipley, when it was his business to paint angels?   I suppose he had to put in devils now and then, but I am sure it gave him no pleasure.   Do you know those lovely angels at Florence dancing in a ring with the blessed souls at the gates of Paradise?

Shipley. Yes, indeed I do. There is plenty of seamy side to the Middle Ages, and I don't see how any honest man who takes them at their own word can deny it ; but such things as Fra Angelico's make one forget it all.

James. This also shall please the Lord better than a devil which hath horns and hoofs.

Mr. Follett. Amen to that, Mr. Etchingham, and you may keep the devils for your restoring architects at Oxbridge.

Margaret. Now, Jem, I trust you are more careful when you call on the Gainsworthys. They are frightfully shocked at anyone not taking the devil quite seriously. I thought your college made you believe in the devil, and renounce Dissenters, and abjure the Pope, and all sorts of things.

James. So some journalists appear to think to this day. We made a Catholic Fellow at our last election.

Shipley. The Queen has promised us lay people with her very own mouth, which for this purpose is the mouth of her Judicial Committee, that nobody can require us to believe in any personal devil. Under your correction, Mr. Vicar, I think that is so.

Mr. Follett. I remember the case, and it was in substance as you say. The Church of England is the least dogmatic of churches in all things that can by any reasonable construction be considered not of the essence of a Christian commonwealth.

Margaret. But is it the same for clergymen, Mr. Vicar? Are you really not expected to believe in the devil?

Mr. Follett. Since you ask me as a clerk, my dear Miss Margaret, I answer as a clerk, that is, with the caution befitting an officer of a body established by law and under discipline. The question you put is between me and—my bishop.

Arthur (entering hastily). Father, here's young Mr. Square and half the Parish Council, and they want you to go and look at those new inclosures at the bottom of Brock Lane.

Sir Richard. Coming, my son. *Panchάyat kά hukm hai.*

B.—*From Sir Richard Etchingham, Tolcarne, to Miss Elizabeth Etchingham.*

Just a line to tell you I find all well on coming back. Margaret and Arthur have kept house together most discreetly: I was sorry for myself to lose a few days of his holidays, but it was better than waiting till they were over and leaving Margaret all alone. Mrs. Tallis has been more than civil to them, and treats Margaret almost like a daughter. Perhaps Arthur found their conversation a trifle dull, but it is good for schoolboys to sit with old ladies now and then. It tempers their robustiousness, and gives them a sort of reverence for antiquity which familiarity prevents them from learning at home. Of course, anybody can teach young people a sort of false external respect by snubbing them at an early age. But that is the way to make the real thing impossible —and very thankful I am to you, not for having done nothing of the sort yourself while you were in charge, for you could not if you tried, but for not having let other people do it.

This morning we (Mrs. Tallis and I) had our perambulation of those little parcels in the hams, with Mr. Follett assisting. Luckily there were no treaties with native princes or chiefs to be considered, and the only question of effective occupation that might have been raised if we chose was who had been accustomed to cut the old thorn-bush in the place where there is a double bank and ditch, so that one cannot be sure of locating the boundary by the outer edge of the ditch in the usual way. It is really quite a simple matter of exchange, and obviously useful to both parties. The only practical doubt is whether we must have in the family solicitor and do it in due form. The Vicar says it is worth thinking of whether we won't just alter the fences and exchange rough plans, and leave lapse of time to make all right. Such things, it seems, are not uncommon. I suppose this is the only country in Europe where quite a large proportion of important affairs, from the Constitution downwards, are worked by just doing the thing you want and saying as little as possible about it even to yourself. As for British India, you know it is a land of codes and regulations and minutes. And to think that there are well-meaning "able officials" who want to carry the formalizing business into our dealings with native States! Well, if it ever happens, my only comfort is that I shall not be there to see the mess.

Parson Follett agrees in your text of the song. The modern editors who print

> " *The* outward senses when the mind
>   Is *or* untroubled, or by peace refined,"

only reverse and break up the rhythm of the whole piece under pretence of making two lines look more regular. Such folk are of the tribe whom Mr. Swinburne somewhere calls deaf and desperate finger-counters.

Perhaps I ought to consult Charles about that exchange: are not such things the speciality of the Chancery Bar? But he will have Clayshott Division on the brain for weeks to come. He threatens to send me his address in draft—on the chance of converting me, I suppose—and it may be here by any post. Good-bye, dear Elizabeth: you see I have almost written a letter.

Your loving
DICKORY.

XIII.

*From Miss Elizabeth Etchingham, 83 Hans Place,
to Sir Richard Etchingham, Tolcarne.*

"Trusty and wel beloved, we greet you well."

"Trusty and wel beloved" you are missed. There was more luck about the house when you were here. Tracy too is missed; and his little empty collar, with its inscription, 83 Hans Place, has now something of the sacred relique about it in Cynthia's eyes. But it was cruel to keep him in London. Spaniels are not the dogs for a town, and I always thought that his frolic humour would land him under a wheel. Now, I suppose, he is racing round and round the lawn, fringes and love-locks flowing in the wind. Does he still pause in his impetuous career to insult Eld in the person of blind old Merlin with belated invitations to play?

I found your notebook after you were gone yesterday hidden away with my sewing tools. I remember you pushed it under a pyramid of embroidery-silks to screen it from Laura's in-quisitorial eyes and then forgot it, careless creature. (No, you are not really careless.) I looked into the book again before sending it after you, and I am half inclined to exchange my derivation of the name Solomon's Seal for Mr. Follett's. His is the prettier as well as the more ancient. The seventeenth-century garden-books explain the name by the circles that show when the root is cut, which " do somewhat represent a seal." The doctrine of signatures has always had a fascination for me. I should like to believe, as I read once upon a time in Cole's " Adam in Eden," that "the fruit of the Pome-citron tree being like to the heart in form, is a very soveraign cordiall for the same." That the walnut, having the perfect signature of the head, is the one thing needful for the brain; that viper's bugloss is an especial remedy against the bitings of vipers and all other serpents, "as is betrayed by both stalk and seed." The author of the book in question is a staunch upholder of the doctrine of signatures, yet he condemns fanciful theorising in others, and will not accept the story "told by a fellow herbalist, Culpeper, I think, of the Earl of Essex, his horses," which being drawn up in a body lost their shoes upon the downs near Tiverton, because moon-wort—loosener of locks, fetters, and shoes— grows upon heaths. Culpeper "was very unable to prove" that moon-wort grew upon Tiverton downs, and the tale of the lost shoes must therefore, in his more cautious contemporary's opinion, be taken with a grain of salt.

It was to-day, was it not ? that Mr. Follett was to guide your steps to Bratton Leys, there to see the " devil's door " in the north wall of the church? I suppose the door is no longer thrown open during the Baptismal service, for the devil to escape at the Renunciation, and carefully bolted and barred on all other occasions? Mr. Shipley visited us yesterday evening. He seemed very sorry to have come just too late to encounter you. I told him that I had heard that when Medievalists met, the devil, who ruled their period, had, naturally enough, taken a prominent part in the conversation, and he answered that the conversation was of angels too. Tell Margaret that I commend her for asking, as, according to Mr. Shipley, she did, how Fra Angelico, who began painting with prayer, could have seen the devil at his worst. She seems to have inquired too, *à propos* of the inferiority of Italian demons to the Flemish variety, if Spinello's devil, who slew the artist that created him by appearing in a dream, and asking the terrified painter where he had seen him looking so hideous as in the fresco, and why he ventured to offer him so humiliating an affront, was not terrific enough. The shock of so unusual an incident naturally killed Spinello, and Mr. Shipley thinks that Margaret has substantiated the claim of the Italian devil to a prominent place in Pandemonium.

Later.—I was sent for by Laura this afternoon, and found the Vivians and Alice Newton in the drawing-room. "I am not again preventing your finishing a letter to Richard, I hope, as he only left us *yesterday*," poor aggrieved Laura said in her huffed tone ; the expression of which hope excited Mrs. Vivian's easily roused curiosity, and, as she does not scruple to put questions when her interest is awakened, I found myself under cross-examination, and when asked what I was writing to you about to-day, answered, "I am writing to Richard about the devil." I wish words would paint the expression of Laura's face. "The devil," Mrs. Vivian cried with increased vivacity, "that's most interesting. Somebody was telling me about the devil the other evening and amused me very much. A man's devil was just the god of his enemy, was he not ? and did not the devil first of all come out of Persia ?" Laura murmured something about the devil and the fruit of the tree of knowledge. "Oh, my dear Lady Etchingham," exclaimed Mrs. Vivian with her sweetest smile, "after your serpent you have to wait centuries for your devil. For your familiar horned, hoofed, satyr devil I feel pretty sure that you have to wait till the Middle Ages. What is the date of the satyr devil, John ?" Mr. Vivian, to whom, as he mechanically stroked Azore, Alice Newton with admirable patience was trying to talk, had not time to produce, if he knew it, the date of the horned, hoofed apparition's first appearance before Mrs. Vivian's tide of words flowed on again. "And I believe that the further cast you go the huger and more hideous the devils become. But Paris was a great place for devils, and Dante went there for his devils, his three-headed devils, as I go for my clothes. And do, Elizabeth, if you are writing, ask Sir Richard if he thinks those dreadful Campo Santo devils—the Campo Santo of Pisa—and those at Mount Athos are cousins? and if they can have flown into Italy from Greece and into Greece from Persia? It's a bore not to know." I was thinking that Blake and sal volatile would have to be rung for on Laura's behalf, and a copy of the Papal bull that teaches the exorcising of fiends for the benefit of us all, but fortunately at that moment in came Colonel Newton, and to my unspeakable relief I soon heard : "You can begin a war without an army, but you can't finish one " ; and Laura's response, " Oh no, of course."

Mrs. Vivian, however, had by no means talked herself out, and went on to demand sympathy in piteous accents on the count of the "frightful, horrible, hideous Christian Death " that had supplanted the " pretty Death " of the Pagans. " Yes," Alice Newton said, " it would be interesting to trace the twin-brother of Sleep to the stern deity of the tragedians and on to the ghastly personification of Death which had little to separate it from the medieval devil. Elizabeth, do you remember the winged figure girded with a sheathed sword, from the temple, I think, of the

Ephesian Artemis? The face is so dreamy and wistful and the hand lifted as if beckoning. It was thought by some, was it not? to represent Eros, and by some, Thanatos. The doubt is attractive." Alice then looked as if she had forgotten all of us till jerked back by Colonel Newton, who broke away from Mrs. Vivian's announcement that the Christian artist's daughter of Herodias and John Baptist's head was just the Pagan Muse holding a mask, to ask Alice if she had remembered to tell the servants that he was dining out. "Jupiter and his eagle were used up, Hugo Ennismore says, for St. John the Evangelist, and the poor Cupids had to be angels," was what I then heard Mrs. Vivian say, for want of a male listener, to Laura. "If Nature is a spendthrift, Art was always economical, wasn't it, Elisabetta?"

Mrs. Vivian sent you a sheaf of amicable messages. She was very sorry not to have seen you. You must come and dine, "just ourselves," when you are next in London. "If Sir Richard had married my daughter," she told Alice Newton, "I should not so much have minded. Sir Richard is charming, very amusing, and original. But I have a son-in-law whose hobby is drains, and whose Paradise is a Trades Union Congress."

Thursday evening.—Your letter has come. Do you remember Harry's trick of tying my hair to the back of my chair when my eyes and attention were riveted to the multiplication table, and then exclaiming "Luna has another bird!" with the object of seeing his sister rise, chair and all, on the strength of a cat's imaginary misdemeanour? Dear, your pronounced references to Mrs. Tallis, who struck 70 the day you were born, somehow remind me of Harry's mischievous proclivities. You may tell Mrs. Tallis from me, that though she treats *Margaret* "almost as a daughter," by a clause in our father's will no one can adopt *you* without my permission, and that permission I have not the slightest intention of granting. After Margaret you belong to me, and I command you, by holy obedience, to resign yourself meekly to the inevitable.

No, I don't think your girl and boy have had the life trodden out of them. I like the natural growth, and never could believe in the crushing beyond recognition of minds and spirits. Nor is there any excuse for it now-a-days, for it is not the fashion of the age to obliterate, as it was more or less in our childhood. The other way is the happier, and, as far as I can see, unwilling obedience is little better than rebellion. "Libertie kindleth love, love refuseth no labour, labour obtaineth whatsoever it seeketh." Nor do I approve the crushing of parents, and if Margaret or Arthur bully you, be so good as to send them to me for correction. You shall not be bullied either (except by one person whose name, oddly enough, happens to be—Elizabeth). You have not yet, I think, heard Mrs. Vivian on the subject of her sons? Reggie, she says, makes her life a burden to her when she takes herself to Eton to see him. He prods and pokes her with his elbow at every turn, lest she outrage the proprieties, and sends her home bruised black and blue. He would rather see her burnt, she informs everybody, than button the lowest button of his waistcoat, roll up his umbrella, or walk down the roadway instead of on the pavement. No woman, she declares, is enslaved by fashion and the opinion of contemporaries to the extent that a schoolboy is. Hugh, when visited at Oxbridge, she finds equally exacting in another direction, and her theory is that, as girls grow free and easy, boys grow precise. Hugh has something of the Methodist or the Quaker in his temper of mind, according to his mother, and is constantly correcting her for exaggeration, whilst himself affixing D.V. to the announcement of his plans. "He dragons his sisters, as though he were a mother of the early Victorian period, and his propriety is something absolutely abnormal."

Charles's address has not yet come our way. Here, for the sake of peace, I ignore his political proceedings. Honest Harry, as we know, thinks sin and radicalism one and the same thing, and considers the family disgraced by Charles's politics. What Charles's politics are I don't myself quite

know, and you should enlighten me. He and
Minnie are in Dampshire now. Mrs. Vivian tells,
that when driving across country and reciting his
speeches to Minnie, Charles, who certainly is a
shockingly bad driver, was jerked out of the dog-
cart. Mrs. Vivian assures me that Minnie was far
too deeply engrossed in thinking out the plot of
her next novel to notice, till the horse of its own
accord drew up, that her husband was no longer
seated at her side, but prostrate in the ditch.

Poor Minnie is in her mother's bad books at
present. She is staying at Clayshott with " a most
horrible, rich, vulgar woman, a Mrs. Potters, who
fawns upon her in the hopes of getting something
out of her : which Minnie, taken in by fulsome
flattery, is too dense to see." (I am again quoting.) The Tory *grande dame* of the place is Lady
Leyton, and the Leytons and the Vivians, though
Minnie apparently ignores or forgets it, are old
family friends. Lord Leyton is a builder of
model cottages and Lady Leyton is one of the
kindest women in the world, "a friend of the
poor," whose pony carriage if not at one cottage
door is at another. Into this Conservative Arcadia
poor Minnie, backed by Mrs. Vivian's *bête noire*—
Mrs. Potters—and armoured with all the courage
that crude feminine Radicalism inspires, is about
to penetrate. Do you think she will escape
intact? Charles, Minnie and the babies were at
Vivian-End in Easter week. Little Harry had

some unusual experiences and came running in
from the garden in hot-haste to say, " Mim, Mim,
I hear the slugs eating Gran's flowers."

The question of the existence of ancient vineyards in Britain is, I see, discussed in one of the
newspapers. There were vineyards at Ely, at all
events, a very long while ago, according to the
Latin rhyme, which was Englished long ago too.
I was too lazy to send the rhyme to the newspaper—but here is the 17th Century English
version for you :—

> " Four things of Elie Towne much spoken are
> The Leaden Lanthorne, Maries Chappel rare
> The mighty Mil-hill in the Minster field
> And fruitful Vineyards which sweet Wines do yield."

Good-bye for now, Dickory, and write again
soon.

" Je prie à Dieu que il vous doint ce que vostre
ceur désir."

ELIZABETH.

XIV.

*Sir Richard Etchingham, Tolcarne, to Miss
Elizabeth Etchingham, London.*

MY DEAR ELIZABETH,

Charles has sent me a proof or early
copy of his address to the electors of the Clayshott
division. There is a long paragraph about ground

values and betterment, the utility of which in a Dampshire farming district is not obvious to my mind; but then I don't understand home politics. Also the inevitable denunciation of frontier wars, which I suspect will not be relished, as a Clayshott man has got his promotion as sergeant-major, and has been writing home enthusiastic letters about Johnny Gurkha (this information is not from my venerable Egeria, Mrs. Tallis, but from the gossip of the last parish council meeting). Also the iniquity of the Indian laws against the native press (there are no press laws and no distinction between native or vernacular and Anglo-Indian publications, and the "Anglo-Indian community" has turned against the Government on that question just because they most properly refused to make any such distinction, but that is a detail which I shall not impart to Charles, as he would not believe a prejudiced official). Also a jeremiad on the wickedness of subsidising land-lords: I believe the landlords in that part of Dampshire happen to be popular. But you will doubtless have a copy of the thing too, with or without official commentary. For my part, I must follow the example of higher Powers by issuing a proclamation of strict neutrality.

Mr. Weekes has negotiated an exchange of duty, to the relief of all parties. I don't much think we shall see him here again.

Tracy is very well and happy, though we cannot

get Merlin to treat him with anything better than dignified acquiescence. Merlin has arrived at the stage of the very holy Brahman who, having fulfilled all his duties as a householder, left a son to maintain the family sacrifices, and mastered all the wisdom of the Upanishads, retires from the world and spends the rest of his life in pure meditation: which, being reduced to terms of canine philosophy, signifies that Merlin has ceased to hunt rabbits, and is almost indifferent to the mention of rats.

If Mrs. Vivian knew anything about Christian art, says the Vicar, she would know that the prevalence of the skull and cross-bones business in churches dates from the Renaissance, rather late in that, and not from the Middle Ages. This, of course, said I, does not alter the fact that any common Athenian stonemason, from the days of Pericles to those of the Antonines (let us say, to be on the safe side), could make a dignified and graceful work of art of a funeral monument, and certainly the average modern sculptor, let alone stonemason, can't. No, says the Vicar, but that is not because he is oppressed by superstitious ideas; it is because he generally has no ideas at all. We agreed that professing and calling oneself a heathen does not suffice to make one an artist; and also, India having taught me to be patient before many mysteries, I submitted to Mr. Follett that we really know next to nothing about the conditions—beyond the obvious ones of available material, adequate skill of handicraft, and a certain superfluity of wealth and leisure—which determine an epoch of great art or good taste. Do we know, by the way, whether the Athenians of the classic age would not have admired, if they had ever had the chance, our inventions which are denounced in their name? Indian princes—able ones too—who live in a splendid harmony of form and colour, the envy of European artists, delight in our musical boxes and childish mechanical toys. So did Italian noblemen in the seventeenth century, as witness Lassels' "Voyage of Italy." And are we not wringing our hands to see the abominations of Brussels and Kidderminster patterns spoiling the design of Asiatic carpets? Bad taste, one fears, is at least as catching as good.

By the way, you have not seen Lassels, at least not my copy: the spoils of Brindisi, where it had drifted somehow to that pleasant little book-shop on the quay where a German couple are delighted to sell you the comic pictures of Munich. I meant to bring it to town, but forgot. "The Voyage of Italy, or a compleat journey through Italy. In Two Parts. With the *Characters* of the *People*, and the Description of the Chief *Towns*, *Churches*, *Monasteries*, *Tombs*, *Libraries*, *Pallaces*, *Villa's*, *Gardens*, *Pictures*, *Statues*, and *Antiquities*. As also of the *Interest*, *Government*, *Riches*, *Force*, &c., of all the *Princes*. With Instructions concerning

Travel. By Richard Lassels, Gent, who Travelled through *Italy* Five times, as Tutor to several of the *English* Nobility and Gentry. Never before Extant. Newly Printed at *Paris*, and are to be sold in *London*, by *John Starkey*, at the *Mitre* in *Fleet-street* near *Temple-Barr*, 1670." An ample title this for a plain squat little book of just under 450 pages. The author was an English Catholic. His highest epithet of praise is " neat ": St. Peter's at Rome, if I remember right, is " exceeding neat." At Florence he heard that there had been such a person as Dante, for he mentions among other famous men whose tombs you may see in the Duomo " Dante the Florentine Poet, whose true Picture is yet to be seen here in a red gown." He seems to have thought that Joannes Acutius, " an English knight and General anciently of the Pisani," ought to have been Sharpe by name, and to have had some difficulty in believing that *Acutius* represents *Hawkwood.* Mr. Lassels was not a very clever man.

What really interested him at Florence was that " by special favour we got the sight of the *Great Dukes fair Diamond,* which he alwayes keeps under lock and key. Its absolutely the fairest in *Europe.* It weigheth 138 *carats*, and its almost an inch thick : and then our Jewellers will tell you what its worth." And wherever Lassels went he was on the look out for such matters as fancy clocks, watches in a walnut-shell, and "wetting sports"—the unexpected fountains which spring up to surprise the unwary visitor in great men's gardens. I have heard that a fine specimen of this Italian jest, which continued in fashion well into the eighteenth century, is extant and in good order at Chatsworth. Why did not the Italian adventurers who left their mark on the domestic architecture and decoration of Indian noblemen introduce "wetting sports" as a regular part of the ornaments that no prince's palace should be without? The princes of the Mogul period would certainly have taken to them. Want of engineering resources, perhaps, though the hydraulics required for that kind of diversion are simple enough.

Jem has been investigating the roads north of London (I think he had some examination or conference at Mill Hill), and sends me a savage growl at the Middlesex County Council for the state in which they leave their roads in those parts. Riding down from Mill Hill to Hendon, he says, is like being tossed in a blanket among sacks full of stones; and the steep places are really almost dangerous, by reason of their roughness, to any one but an experienced rider—not merely "dangerous" in the danger-board sense, which, in the home counties at any rate, means, with very few exceptions, that you can ride down with care in ordinary conditions of weather and surface.

Jem also says that he is pleased with Arthur's promise of scholarship, which he took some little pains to look into. He greatly approves the old Eton plan of letting boys read the classics in considerable masses and acquire a feeling for them as literature, instead of treating them as repertories of linguistic puzzles. There is plenty of time at the University to find out how hard the hard places of easy authors really are. But, Jem says, there are really no easy Latin authors and very few Greek.

I wonder whether Tennyson's "Promise of May" contains a cryptic allusion to May weather. It is strange that the name of that poetic month is conspicuous in the two least good pieces of work he ever did (the other being the May Queen). Mr. Follett remembers Tennyson once saying, a long time ago, that an English summer was like living in an undressed salad. All the neighbours are grumbling at the unseasonable weather. I think of what the sun is now in the desert round Bikanir, and feel like Anson's sailors when they hailed the "chearful gray sky" on the Peruvian coast after a long baking in the south seas.

Your loving brother,
Dickory.

P.S.—I must send you Lassels by post. He will amuse you.

XV.

Miss Elizabeth Etchingham, 83 Hans Place, to Sir Richard Etchingham, Tolcarne.

DEARLY BELOVED DICKORY,

I feel crosser than words can say. So enraged indeed have I become that fortunate for you is it that you are not within reach. I have pent-up grumbles and growls enough to last from to-day till Christmas, and were you here you would think that the state of the stone-deaf was not without compensations. My temper, I find, is not of the kind that improves with keeping, and I make up for persistent self-control by indulging the accumulation of the very spirit that I long resisted. You know how I have preached, if you don't know how I have practised, forbearance with Laura since we came to London. I really have toiled and moiled to throw oil on the troubled family waters, and have found a thousand reasons that don't exist for Charles's lapses in the way of visiting his relations, for—for everything, in short, of which Laura complains. And now, suddenly I see myself wishing to stir up every dormant evil passion and embroil each member of the family. Restraint evidently does not suit my temperament.

I begin to think that you were right in suggesting

that existence with Laura is unworkable. We shall never amalgamate, and you cannot imagine how extraordinarily jealous she is in the pettiest matters. At present, you away, she has fixed upon my relations with Harry as a personal calamity. Harry has reached the point in his falling in love process at which, if he cannot talk to Cynthia, he must talk of her, and, as even the dumb speak when thus bewitched, Harry, who in normal frames of mind is not taciturn, now, whenever the opportunity offers, pours forth a perfect torrent of words on the subject of Cynthia's perfections. Mrs. Vivian now-a-days, or rather now-a-nights, takes Cynthia to and fro pretty often (Cynthia and Blanche have struck up a friendship), and the evenings that Harry and I spend at home he looks upon as hours set apart for the expounding of his hopes and his fears. And here comes Laura's latest and largest grievance. She bitterly resents my sitting below with Harry and his cigarettes after dinner whilst she writes letters in the drawing-room. Why, please, may not I sit with my own brother, or with anybody else's brother, for all that, and not be treated as if I had broken every law, human and divine? It is absurd. If Laura chose to use the sense with which I suppose an indulgent Providence provided her, would not she know that you, Harry, and I must be more to each other than she is to us? But she will not acquiesce.

When first we came to London Harry did not trouble about her one way or the other, but accepted her as he does the stair-carpet—as part of the furnishings of the house, though the stair-carpet happily does not rise up and require of each wanderer who returns a map indicating with Ordnance Survey exactitude the course of his wanderings. But during the last week or two Harry has come to consider Laura the personification of his life's evil. He thinks she means to marry Cynthia to Sir Augustus. And really I don't know that she does not.

Laura, as befits her unimaginative nature, has the greatest possible respect for this world's goods; a "comfortable establishment," massive diamonds in obtrusively solid setting, powdered footmen, and carriage horses, with bearing reins stupidly, cruelly tightened, are all things for which, in her opinion, to give thanks kneeling in church. The crowned peacock crests poised upon the Pampesford-Royal gates, and let into every available stretch of bricks and mortar—Sir Augustus has shown us photographs of Pampesford-Royal—would not bore her or have anything of the ridiculous about them to her eyes. Cynthia is her niece, and her pretty-well penniless niece, and I am by no means sure that, from Laura's standpoint, the marriage is not only desirable, but supremely advantageous. If Cynthia were of Laura's fibre, it might not be wholly disastrous, but

Cynthia, as women are apt to do more or less, inherits her father's temperament, and to Colonel Leagrave loaves and fishes never counted for much. I don't know what to do. The fact that Harry is my brother both drives me on and holds me back. Harry is a poor man, and to marry Harry would be, in the judgment of the vulgar world and all who serve Mammon, a poor marriage. And that thought restrains me when I feel I must go to this motherless Cynthia and tell her that she had better fling her life into the gutter than marry some one for whom she does not care. But then in the case of such an unsophisticated child it seems criminal to stand by and let so mercenary a marriage come to pass. If Harry were not in the running, or were I wholly sure that Cynthia is one of those to whom the things which money-bags cannot pay for are the worth-having things, I would make over my opinion to her forthwith; but as it is, I don't know about bringing pressure to bear? She is open to influence, readier to succumb than to oppose, and my words possibly might carry undue weight. Do please tell me what you think.

I unfolded the story of my own encounters with Sir Augustus to Harry. I thought that the present turn of affairs demanded that I should. At first he laughed loudly, and then, poor fellow, he slid back into gloom, and said in doleful accents, " The ass evidently means to marry."

Sir Augustus at present "waits" upon us (no other word seems to fit the grandiloquent proceeding) with the superfluous regularity of General Leite when, with his suite, he came daily to ask the Duke of Wellington how he had passed the night, even when the Duke's night had been passed in the trenches. And he is received by Laura with a far fuller measure of cordiality than the politeness of the Spanish Commander-in-Chief drew from the Duke.

When I attempt to sound her as to the object of the surplus visitations, she looks mysterious and rings the bell for Blake, with some such excuse as that she needs eau de Cologne, or wishes to change her shoes. You will probably think that it is impossible for Cynthia to accept Sir Augustus, as you only know him as a pompous, middle-aged (or to quote Mrs. Vivian) medieval bore; but I don't know that Cynthia is not young enough and undeveloped enough, morally and mentally, to marry, at Laura's bidding, almost anybody. She thinks Sir Augustus "very good natured." She thinks Harry "very good natured," too. She is right, but it is not good nature that forces Sir Augustus, puffing and panting, up these stairs daily, nor is it good nature, in the ordinary sense of the word, that sends Harry from his soup to the front door if, in answer to Cynthia's inquiries at dinner-time, Turnbull reluctantly admits that Trelawney was seen to go up the area steps, but not to come down them again. I witnessed another instance of Harry's imperturbable good nature yesterday. Instead of keeping an appointment at his club, he held the feathered forms of Blair and Atholl whilst Cynthia, armed with gilded scissors in the form of a stork, shortened the claws of the beloved birds.

Now I have your letter. Thank you for it and for the book. You may disclaim all knowledge of European politics, but the science of conveying your opinion upon the politics of others seems, my dear Richard, within your ken. From the comments accompanying the extracts from Charles's address, I don't somehow fancy that the balance of parties is likely to be changed by our brother's Dampshire exploits.

I wonder if our nineteenth-century handicraft monstrosities will be the curios of the twenty-second century? Time can hardly succeed in making Kidderminster carpets and early Victorian furniture beautiful, but Time may make them quaint. Even the portrait of a provincial mayor, when 300 years have passed over its head, may come to have a certain cachet. I don't think that some of our old Etchinghams of the sixteenth century, grim Sir Nicholas with his thumb in his magnificent chain for example, can have beautified the walls when first hung.

Perhaps at last will be discovered the laws that

govern artistic achievement, and the conditions that help or hinder the sowing, the flowering, and the seed-time of art. What a thing it would be if research enabled the chemists to furnish the London County Council with soil and even climate, congenial to the æsthetic growth. Can soil influence the choice of medium? Pastel should flourish on chalk, water-colour on sand or gravel, and oil on clay, talking nonsense, it seems to me.

Minnie, guided by Mrs. Potters (of whom Harry irreverently speaks as Mrs. Potters' Bar), addressed a Clayshott mothers' meeting, I hear, and spoke to the "mothers," a body of substantial and comfortable women, of the abomination of female out-of-door labour. The worthy mothers were greatly incensed, and met the expression of Minnie's sympathy for women field-workers as would Laura, did Mrs. Vivian include her when commiserating the hardships of washerwomen.

Stephen does not forget, if you do, his wish to visit Tolcarne. He is quite pleasant, and I think that he and Minnie would amuse one another if under your roof at one and the same time. But that is your affair, not mine. Stephen thinks to glean some West country-folk lore from Mr. Follett, some of the legends that dub Sir Francis Drake with a wizardry akin to that with which the Italian peasants endowed Virgil. From me he can get nothing but the well-known superstition that Sir Francis leads the Wild Hunt over Dartmoor, and rises to join in the revels at the beating at Buckland Abbey of the drum he carried round the world. With this old epitaph Stephen's monograph is to close :—

> " Where Drake first found, there last he lost his name,
> And for a tomb left nothing but his fame,
> His body's buried under some great wave,
> The sea that was his glory is his grave."

Now Alice Newton has fallen ill, and your friend Mr. Shipley is unhappy about her. Colonel Newton so far has not realized that wailing robes with reason might be donned. I felt sure that she would collapse. She was always a fugitive creature, and of late she has looked intangible as one of Maeterlinck's dream-women. She said to me the other day, "You see, one can be dead and be still going about and people don't know that one is dead. That is the curious part of it." Her old nurse, who was the child's nurse too, appeared when I went to see Alice yesterday, and, though I tried to stop her, she persisted, undeterred by Mr. Shipley's presence, in telling me of Alice's misery since the child died. "Mrs. Newton, M'm, she would come wandering up into the room that was the day-nursery, at three and four o'clock in the morning, and walk up and down and cry by the hour. No health could stand such goings on." Mr. Shipley is devoted to his sister, and I am very sorry for him. When you come to London you must hold out the hand of friendship to him. He asks for Tolcarne news frequently.

Would you welcome a copy of Willughby's Birds—"The Ornithology of Francis Willughby of Middleton in the County of Warwick, Esq."— the text in English, London, 1678? Laura met me the other evening on the doorstep with the book under my arm. I saw it lying in a dim, dusty shop to which I repaired in search of something else, and I had not the heart to leave it. Laura hates old books, looking upon them but as dust-catchers and germ-carriers. When reigning at Tolcarne she put John Florio into a room with a sulphur candle, to my intense indignation. (Poor John Florio to be disinfected at this time of day.) The Willughby is hardly a pocket-volume, and I could not conceal it, as, to save an argument, I would have done. "What in the world is the use of such a book to you, Elizabeth?" Laura inquired. "I shall give it to Richard," I said ; so don't turn me into a liar by refusing it. The Willughby will be happier at Tolcarne than in Hans Place.

Publication brings strange shelf-fellows, I thought, as I glanced at the books in our bookcase this morning. Laura's Marie Corelli, Edna Lyall and then Herrick, and Catullus all in a row. If contrast is attractive, Maeterlinck and Dr. Johnson, cheek by jowl, as we have them here, are desirable. (Dr. Johnson: "Sir, you are a fool." Maeterlinck: "I am not happy. I am not happy.") For myself, as in the long run I prefer a chime to a clash, a harmony to a discord, I have half a mind to carry Maeterlinck to Mr. Vivian presently. Mr. Vivian (a figure of silence not of speech, to quote his wife) buys a Burne-Jones whenever he can get one. When Burne-Jones is on the wall Maeterlinck should be in the book-case. Do invent a conversation between M. Maeterlinck and Dr. Johnson, and mention too what M. Maeterlinck would say to a Hogarth, and Dr. Johnson to a Burne-Jones.

Now, good-bye. I have rather written out my evil temper and no longer feel that everyone is trying to beat the record of his or her past trouble-someness. I begin to reproach myself also for my denunciation of Laura. However, it shall go (there is nothing like a remorse for paring down ill-temper to reasonable dimensions), and please don't be a hundred years answering. I am impatient to hear what you think about the Harry-Cynthia-Laura-Sir Augustus affair. I am rather inclined to expect the worst—Cynthia being a childish creature, used to authority, and of the stuff of which victims are made, whilst Laura, in her quiet way, is obstinate as the Pope's mule. Sometimes I wish that Harry would propose to Cynthia, and have done with it. But he thinks by so doing he might lose the little he has got.

I don't, as you see, know what to say or to leave unsaid, and don't agree with myself for five minutes consecutively.   I shall try and reduce my thoughts to order by reading your little old book.   Laura dines with Mrs. Carstairs to-night.   Harry is bidden somewhere whither Mrs. Vivian is conveying Cynthia.   Sir Augustus is decorating with his presence a Primrose League Entertainment, so the family and the family's adjunct are happily disposed of, and I shall spend the evening with Trelawney and "The Voyage of Italy."

Your obedient servant, your loving sister,

ELIZABETH.

XVI.

Sir Richard Etchingham to Miss Elizabeth Etchingham.

MY DEAR ELIZABETH,

You shall have a short and prompt answer for once.   Why can't you send Cynthia here along with Stephen?   It would put her out of harm's way for a while at any rate, and give you time and occasions to test your conjectures.

This is sickening stuff about poor marriages. What had Maggie and I before we married, and what had we not afterwards?——There—you know there are some things I cannot put on paper even to you.

Don't be worried out of your evening sessions with Harry, whatever you do ; and be firm. The head of the family is with you for whatever that office is worth in this present *Kali Yug.*

Yours ever,

R. E.

XVII.

From Lady Etchingham, 83 Hans Place, to Sir Richard Etchingham, Tolcarne.

MY DEAR RICHARD,

I have not seen your letter, but I understand from Elizabeth that you have kindly invited Cynthia to Tolcarne for Whitsuntide.

I am sure that Cynthia would be very pleased to be with Margaret, but I am afraid that I do not quite see how it can be managed just at present. Elizabeth, who has been very much taken up with Mrs. Newton lately, proposes, I now suddenly hear, to start off with her to the sea for a few days next week. You know what Elizabeth is when she takes people up violently, and how impulsive. Mr. Shipley, Mrs. Newton's brother, called last evening to say that the doctors suggest change of air for Mrs. Newton, whose health has been, I believe, very unsatisfactory lately from insomnia and nervous exhaustion, and would Elizabeth be persuaded to go too, as his sister had an invalid's fancy to have Elizabeth with her. I do not myself see the need, as if Mrs. Newton does not consider her husband sufficient escort, there is a sister-in-law—a Mrs. Ware—quite willing to be of use and accustomed to illness. I remember her telling me the first time I met her that Mr. Ware had been completely paralysed for five years before he died. Also, as I told Elizabeth, I think it quite possible that Mr. Shipley just suggested her accompanying Mrs. Newton, thinking she might enjoy the trip. She often speaks of her dislike of London, which is, I think, a mistake. Mrs. Newton, I fear, is on the verge of melancholia, and would really be best left with her husband, who no doubt understands her temperament.

If Elizabeth is to be away for several days with her friend, I feel quite sure that Cynthia would not consent to leave me wholly alone, much as I should like her to have the pleasure of a visit to Tolcarne. My eyes have troubled me a good deal lately, and I have rheumatic gout in my hands (from weakness, Dr. Bowles says), and to sit alone, unoccupied, though I am willing to undergo it if Elizabeth thinks it will amuse her to be with Mrs. Newton, is not, I know, what others would choose for me. I really quite think also that for Cynthia's own sake it is better for her to remain quietly at home till the weather is more settled. You have had heavy rains I hear

from Mrs. Follitt, and dear Tolcarne, of course,
is damp. I always considered the roof faulty.
Hoping you have had no recurrence of your old
attacks, and with love to Margaret and yourself,
Believe me,
Affectionately yours,
LAURA F. ETCHINGHAM.

XVIII.

*From Miss Elizabeth Etchingham to Sir Richard
Etchingham.*

DEAREST DICKORY,

Thanks very much for your letter. It
was just exactly what I wanted, and it has stiffened
me. Cynthia would be perfectly content at Tolcarne
with Margaret and Stephen, and he and she can
travel down together. I will propose it at once,
and I should hardly think that Laura's hard-
worked team of phantom lions could be trotted out
to block this path.

I am summoned to the drawing-room, and
rumour reports Mr. Shipley's arrival with a message
from Alice. So here endeth this epistle.
Yours,
ELIZABETH.

P.S.—Send me a supplementary letter soon, and
in it wrap up a recipe for patience and a right
judgment in all things.

XIX.

Sir Richard Etchingham to Miss Elizabeth Etchingham.

My dear Elizabeth,

Let a pleasant thing come first. I shall be delighted to have Willughby's Birds; the rather that I had almost forgotten what home birds are like. Did I ever tell you that among the great Akbar's accomplishments was a lively interest in the natural history of Hindustan? The work of encyclopædic Indian statistics (or as near statistics as Asiatic scribes could get) compiled under his charge includes elaborate figures of Indian plants. I wish the ingenious Mr. Traill would add a dialogue between Elizabeth and Akbar, wherever they ought to be, to his "New Lucian." Akbar deserves to be in the eagle's eye in the sphere of Jupiter, whether Dante's principles could make room for him there or not. I am not so sure about Elizabeth. Akbar could have taught her not to scamp the supplies of stores and ammunition to her fleet. If ever the Government of India gets a piping time of peace before the coming of the Cocqcigrues, there ought to be an adequate life of Akbar produced by a combination of European and Indian scholarship. He wanted, like Frederick II. some centuries earlier, to do more than was possible for any one man, including the foundation of a universal religion.   But he was a magnificently ambitious prince, and his peccadillos were trifling as the sins of Eastern despots go.   There should also be a great publication of his architecture at Fatehpur-Sikri, that city of palaces which stands to this day deserted, but not ruined.   It is more impressive in some ways than any of the show monuments of Delhi or Agra.   Some publication there has been, but with the curious shyness of official publications, almost amounting to concealment.   I want a monumental work, more like what the French would do if they were in our place.

The British public does not appreciate the "New Lucian," I fear, perhaps never will.   Mr. Traill's humour is too subtle for the general.   But there will always be a select number to delight in it.   His work, if it is not so brilliant as Landor's, is free from Landor's prejudices and crankiness, and the violent disproportions introduced by them into Landor's Imaginary Conversations; and sometimes it rises to a note of historic tragedy, as in the dialogue between Alexander II. and Peter the Great.   If you ever meet with the comments of the Canaanitish press on the Exodus —written by Traill before the outbreak of the Russo-Turkish war in 1876—grapple those few leaves without fail.   But you won't, for it has become one of the really scarce pamphlets of our time, and I doubt if it is to be had for money.

Sir Augustus's proceedings are very dark to me. There is nothing impossible in a vulgar ambitious man being captivated by a fresh pretty face ; and yet I fancy somehow that his ambition is more calculating, and can hardly conceive that ruling passion being dethroned. Watch, I say again, and keep Harry out of despondency if you can. Cynthia is unformed, and may change her mind once and again before she fixes it ; I cherish hopes that the final direction may be right.

Stephen Leagrave has settled to come here next week, with a quite neat and official disquisition on Secondary Education thrown in. Charles may tackle him on that subject if he likes, and give the Clayshott electors the benefit of the result. It will be about as useful and intelligible to them as the other matters Charles is committing himself to in his address. Here come by the same post your note, and a gushing billet from Minnie, omitting to specify the date of arrival, for which I particularly asked, so there will most likely be a morning of telegraphing ; and a letter from Laura, who is verily of the tribe of the Dúzakhís, if odious virtues ever made anyone so ; I enclose it for your edification. You see she is too many for us as regards my little plan about Cynthia. She carefully misspells Mrs. Follett's name. If there is a thing I detest it is misspelt names.

I have had to explain to several people that Wei-hai-wei is not in the sphere of the Indian Political Department, and that a smoking acquaintance with cheroots does not make one an authority on Manila. But my comparative study of the Parish and the North Indian Village is going to be a great work.

Your loving brother,
RICHARD.

XX.

From Miss Elizabeth Etchingham, 83 Hans Place, to Sir Richard Etchingham, Tolcarne.

DEAREST DICKORY,

Cynthia has refused Harry, Trelawney is lost, and Sir Augustus has gone away to bury a relation. If Niobe left a recipe for preserving furniture from mildew, please send it. We are very damp here. Had Trelawney not strayed, there might now be no new misadventure to report; but Trelawney left his family on Monday, and has not since been seen or heard of. Wherefore what follows.

This not being the first time that Trelawney has absented himself, Cynthia, till this morning, buoyed herself up with hopes of his return. This morning, however, Blake, with her race's love for harrowing, went to Cynthia with a chapter of cat accidents, derived from the milkman—kidnappings, poisonings, &c.—the scene of every one of these catastrophes being this neighbourhood, the time the present. Cynthia carried the depressing intelligence about with some stoicism for an hour or two, and then, suddenly succumbing, wept. Harry, like you, has no armour against tears, and Cynthia smiling having of late disturbed his equanimity, Cynthia weeping was altogether too much for the poor fellow. From offering consolation and seeking to inspire hope, he went on to tell the story of his heart ; and presently he came to my room, looking sad enough and white enough to frighten me. (Of course, before he spoke my thoughts suggested a telegram with bad news from Tolcarne. I always think that something will happen to you, because it would obliterate me if it did.) Harry, blaming and banning himself the while, then begged me to go to Cynthia, who was crying, he said, in the drawing-room, and whom he had frightened, "clumsy boor" that he was.

Until I beheld Cynthia I felt almost angry with her as the cause of Harry's distress ; but no sooner had I seen the creature's scared, woebegone aspect than I found myself commiserating her almost as much as I commiserated Harry. She clung to me, weeping, and said, as well as she could for her tears, that she was very horrid, she knew ; that we should all hate her ; that Major Etchingham was

very kind, but—but she did not want to be married.
With this pretty, absurdly pathetic-looking child
clinging to me as if I were a rock of defence, my
sympathies were equally divided; and, while I
was doing my best to quiet and reassure her, in
walked Laura—come to see if the blinds were
drawn down, lest the sun should injure the
furniture.

(It was long since proved to me that the Fates
were humourists. Of late I have suspected that
these ladies are not only humourists, but practical
jokers.)

When Cynthia looked up and saw Laura she
instantly took to flight, and left me to tackle our
stepmother single-handed; and Laura straightway,
in frigid tones, inquired if it would be an imper-
tinence to ask the cause of Cynthia's emotion.
"Of course, I have no wish to force anyone's confidence, or to come between you and my niece."
As Cynthia is not only Laura's niece, but her
ward, and as Harry is my brother, I considered
Laura entitled to an explanation. In another
very few minutes I wished that my temper were
sweeter; and in still another very few minutes I
wished my *de profundis* wish—that you were
present. Laura can be perfectly detestable; and
I am not one of those to whom the inheritance
of the earth is promised. At this juncture
whom should Turnbull, suddenly jerking open
the door, announce but Mrs. Vivian, who flitted

in with her charming smile and air of graceful well-being.

"Oh, Lady Etchingham, I did not know that you ever appeared upon the scene so early," was the propitious beginning. "I came to see Elizabeth about——" (the boarding out of London children at Vivian-End). It was as if the Mother of Mischief were prompting Mrs. Vivian's chatter. In response to Laura's statement that however far from well she might feel she considered it her duty to take her place in the house, Mrs. Vivian airily recommended her to try Christian Science for her ailments. "I think you might like it very much. Don't you think, Elizabeth, that Lady Etchingham might be very much amused by Christian Science ? It's not half so nasty as the Salisbury beef cure nor so dangerous as German baths. Lady Clementine Mure says it's done wonders for her, and she means to stick to it, and not try the new fresh air treatment. Not that Lady Clementine had anything but *malade imaginaire*ism the matter, and as Hugo Ennismore says of Christian Science, imagination cures what imagination creates. (I think you would like Hugo Ennismore, Elizabeth ; he is thought clever.) Then there was Tessy Graham-Gordon, who lay upon her back for two years and would not see a soul, and now she cycles twenty miles a day and takes fencing lessons. I always said if that poor unfortunate husband of hers, who is so weak as to be

almost wanting, had only had the strength of mind
to set the house on fire it would have got her off
her sofa before. But Christian Science did equally
well, and made far less mess than deluges of water
and flames and firemen's dreadful heavy boots
trampling over everything. Do give it a trial. It
is sure to do your nerves good if it does not drive
you mad."

"Dr. Bowles considers that my nerves have
stood the strain to which they have been subjected
peculiarly well," Laura answered, in her North
Pole voice. After half an hour of this and other
equally pacific matter, it seemed prudent to leave
the room when Mrs. Vivian did; and having seen
her off the premises I sought out Harry, whose
dejected looks haunted me. I hope I succeeded
at last in convincing him that Cynthia's health
and happiness are not permanently blasted by an
offer of marriage from a good man. He was very
grateful for nothing, but very sad. "Send somebody out to look for that brute of a cat: it is all
she cares for," were his final words. I dared to
say that perhaps it was not all that she would ever
care for, and poor Harry patted me on the head
and departed with a sigh. (What I write is, as
usual, for you only; for you who, in the matter of
confidences, are a *cul-de-sac*.)

The disquieting Cynthia I think had best take
advantage now of Mrs. Gainsworthy's invitation,
and stay at Oxbridge till we go north. As to that

letter of Laura's which you return, I believe pique prompted it. Why invite Cynthia to Tolcarne and not herself? Between you and me it is safe to ask her. She wishes to be asked, but she does not wish to go. I am very sorry that my possible absence next week afforded an excuse for keeping Cynthia here to play companion. But if Alice Newton wished for me I would not refuse. Long ago, soon after she was married, when once she was very low and wretched, she made me promise that I would always befriend her if I could. I can be of no real use, but for a greater thing than a whim of Laura's I am not disposed to say " No " to Alice, who is unhappy and ill. Yes, would not Mrs. Ware, who related every particular of her husband's fatal illness on the occasion of her first meeting with Laura, be a congenial companion to some one who is bruised? As it turns out, Alice is too ill to go anywhere. I visited her this morning and found Colonel Newton fussing and fuming, and not in the least amused by a charge in a solicitor's bill—" rectifying error caused by our own carelessness, 13s. 4d."

After the commotion of the day I went in search of a sedative to St. Paul's Cathedral. Evensong and anthem, as every afternoon of the week given there, are the best nepenthe I have yet discovered in this vast kingdom of London. And then at St. Paul's Cathedral we do not see half the people we know crowned with their best bonnets, and best bonnets and the Confession never somehow seem to agree. (Mrs. Vivian says that while she can imagine the Apostle Peter admitting a beggar to the precincts of Heaven, "I can't quite see him letting in Lady Etchingham in her Sunday get-up.") But the patterning of St. Paul's is disturbing. There is rest and relief to my eyes after the plague of patterns from which we suffer in the cold, white bareness, unfretted by device or design, and I trust that this superfluous patterning will not encroach very far. For an understanding of the value of blank spaces, we look, as a rule, in vain to the art of the West. It is realised in Japanese art. Also where patterns are, there the full play of light and shade is not; and to turn from St. Paul's Cathedral and from the art of Japan to dwelling-house decoration, the shadow of flowering bough or foliage thrown upon homely whitewash is beautiful, but throw the shadow upon a patterned surface, and however fine the fabric, the beauty of the shadow line is lost. Do you go with me in preferring whitewash to the meaningless scrawls and imitation anythings with which walls are often hung?

I heard from our cousin, Arthur Etchingham, by the last mail. He is very hot and rather depressed, poor man. The Bombay winds have been all wrong, and the winds they have a right to expect to come off the sea have never come—a condition of things bad for man, beast, and temper, he says. The prayer for the plague has been used, he tells me, in the Bombay churches for the last six months. "If you look at it you will see how futile it sounds on an occasion like this, and like an attempt to appease one of the hundred-armed Hindoo avenging deities. Don't you think that parsons should adapt themselves more to the times?" The letter breathes carbolic, and Arthur is homesick, I fear. He speaks of the parks and of the flower-beds "which are such feasts for Indian eyes after years in this country." If I had my wishing-carpet, I would spirit Arthur back. "Tell Richard to bring you and Margaret out for the next cold weather," he says. "Oh, that 'twere possible" after being pent up here with poor Laura to go ever so far away. I wonder if you too sometimes feel an acute desire to hurry to the further side of space and see nothing for a hundred years that you have yet set eyes on?

Mr. Traill would not, I imagine, covet the British public's appreciation of "The New Lucian." When I tried Laura with "The New Lucian," she said, "Where is the joke? Is it meant to be humorous?" To continue my researches into the recesses of the human mind I then plied her with a translated extract from "The Sale of the Philosophers," but when she interrupted the reading to suggest gravely that probably the chronic weeping of Heraclitus arose from inflammation of the tear-duct—she had suffered from it herself, and it was very troublesome and difficult to cure—I thought we had gone far enough.

Let me hear the tale of Charles's and Minnie's visit. The weather will, I hope, permit of the airing of theories out of doors. To be shut up with adverse opinions makes a long day. Has Minnie, as she threatened, asked your leave to dedicate her new novel to you? She says that your encouragement has been such a great help to her in her writing. The title of the novel, on the dedication page of which she proposes to print your name, is "A Tribute of Tears." When she told me that you had encouraged her to write, I felt disposed to say, "Richard is too wise to encourage a woman to do anything." In Minnie's absence and by her leave, I repair rather often to Lower Berkeley Street and sit in the nursery with the small boys. And here is Dicky's description of his first flash of lightning and first thunder clap: "I saw an angel go into Heaven, and bang the door after it." (Mrs. Vivian says, "The child never said anything of the sort. It's just one of Minnie's second rate literary ideas.")

It is very, very late. "The time of night when

Troy was set on fire," and I am cold and tired.
So good-bye for now.

Your loving sister,

ST. ELIZABETH (not of Hungary, not
of Portugal, but of Hans Place).

Not your saint, your sinner.

Thursday morning.—I open my letter to tell
you that Trelawney has just sauntered in with
an air of perfect unconcern. It was Turnbull,
not Harry, alas, who opened the door to him.

XXI.

*From Sir Richard Etchingham, Tolcarne, to Miss
Elizabeth Etchingham.*

DEAR AND MUCH TRIED LADY SISTER,

She is a little goose ; little, because her
age gives her the privilege of that mild and
endearing diminutive ; if she were five years
older she would be a great goose. If she likes
no one else better—and I see nothing to show that
she does—it may come right yet, with patience
and leaving alone. Acting on your hint, I have
sent an invitation in due form to Laura. If she
accepts, I must invent some new form of the old
Eton " Friday fever," when Friday was the heavy
day of the week, with every one from sixth form
to lower division (*i.e.* of fifth form) doing the same

seventy lines of Horace : and there was something in that old fashion of taking our classics in good lumps, as I think I said on some occasion a while ago. But, as you wisely observe, Laura will not accept. I should like to see her try "Christian Science," of which the Christianity is even more obscure to me than the science. I understand it to consist in believing very hard that there is nothing the matter with you ; and when there is nothing the matter, as is often the case with people who have nothing else to do, I do not doubt it may be an excellent way.

Also part of their scheme is to believe that matter is nothing, a doctrine of which the Christian Scientists appear to suppose themselves the first inventors—they are only some few thousand years late. This may seem, if it could prove anything for their purpose, to prove too much. For if your body is nothing real, then health and sickness are alike illusions, and an ache more or less in your tooth or your stomach is merely indifferent, and it is not worth while to be well even if it is to cost you no more than the pains of thinking so. And so forth in an ever-increasing tangle of absurd consequences, if you begin to converse with such folk according to the folly they have confounded with a little bad science and a little even worse philosophy. Speculation about the remote or ultimate nature of things really makes no difference at all to actual experience. Stones, and my head, and gravity, may be all illusions in some sense. All the same, a man who does not desire the illusion of breaking his head will keep up the illusion of not falling on stones. But Lord! to think of the patronising contempt the smallest Yogi would pour on these pale, far-off imitations of the old, old Eastern tricks! And of our bishops confronting Shiva with their polite and reasonable Anglican prayers! The doctors seem to have all their work to do to stand up to him.

Our enlightened brother Charles and Stephen Leagrave are dosing me with the latest wisdom of the West. The very night of their arrival Charles went off on the iniquity of voluntary schools (there being no Board school at Clayshott, and not the least demand for one), and Stephen gave us a lecture of an hour and a half on Secondary Education. Margaret nobly came to the rescue by insisting that the whole Education Department and all the electors of the Clayshott division should not deprive her of her revenge on me at piquet. We find it a fascinating game: it seems more human than whist. I could never rise to the height of the men who can play a good hand at whist in the Red Sea, with a following breeze that makes a dead calm on the ship, and the thermometer steady at 90°. When I say more human, I mean that one gets a more faithful image of life in the alternation of elder and younger hand, in the power of the lead to dominate the adversary's cards, and in the chance of taking the tide at the flood and making one's fortune by a judicious discard. I believe, by the book, in very bold discarding; our practice, I suspect, would be considered feeble and pottering by good players. Then piquet is adventurous, as whist is not, and as life can be in the East at any rate, and used to be before John Company came sweeping and garnishing and stickling, Mrs. Battle's way, for a clean hearth and the rigour of the game. What is there in whist to come near the emotion of a repique, or the fearful joys of manœuvring to save a capot? On the subject of whitewash I partly sympathise with you; but I have had a dose of orthodox æsthetics too, and am crushed.

Leagrave is what they call a good fellow, but I fail to get any satisfaction from him. He is educated: doth he not serve My Lords who educate us? and they can pick and choose their servants among the best University men. He is trained and able; he can write a neat and perspicuous minute. He is always ready when wanted, never at a loss for something to say, and what he says is mostly appropriate and never absurd; good-tempered, an easy companion, altogether a desirable and safe member of a party or an excursion; active enough too, short of competing with younger men. I believe he has done some respectable mountaineering within the last few seasons. And yet I find myself asking, Where is the real man?

or even, Is there any real man? There is something he wants ; perhaps, morally and figuratively speaking, it is a good shaking. If, now, he had been sent to hunt dacoits in Burma instead of analysing school returns, or whatever else he does in Whitehall, he might have grown in some directions. Or if it should occur to a young woman to think him a real man, perhaps, on the principle of your Christian Scientists, it might make him so. But then I don't see how, at best, it could make him more real than the young woman herself; and I should hardly expect the young woman who takes a fancy to Master Stephen to be of the most real sort.

Meanwhile, our neighbour Square (not old Mr. Square, but his son, who is active in promoting local good works) had got wind somehow of Leagrave being a man of letters, and caught him to give a lecture on English poetry at the Little Buckland Working Men's Club. Charles pleaded multitude of correspondence and arranging meetings in Dampshire—when he leaves this it is for the final campaign—and Minnie could do no less than stay to help him. So Margaret and Leagrave and I jumbled down to the fat pastures of Little Buckland, which we half envy and half despise, and Leagrave held forth in the orthodox modern manner on modern poets. He left one the impression, though he never said so, that Wordsworth is antediluvian, Tennyson obsolete, Browning uncouth, and the history practically begins, for this generation, with Rossetti, being continued even unto—Mr. Biggleswade, of whom he spoke with apparently sincere respect. The only thing the audience seemed to care for was a piece of Kipling, which he introduced in a sort of rather deprecating way, as if not sure whether it was good form or not (by the way, I am bound to say he reads well enough). Most of it was received with a respectful desire for instruction, and assumption that what he said must be all right: and those who preach week-day sermons surely need not complain of being treated no worse than the parson. What really bored them, being, then and there, entirely puzzling to them, was a passage he had evidently taken special pains with, about Omar Khayyám and Orientalism, and the reactions of Eastern and Western mind. I listened with a grim inward chuckle, knowing that the young man's father, the Colonel, who does not pretend to be literary, could have told him, if he had the wit to avow his ignorance and ask, some things a good deal more to the point on that subject.

And so vote of thanks to lecturer for most interesting lecture, to worthy chairman for presiding (they had made me take the chair), and our party back up the hill, feeling virtuous and rather empty. Leagrave wanted to convert us to some of his new little poets—must we not admit a delicately fervent passion in Huiteau Ledache's ballads? "Margaret," said I, "what was that opinion somebody gave us of Huiteau Ledache? I never read him." "Oh yes," answered Margaret, with a shade of hesitation, "was it Jem? No, it was Mr. Shipley. He said the creature was fit— yes, just fit to put in Rudyard Kipling's pipe, and bad tobacco at that." Leagrave tried an attack at another point by claiming recognition—an adequate though not extravagant recognition—for the speculative charm of Exon Versine and the intellectual frankness of Biggleswade, his latest "Omarians." This was too much. "They have not enough stuff among them," I protested, "to make a clout for the left shoe of old FitzGerald, whom your father and I knew by heart in India before they were born." So Stephen Leagrave and I don't agree on the most modern poets: we don't quarrel, neither, for he is well bred.

Charles, for all I can see, is organising a certain defeat for himself, but I know nothing of election tactics.

Your loving brother,
RICHARD.

P.S.—You may discount what I have been saying about Stephen L. to any reasonable extent. Strike off from twenty to thirty per cent. if you like. The confident polish of the home official has a peculiar effect in rubbing us old Indians the wrong way. Stephen is a scholar, and not pig-headed when you reason with him. I have just made him admit that one of Tennyson's later minor poems, a pretty late one, which I fancy the general public never cared for, is as absolute a piece of workmanship as can be found in any modern author for language, verse, and felicity, and that no other man could have done it. Now guess which it is, and you may take three guesses.

R. E.

XXII.

From Miss Elizabeth Etchingham, 83 Hans Place, to Sir Richard Etchingham, Tolcarne.

Good morning, Dickory. How do you find yourself to-day? Well, I trust. You need never trouble to be ill, thank you. Illness is a grave fault and one it would go against my conscience to tolerate in you for a moment unless it gave me the chance of keeping my hand in as sick nurse. And of me in that capacity you had best beware. I should treat you very harshly, forcing a new-old book upon you every day and refusing, without consulting the patient, all garden-party invitations that the Bucklands might afford. Ordination only should compel male attendance at a garden-party. Have you ever noticed the sown broadcast smile —pathetic almost in its want of focus and concentration—which the typical clergy assume at a garden-party?

Why are tiresome Mrs. Mammon people even yet more tiresome and impossible when under a tree than when under a roof? Is failure to adjust themselves to environment at the root of it? And does a garden full of women in garden-party attire vaguely expressing admiration for their hostess's shrubberies and flower-beds make you long to hybernate? It does me. First Person Represented: "What a charming effect: pink geranium and white viola. I wish my gardener, &c., &c." Second Person Represented (languidly and with eyes at the back of her head, as otherwise the charming effect has not come into her line of vision): "Very, very charming. Mrs. Bowanbore has such exquisite taste. Everything is so perfectly kept. (With sudden vivacity) Oh, Mrs. Bowan-bore, we were just saying, &c., &c." Richard, how deadly, deadly dull to hear people applaud what they don't admire. Please I will fall asleep and dream of something real till they have quite done.

Would you have me try Christian Science upon Laura's huffs or upon her rheumatic gout—which, however, she now says is not rheumatic gout at all but neuritis—"A far more likely complaint for me to suffer from, Elizabeth, after all this strain." I don't think Christian Science moves huffy temper. The prefacing formula of huffy folk is "I am not annoyed, but still——" The persistent disavowal of annoyance according to Christian Science doctrine should dispel it, whilst in reality the disavowal seems to feed the distemper. Mrs. Vivian's friend, Lady Clementine Mure, has, I admit, bettered her state by conversion. A forlorn, kind, backboneless creature of the sort only comfortable under a despotic form of government, after that very decisive and slightly tyrannical Mr. Mure died she drifted aimlessly till a Christian Scientist took her in tow. When her husband had no further use for her services she was thrown out of work, poor soul. (Maud Mure carries the rebutting of her mother's good offices to the point of seeming to resent Lady Clementine's existence.) And what excuse in the way of vagaries and depression of spirit is not to be made for the unemployed? The old divine who said he had known a man come home in high spirits from a funeral merely because he had had the management of it, had the rare gift of seeing cause and effect. A fanatical *culte* is essential to the happiness of women like Lady Clementine. Those of her type and of an earlier generation found comfort, I imagine, in sitting under Evangelical clergymen and strewing tracts on the efficacy of prayer in paltry mundane matters. (How aggressively determined to have their own way with Fate some folk are.) For the derivation of the term Christian Science, I give you Mrs. Vivian's explanation: "They call it Christian Science though it's neither scientific nor Christian, because two negatives make an affirmative."

But now to business. You were always obliging, and may I ask you to do just one commission for me? Box your own ears, dear (not brutally). That postscript to your last letter can't go unpunished. Had you told me to guess by word of mouth and while I could drag the riddle's solution from you after five minutes' suspense, I should have looked upon it as a trial of patience. But to be told by post to guess, and left for days to seethe in torment-ing perplexity, I could not have believed it of you, and the deed throws a new and lurid light upon your character. And to treat me so, for whom you profess a very especial kindness. Heaven defend those whom you do not pretend to favour. That they may die before they meet you will be my prayer. And the expense, too, to which you put me. We have no Tennyson here, and curiosity drove me to the bookseller and brought me back again the richer by a fat emerald-green volume, and the poorer by *7s. 6d.* Refund the money, please. Not that I meant to guess. Canny folk, like your sister, not only never sign anonymous letters, but never guess without sufficient evidence for the forming of a correct opinion. It was Goethe, I believe, who said that women have very weak ideas about poetry and think of nothing but the feelings and the words and the verses. I would not for the world put the dead in the wrong—an even baser treachery than speaking ill of the dead—and I should be sorry for Goethe's verdict to find itself challenged by any brilliant poetical criticism of mine. So take notice that I offer what comes as proof, not confutation, of Goethe's dictum.

The Tennyson poems, latterly published, that I think I like best are, the "Hymn to the Sun," with which ends "Akbar's Dream" (write a life of your friend Akbar yourself), "Silent Voices," and "Early Spring." Don't you think the "Hymn to the Sun" exquisite? It seems to me born, not made, and excellence of workmanship or workmanship at all is not suggested by it. If we can separate the thought and the phrase, has not phrasing failed to go as far as felicity of phrasing can? The two should be indissoluble—the word the only complete manifestation of the thought ; as a snowdrop can be only manifested in the form of a snowdrop, a rose in the form of a rose.

On Stephen's return to London I will preach the Gospel of Wordsworth, Coleridge's "Friend of the wise and teacher of the good." I may not get Stephen to endorse Matthew Arnold's eulogy, but I will make him admit here and there a measure of beauty which brings Wordsworth near Shakespeare. There is one thing, though, for which I don't forgive Wordsworth. The sonnet—"Why art Thou Silent," that enshrines the lovely imagery of "a forsaken bird's nest filled with snow," should come from a man to a woman, or a woman to a man. Not from man to—I suppose—Coleridge.

But who can throw a stone at Stephen if he has passed Wordsworth by? The days don't grow longer, and the roll of poet names does. Further than ever removed are the times "When all found readers who could find a rhyme." Paid readers will soon be a necessity and Mæcenas will subsidise his *protégé*, not to produce verse, but to read his patron's. As to quality, for another Golden Age of Literature shall we have to wait for another Age of Calamity? Does the Tree of Letters need a winter, a black frost, a severe check, a stern repression? The reign of Mary came before the reign of Elizabeth. The triumphal Elizabethan days followed the days of persecution, which drove many scholars out of the kingdom and made the pursuit of learning dangerous to those at home. Were a law passed making death the punishment of publication, or even composition, on the law's repeal—perhaps sooner—we might again get something supremely poetic.

Stephen improves on acquaintance, and it looks as if a very real young woman, Blanche Vivian, takes sufficient interest in him to shake him into activity. Blanche is delightful—frank and unaffected as a pleasant boy, and yet not a hoyden. I can't agree with Mrs. Carstairs in her condemnation of the young girl of the present day and her pastimes. I would rather see, as more hygienic, time spent in cycling and playing hockey than spent in painting china tiles and playing the piano—sheer waste of energy when there is no prospect of excelling in paint-box or piano work.

To return to Stephen, his *fainéant* manner is, I think, a pose, and he schools himself to in-difference. He does not lack grit, and if some pretty stories cherished by Colonel Leagrave of his school days tell truly, he has pluck enough to be no disgrace to his "for valour" decorated father. And I like his courtesy. "Know, dear brother, that Courtesy is one of the qualities of God Himself, who, of His Courtesy giveth His sun and His rain to the just and the unjust; and Courtesy is the sister of Charity, the which quencheth hate and keepeth love alive."

While looking into Maeterlinck I was reminded by his chapter on silence of the story given in the "Fioretti," of King Louis and Brother Giles. When King Louis met Brother Giles the two spoke not the one to the other, but knelt down and embraced with "signs of love and tenderness." And when the Brothers upbraided Brother Giles for discourtesy in having refrained from good words, he answered that looking on each other's hearts they read each other far better than had they spoken with their mouths, and sought with the weakness of human speech to show forth the feelings of the heart. But in what Maeterlinck says of silence, etiquette and habit have to be taken into account. I dare to be silent whilst watching Enticknap's potting operations, nor feel as if without a frantic wrench and speedy flight by the vehicle of speech we should find ourselves on the threshold of "the great kingdom of the dead," or a realm mystic as Omar Khayyám verse. Possibly though, Enticknap on such occasions is not equally unmoved, and, in his queer guttural sounds and half-articulate expression of disgust at the cussedness of things, we have his efforts to escape from the uncanniness fast closing him in.

Do you know Archbishop Secker's first rule of conversation—silence?

Colonel Newton is making his cure at Carlsbad, and I can't help wishing he might continue the process till the end of the chapter. Alice, unmolested, has gathered herself together more or less. She mobilised her forces sufficiently to dine with us last night. She still looks young, and she still looks as if it were possible that life might have something better to give her than the power of enduring distress. Mr. Shipley, for the time being, has taken up his abode with her, and the plan works well. I think she would be glad for him to marry, although his marriage would take him from her to a certain extent. The other day she was saying that she wished he might find himself a wife if only he found the right woman—

"someone who would care for him most for what is best in him, though his merits might interfere with social success and the amassing of riches." Alice admires excellence—admires it far more than she admires the diamonds with which Colonel Newton, when first they were married, stored an iron safe of dungeon-like proportions. She has never learnt to endure the way he ill-uses his dogs and bullies his subordinates. I found her once crying over the parting with her dog. I asked her why she sent him away. "Because Hubert kicks him when he is out of humour with me," she said. Colonel Newton used to think to allay her indignation with presents, and now the presents have ceased, and I think she is glad of it. (Who is it who said " Death, alone of all the gods, loves not a gift " ?)

Laura is happily occupied in finding reasons for not accepting your invitation to Tolcarne. Certainly, at her pace of travel-preparation, if we mean to cross the Border any day this month, we must before going north turn neither south, east, nor west. She is one of the people who prepare and provide for every possible contingency, and to avoid minutes of trifling discomfort, spend hours in painful precautionary measures. Harry, whilst admitting that camel-corps business is child's play compared to the getting of Laura from London to Edinburgh, bids me bear in mind that Land-Transport has been acknowledged by high authority to be a most difficult question. He tells me that in view of the coming campaign he feels bound to remind us that it is thought unadvisable for a convoy to occupy more than one mile of road, which would allow it to consist of from 60 to 180 wagons. "And on no account forget that if oxen are worked in larger companies that 80 wagons you will find yourself in grazing difficulties, Elizabeth. Leave your pack elephants undisturbed if possible from 9 A.M. to 3 P.M. daily. Remember that Blake, when loaded up by Laura, will take about as much room as four loaded camels. Send Blair and Atholl if sick or wounded along the Line of Communication as quickly as possible to the Base," &c., &c., &c. He recommends Mrs. Carstairs for Intelligence Department work, since there is nothing sanguine about her disposition, it being rather of that calm and distrustful order which is acknowledged to be most efficacious for such employment. He promises, too, a list of necessaries. The necessaries to include hand hatchets, felling axes, lashing ropes, shovels, crowbars, &c., &c. In discoursing after this fashion he amuses himself, then he strokes Trelawney's coat meditatively, and, poor Harry, sighs. He is taking his repulse to heart.

I shall be thankful, as far as the background goes, to get away from London. The long, hot days in London are very long and hot, and when

Pan sleeps there is no hush of omnibuses. I hope that change of air will do Laura good. She has unfortunately for herself lost her voice, and so, when she is huffed, we don't hear much about it: a state of affairs Harry likens to artillery without ammunition. Since Laura's dumbness supervened, Admiral Tidenham, whom previously I had on her behalf cultivated, is unavailable as a safety-valve. I thought there was no safer harbourage for her lamentations and grievances than Admiral Tidenham's ear-trumpet. She tempered them for transmission by ear-trumpet. (You can't with graceful ease accuse those of your own household of heinous offences down an ear-trumpet.) Admiral Tidenham is a kind old fellow, and his talk of armoured cruisers, food supply in war, Russian naval expenditure, offends no one that I know but Charles. Sir Augustus, rumours report, is at Pampesford-Royal, and contemplating alterations of the house. If ever there was a dwelling deserving of the house agents' objectionable term of mansion, I feel it is Pampesford-Royal.

Rumour further says that Mr. Biggleswade is now at Oxbridge. (The Gainsworthys are his despised relations.) If Cynthia sees him, his rather impertinent attentions may, by force of contrast, do Harry a good turn. "Put your mind at rest; you have made it plain to me that you have no prejudice against sin, and you may as well let the subject drop," Mrs. Vivian told him when last

I saw them together. " I see from the publisher's advertisements that you are in eruption again," she went on to say, and further informed him that she thought she preferred the Elizabethan " frankness " to his. " Yours, you see, Vicar (the Vicar form of address she knows is abhorrent to him), seems an anachronism, and theirs was in keeping with the manners of the age. The coarseness of their verse and sports and jokes, Hugo Ennismore says, tallied." Before he appeared upon the scene she had told me that the title of his new volume is " Love in a Mist," and she wished there was more mist.

What you say makes me disposed to learn piquet. I have gone the length of looking into the book of the game, and the first rules I came across were those that I wish Providence had adopted when framing the rules of life : " Cards accidentally dropped may be retaken." " If the cards are dealt wrongly the error may be rectified before either player has taken up his hand." The following would tie the hands and tongues of meddlers and busybodies : " A bystander calling attention to any error or oversight and thereby affecting the score, may be called upon to pay all stakes and debts of the player whose interest he has prejudicially affected." Poor Mrs. Carstairs, poor countless old women, were this rule of piquet the rule of human existence. " For he that hath to him shall be given, &c.," seems the idea of piquet as of life. Is piquet the sword-game, do you think ?

At last, at Alice Newton's bidding, I have read "The Secret Rose." Owing to your brotherly munificence I am the owner of sundry Indian necklaces, strings of cut and uncut, many-hued stones. If among these I threw a tassel or two of seed-pearls, of gold-dust, of amber, of jade, of crystal, as much, Sir, as you will ; if to these I added a raven's feather and the feather of a swan, "a lily pale," a damask rose (crimson), a sprig of funeral yew ; and if then I could dream of a rainbow reflected in silver mirror and stars reflected in cypress-circled pool, I should get the feeling that I had read "The Secret Rose." You would esteem the curse of Hanrahan the Red. I quite enter into the sentiment of it and the insufficient reasons for the various damnations please me. In certain moods I feel disposed to call down fire from Heaven and consume someone, because in my mind's eye I always see her in a bonnet of an unbecoming hue, or upon another because, when I am impatient to be gone, he is rather longer over his dinner than is a dog.

Which day do you come to London ? It must be before we go. Don't let us have for stage directions again, Exit Elizabeth, Enter Sir Richard. I really *must* see you, and there are plans to discuss. The present situation is untenable, and somebody must retire or show a change of front.

But I won't give an opinion in family conclave till I have heard yours. Harry says, "Chuck the whole thing up," by which he means "chuck up" Hans Place, and he speaks of a flat at Albert Gate or in Sloane Gardens for the two of us, or if alone, his old quarters in Duke Street. I, however, am partly responsible for the rent of this house, which we took on a seven-fourteen-twenty-one years' lease when Laura seemed to wish the future to be a fixture as far as we could make it one ; and I do not feel free to leave with a month's notice. We might let the house. Houses let in this part of the world, and Laura could put herself and Cynthia into a smaller dwelling-place if she would. Aunt Jane says, "You and dear Harry have always a home in Chester Square." But nothing would induce Harry to go there. Aunt Jane is very kind, but her sympathy and partisanship have of late become rather too marked for the preservation of peace. Since her talebearing old maid learnt from Blake that "her ladyship wants so much waiting on that she can't do Miss Etchingham justice," Aunt Jane's bearing is that of benevolent aunt to Cinderella ill-treated by a stepmother. "Dear Elizabeth was always used to this and that," she tells Laura pointedly, and Laura in consequence no longer considers Aunt Jane in need of a champion, and shamefully neglected by every member of the family but herself.

Now write " before three suns " and tell me which is your Tennyson poem, and let the letter be a " best selected " letter. Those letters that can be read aloud to Laura or carried round to Chester Square are nothing very much to me. I like the letters from you that I understand, but which, did they fall into the enemy's or the uninitiated's hands, would provoke the enemy or uninitiated to say in irritated accents, "What in the world is all this about?" A letter, not of commerce, should but be possible from its sender to its recipient, and should bear the impress of both like a gift.

Farewell, Dickory. "Yours in that which no waters can quench, no time forget, nor distance wear away."

ELIZABETH.

P.S.—Blair and Atholl have not been quite themselves, but are now convalescent. They send you a message: " In thought we gently ruffle ourselves against Sir Richard's hand." Trelawney, cat of my heart, on hearing this, and not to be outdone in dutiful affection, said, "When I think of Sir Richard I purr involuntarily."

XXIII.

*From Sir Richard Etchingham, Tolcarne, to Miss
Elizabeth Etchingham, 83 Hans Place.*

My dear Elizabeth,

Speak not of garden parties, or rather
do, for Mrs. Follett is much comforted by your
opinion of them. Last week she was set upon in
intervals of tea and croquet, within about half an
hour, by six other clergymen's wives, who wanted
to know exactly why that excellent young man
Mr. Weekes had gone away; likewise Mr. Follett's
opinions on ritual. She gave them six different
and wildly inconsistent answers, and hopes they
will be edified when they compare notes.

We agree pretty well about Tennyson's latest
poems, I think. But the one I had in mind is not
of that set; it dates from several years before. I
mean the lines to Virgil written at the request of the
Mantuans. (Stephen Leagrave must needs write
Vergil with an *e*. I will not alter a name fixed in
English literature for centuries, because the true
Latin form has turned out to be Vergilius, any
more than I will write Muhammad for Mahomet
or Qurān for Koran when I am writing English.)
There is to my thinking no more perfect example
of Tennyson's mature art. A novel and impressive
metrical form, which would alone have gone far to

make a new poet's reputation, is the least of its perfections. It is full of Virgilian scholarship and exquisite Virgilian echoes, and there are lines in it which for pure harmony cannot be surpassed even in "Lycidas." This, for example, which I see people are beginning to use as a quotation :

> " All the charm of all the Muses
> often flowering in a lonely word."

Still more choice, perhaps, is this :

> " Summers of the snakeless meadow,
> unlaborious earth and oarless sea."

And then the delicate conceit of the Italian form brought in at the end ; something of risk in it, if you will, but such risk as only the consummate masters of language know how to take and use :

> " I salute thee, Mantovano,
> I that loved thee since my day began,
> Wielder of the stateliest measure
> ever moulded by the lips of man."

Just so would Virgil, if called on to celebrate a Greek poet, have delighted to play with some rarely sounding Greek name like his *Actias Orithyia*, or close on some fuller half-exotic cadence like that of his wonderful line—

> " armatumque auro circumspicit Oriona."

Not that the lines to Virgil are Tennyson's

greatest work, or in the strict sense a great poem. But they are a jewel of workmanship in a difficult kind, absolute in its kind, and such as Tennyson alone, in our time, could have wrought with such a combination of high dignity and minute felicity.

Now and then I wonder why Tennyson did not strive to emulate Virgil and Milton in their use of proper names to ornament verse. Perhaps he felt that Milton had done it in English once for all. Mr. Swinburne, I suppose, is of the same opinion. He knows Victor Hugo's work intimately, as Tennyson did not; and I believe Victor Hugo is the only modern poet who has habitually aimed at that sort of effect. It would be unkind to ask Mr. Swinburne whether he thinks Victor Hugo succeeded, as unkind as to ask us oldish fellows, who were carried off our legs by "Songs before Sunrise" a quarter of a century ago, to go back on it now and pick out the inequalities. My own feeling, with submission to French critics, is that Victor Hugo did not succeed with his proper names on the whole. They are imposing only by chance; he could not handle them with Virgil's or Milton's perfect choice and sureness, and sometimes he gives us nothing but a jaw-breaking catalogue for the space of two or three couplets. Leconte de Lisle (a poet whom English scholars ought to be better acquainted with) occasionally gives signs that he could have achieved more in

this line if he chose. All this without prejudice
to maintaining old father Hugo's fame, in other
respects, *contra mundum.* Have you still that
precious, thumbed, bedamped, bedusted, pencil-
marked, travel-beaten volume of the " Légende des
Siècles," in which we read his masterpieces together?
I shall never get so much pleasure from the final
ne varietur edition : the pieces are all shuffled
about, as I found the pictures at the Louvre, and
I can't lay my hand on an old favourite without a
hunt. But Lord! (I thank Mr. Pepys daily for
that convenient form of breaking off) to think how
few English people know that French poetry is a
kingdom of itself, and richly worth taking the
trouble to enter into. Perhaps M. Rostand may
be the destined missionary. So many English
folk have bought " Cyrano de Bergerac " that I
suppose a good many must be reading it who
never read any French verse before. And M.
Rostand's verse—leaving it to the French critics
to settle the precise degree of excellence—is
certainly very good.

Maeterlinck, Maeterlinck, and Maeterlinck !
Stephen Leagrave has been preaching him to
Margaret and me. We feel rebellious. There
are pretty things, some fine ones, and Maeterlinck
has doubtless made a manner of his own. But
can you believe that this modern mysticism will
come to more than a curious literary phase to be
chronicled in the school books of the later twentieth

century? Real speculative mysticism is lofty and splendid while it holds together—and perhaps more of it is true than the formal philosophers allow. In decay it is odious. By no means is it the case that "*les morceaux en sont bons.*" The bits, when it breaks up, relapse into disgusting superstition. I have seen "The Secret Rose," too; it gives me more pleasure than Maeterlinck. And I don't see why it is not quite as good work. I believe, however, that they do these things better in the East, and I doubt if the clever young men of our day can get into anything but a backwater by competing with the East or even the Catholic Middle Ages.

Piquet does seem to be connected with the Italian *picche*—which became *pique* in French, as for us the equivalent *spade* became the suit of spades; but the connexion is none too clear. I can only refer you to Cavendish's historical introduction.

The enclosed letter from Jem will have some interest for you. I am not sorry about Cynthia. She may appreciate a gentleman better after having to suffer a pretentious cad. I add a translation of the curse

Our brother Charles is off to command his fate, if he can, in Dampshire. After this week I am free for London when you please. Let me have your orders accordingly. Margaret is keen on hearing some good music; there are not even any musical people here. The Folletts would like to be, but have no time to keep it up.

Your loving brother,
RICHARD.

XXIV.

(Enclosed in No. XXIII.)

From James Etchingham, Silvertoe College, Oxbridge, to Sir Richard Etchingham.

MY DEAR SIR RICHARD,

Our young friend Arthur's work will do, I think. When I was at Eton last week—a mighty pretty ride from Oxbridge—Lytewell let me see some composition of his, which was really·well turned, and showed a good grip of the language for his age.

I have been meeting another young friend of yours at the Gainsworthys', a Miss Leagrave—immature, but pleasing so far as she goes, and she seemed disposed to expand. I dare say she was hampered by the formal, old-fashioned ways of her well-meaning hosts. They bristle with prejudices and find something to be shocked at in every new person who makes their acquaintance, unless he or she comes to them with some sort of reputation, in which case they assume with the most touching simplicity that it must be all right. So they tolerate, or more than tolerate, that intolerable ass and impostor Biggleswade, whom Aristophanes would have called—— [*Marginal note by Sir R. E.* Here follow some epithets which, being Greek, you could not read, nor should I recommend most of them for your reading if you could. So I have cut off those few lines at the bottom of the page.]

Pity that such corruptions breed in the sun of learning at times. The beast was rather offensively attentive to Miss Leagrave. I am bound to say for her that she seemed to dislike it thoroughly ; her mind is unformed, but I guess her instincts are pretty sound. If Mrs. Gainsworthy had been a person of any gumption she would have rescued the poor girl. But she smiled and looked on fatuously, no doubt supposing that Miss Leagrave was much honoured by the conversation of a distinguished author. What d——d idiots good people can be !

Blunham and I have been cursing the common dog for the last fortnight. Hunter, one of our promising scholars (a history man, so I don't see much of his work myself), was out cycling with Blunham, and as they were coming home a big loafing village dog turned right across Hunter's wheel and brought him down with a broken collar-bone. Wheeling, like mountaineering, has some unavoidable accidents besides the $(n+1)$ avoidable ones. Lucky it was not Blunham, who is in for the Schools this term, both for himself and for the College ; and it was one of the first remarks

Hunter made, which does him credit. He is a cheerful man, and has been finding amusement in learning to do as much as he can with his left hand. I suggested a trial of Leonardo da Vinci's trick-writing, reversed from right to left, to be read in a mirror; and he finds it really comes easier to the left hand that way. Blunham and I revisited that village within a few days and found the dog as fat and well-liking as could be. He was too large to be run over, and seemed not to have minded at all. So we could only relieve our feelings and Hunter's with a curse. I got it a little touched up by Shipley one day when we met in town; of course he would have done it better. Still, it may amuse you and Mr. Follett.

Incipit excommunicatio canina.

Maledictus sit canis ille impudentissimus qui scholarem nostrum de rota eversit.

Maledictus sit cum omnibus malis canibus qui a principio mundi maledicti sunt.

Maledictus sit cum canibus Samaritanis qui carnes reginae Iezabel comederunt.

Maledictus sit cum latratore Anubi et ceteris daemonibus cynocephalis quot unquam in Aegypto latraverunt.

Procul sint ab ipso omnes benedictiones quas boni canes meriti sunt in caelo vel terra.

Minime videat annos Argi, neque cum angelis ambulet sicut canis Tobiae.

Maledictus sit per canes caelestes Sirium et Procyonem et Canes Venaticos.

Maledictus sit in triplici maledictione per Cerberum canem infernum et per tria capita eius.

Maledictus sit coram domina regina et coram comitatu per omnes constitutiones de capistris imponendis.

Maledictus sit etiam per omnia rotabilia quae fecit Dominus, per primum mobile firmamenti et per gyrationes eius, per stellas, per planetas, et per polum, per solem, per lunam, per terram, et per omnium angelorum potentiam qui revolutiones ipsorum regunt.

Maledictus sit in ventorum circulis et in oceani gurgitibus.

Maledictus sit per rotam motricem universi quae est materia et per rotam directricem quae est spiritus et per catenam quae est ipsorum harmonia praestabilita.

Maledictus sit per rotas animalium alatorum quae vidit Ezechiel propheta et per eorum volubilitatem in saecula.

Opprimat cum Fortunae improbae rota et semper in infimam sortem deiciat.

Torqueatur super rotam Ixionis et frangatur sicut rotae curruum Pharaonis.

Maledictus sit in orbe rotundo ac perfecto maledictionum.   Fiat, fiat.

Explicit.

Otherwise the chief news of this ever-being-reformed University is that we have been without a burning question for two whole terms.

Yours ever,
JAMES ETCHINGHAM.

XXIV*a.*

(Enclosed in No. XXIII.)

Translation.

Here beginneth the excommunication of the Dog.

Cursed be this dog of infinite wickedness who upset our scholar from his wheel.

Cursed be he with all evil dogs which have been cursed from the beginning of the world.

Cursed be he with the dogs of Samaria which ate the body of queen Jezebel.

Cursed be he with the barking god Anubis and all other dog-headed devils that ever barked in Egypt.

May all the blessings earned by good dogs in heaven or earth be far from him.

Let him in no wise see the age of Argus, nor walk with angels like Tobit's dog.

Cursed be he by the heavenly dogs Sirius and Procyon and by the Hunting Dogs.

Cursed be he with a threefold curse by the hell-hound Cerberus and his three heads.

Cursed be he before our Lady the Queen and before the County Council by all and every the muzzling orders.

Cursed be he likewise by all wheeling things which the Lord hath made, by the prime mover of the firmament and his rotation, by the stars, the planets, the pole, the sun, the moon, and the earth, and by the power of all the angels who govern their revolutions.

Cursed be he in cyclones and cursed in whirlpools.

Cursed be he by the driving wheel of the universe, which is matter, and by the steering wheel, which is spirit, and by the chain, which is the pre-established harmony thereof.

Cursed be he for ever by the wheels of the winged living creatures which Ezekiel the prophet saw and by the swiftness of their rolling.

Let the wheel of Fortune in her wrath crush him and ever cast him down to the meanest fate.

Let him be whirled upon Ixion's wheel and broken even as the wheels of Pharaoh's chariots.

Cursed be he in a whole and perfect round of cursing. So be it. A true version.—R. E.

XXV.

From Miss Elizabeth Etchingham, The Hotel, Glenfearn, N.B., to Sir Richard Etchingham, 83 Hans Place, London.

Wonders, Dickory, will never cease ; we have actually survived the hardships of a journey from London to Edinburgh and on from Edinburgh to Glenfearn. Certainly we have left from Laura's point of view most necessaries of life behind us, but as we have not left ourselves, that need not trouble you—who need Hans Place house-room. I really did think we should never get Laura off unless we dug her out with a spade. She seemed as firmly rooted to the ground as if she were a tree. It was, you know, that last visit from Sir Augustus that finally set her in motion. What arguments can he, of all people, have brought to bear to get her to the starting point ? The matter is full of mystery ; however, while I can see the hills, range beyond range, still topped with snow, and breathe this delightful moor-scented air, I feel as if Sir Augustus and all his works weren't worth the fraction of a moment's thought.

I am glad to escape, and waste time wondering why anyone lives in London who can live elsewhere. Do you remember in "Fumifugium" the story of the merchant who had "so strange an antipathy to the air of London" that when he came to the Exchange he "within an hour or two grew extremely indisposed," and was "forced to take horse and ride as for his life till once more he came into the fields"? My mortal frame is not so sensitive to maleficent influence as was this gentleman's, but I think my spirit's antipathy to the air is unconquerable. John Evelyn had no patience with the "presumptuous smoke" which "spreads a yellowness upon our choicest pictures and hangings," "kills our bees and flowers," and "sticks on the hands of our fair ladies and nicer dames." "Where is there such coughing under Heaven as in the London Churches?" he asks. London, he says, killed Old Parr, and he likens the city to "the Suburbs of Hell."

Glenfearn does not quite match my old recollections. There is more snow upon the hills and there is more water in the burns than I remember, and where I used to see scarlet hips and haws wild white roses now are blowing. The thicket of rose-briers at the head of the loch is white with blossom, the whin on the brae glitters in cloth-of-gold, and, as is seemly in Scotland, bluebells—"the azured harebell" like Fidele's veins—are everywhere.

Crossing the border would not, I suppose, enable the Ethiopian to change his skin nor the leopard his spots, and this side of Tweed Laura is Laura still. The poor "Camelry," as Harry christens Blake, has therefore been busily employed running

to and fro on telegraph business to the post-office
—a queer dim little room in a road-side cottage
overshadowed by fir trees, its whitewashed walls
garlanded with *Tropæolum Speciosum.* Things
telegraphed for include green glazed calico and a
green lampshade to exclude the light of day and
night, a square of mackintosh, "as her ladyship
thinks now, M'm, that the damp will rise when she
sits out," a tray on which to bring breakfast upstairs that will not crush beneath its weight the
Breakfaster in bed, beef-essence, peptonized cocoa
and milk, meat lozenges, a filter, &c., &c. Our
stepmother has already changed her room three
times. In the first room the noise kept her awake
late, in the second the light awoke her early, in
the third a most pestiferous (and, I fancy, imaginary) odour prevented the closing of her eyes
all night. Blake was caught red-handed by Mrs.
McPhail pouring Condy's fluid into a gully outside
this last-mentioned room. Had Laura ordered
the breakfast to be thrown down the gully Mrs.
McPhail's feelings would have suffered less. We
ran indeed, thanks to Laura's passion for disin-
fectants, a narrow risk of being turned out of
"The Hotel, Glenfearn," bag and baggage. "That
woman's fou o' fikes, I canna be fashed wi' her.
The drains was a' richt afore she cam—naething
short o' Scone Palace and a French shaif wadd
plase her," was what Mrs. McPhail did not mean
me to hear. However, I had not a father in the

diplomatic service and a brother in the political department for nothing, and, though our tenure is precarious, here we remain.

Laura, too, is slightly better content. The hotel omnibus yesterday brought a woman of London aspect accompanied by many substantial-looking trunks and an unsubstantial-looking maid tottering under the weight of a big dressing-case and a bigger dressing-bag. When Laura found the new-comer's name to be Mrs. Le Marchant and her address Lowndes Street, dejection gave way to interest. Later in the day I was thankful to see her venture so far as to seat herself beside Mrs. Le Marchant on a bench in the dank and diminutive garden of the inn—a garden where a paling, a privet-hedge, and a dilapidated water-butt conceal every vestige of the view, which is wide and magnificent. The Birds of a Feather fell almost immediately into conversation, and talked on and on with decreasing suspicion and increasing civility till nearly dinner-time. "She seems to know a good many people that we do," Laura told me afterwards, with far more approbation in her tone than I had heard since we left home; and her "leddyship" and her "leddyship's" latest find have now gone to drive together in Mr. McPhail's largest landau; and on and on they will drive, the eternal hills around them, too conversationally occupied in the quest of mutual acquaintances to see anything but each other's veils.

If you think it would not be indiscreet, you might let Harry know that *la dame de ses pensées* is auspiciously sad. Her Oxbridge adventures have done my dear Harry's cause good. Jem is right about Mr. Biggleswade and right about Mrs. Gainsworthy too. She is fatuously unconscious of the obvious—of the obvious which was not the obvious in her youth—as advancing years and increasing bulk make many a worthy woman. There are exceptions of course, but age does dull women more than it dulls men. The dullards of your sex at least retain some shred of interest in their past, but those of mine seem to become the next thing to comatose. What a good fellow is that man of many jests but few spoken words, Jem. He seems to have played the friend in need to Cynthia once or twice, particularly once when Mrs. Gainsworthy sent her home from some house where they were dining under Mr. Biggleswade's sole escort, and Jem, for all his shyness and avowed dislike of women's company, voluntarily went too. Cynthia's instincts are true enough, and I doubt that she will be as easy to move in the marriage-way as, with less evidence at my disposal, I judged. And for this I thank Heaven.

In Edinburgh I paid a visit to one of the old bookshops. I bought myself a copy of Hobbes' "Leviathan." Tell me if you are an admirer of Hobbes, but don't tell me I can get "Leviathan" in "Morley's Universal Library." I see their value, but I detest wonderful-at-the-money re-prints, and would as soon read Hobbes in such guise as see him himself portrayed in deer-stalker and shooting-jacket. Then, to add to your song-books, I bought a little second-hand but not old book of Canadian songs, taken down from the boatmen. I can't suppose they will satisfy your fastidious taste, but approach my gift in a com-placent attitude please, at all events. The first in the book, "*A la claire Fontaine*," seems to me pretty—

> " A la claire fontaine
> M'en allant promener,
> J'ai trouvé l'eau si belle
> Que je m'y suis baigné.
> > I'ya longtemps que je t'aime,
> > Jamais je ne t'oublierai.
>
> " Sur la plus haute branche
> Le rossignol chantait,
> Chante, rossignol, chante,
> Toi qui as le cœur gai.
> Chante, rossignol, chante,
> Toi qui as le cœur gai :
> Tu as le cœur à rire,
> Moi je l'ai-t-à pleurer.
>
> " J'ai perdu ma maîtresse
> Sans pouvoir la trouver,
> Pour un bouquet de roses
> Que je lui refusai.
> > I'ya longtemps que je t'aime,
> > Jamais je ne t'oublierai."

And the tune of "*A la claire Fontaine*" is attrac-tive.

Still further did the Edinburgh bookseller tempt me, and I bought a collection of old Scotch songs. In England the song-makers are in want of a "little language," and the Scotch have the better of the southerners there. The English are not quite happy in diminutives, and to talk affectionate nonsense it is well to have another tongue.

As to what you said once about the decorating of English verse with proper names, do you know Drayton's "Poly-Olbion?" Look into "Poly-Olbion" when you return to Tolcarne. You will find it beside the Crashaw in the library. Drayton gives delightful pictures of birds and of fishes, to say nothing of the descriptions of "tracts, rivers, mountains, forests, and other parts of this renowned isle of Great Britain."

And tell me this. Do you agree that for melody pure and simple there is no English poet that excels Crashaw when Crashaw is at his best? Do you remember the lines entitled "Love's Horoscope," and also the " Hymn of the Nativity?"

> " Proud World (said I) cease your contest,
>   And let the mighty Babe alone,
>   The phœnix builds the phœnix' nest,
>   Love's architecture is his own ;
>   The Babe whose birth embraves this morn
>   Made His own bed ere He was born."

The St. Teresa lines, too, which Coleridge says were in his mind when writing the second part of "Christabel," have magic in their cadence. And when you are about it tell me your opinion of Henry Vaughan.

From Henry Vaughan and Crashaw, the mystics, my thoughts turn to Alice Newton. Beg Margaret to go and see her, or rather go yourself. I think somehow she might get on better with you than with Margaret. Margaret is both too old and too young, and therefore too literal, for the dovetailing of her sentiments with Alice's. Alice was never matter-of-fact, and her troubles have accentuated her taste for parable and metaphor, *l'excès du malheur l'avait fait en quelque sorte visionnaire.* That is what *l'excès du malheur* is apt to do if it has any thread of mysticism to work upon. The Temple of Mysticism and the Cave of Adullam I always fancy in the same street.

Last night's post brought me an ecstatic letter from Minnie. "We are most sanguine. Everyone is as cordial as possible, and it has been quite a triumphal progress for Charles. Mr. Baxter" (the Tory candidate and Lady Leyton's nephew) "is ridiculously blind to the needs of the times and to the fact that country electors are not fossils. The poor man seems to tread, too, on everyone's toes to an extent that would be ludicrous if it was not pitiable. I am really sorry for him, and his agent is most unpopular—a regular tactless bear." . . . "I have been doing a lot myself, and am nearly dead; but I don't grudge it a bit. Women can do so much—though I must say I think the Primrose League tactics perfectly shameful." Charles, she says, is hourly receiving most flattering telegrams from the leading lights of the Radical party. "It does not do, of course, to be too sure, but I have not the slightest doubt myself that the majority will be enormous. The poor people are so touchingly glad of sympathy and I am getting a great deal of 'copy.'" Minnie winds up by saying that Mrs. Potters is very kind and not half as vulgar as she looks. Then in came a letter from Mrs. Vivian, asking me if I see my way to going with her to Marienbad next month. "Blanche goes to Norway on her own account, and I want someone to walk about with John. Come if you can, and I won't trouble to look out for anyone else. It would do Lady Etchingham a world of good to run her own errands and shift for herself." And this is her view of the Dampshire election case: "It's a comfort to reflect that Minnie's time for making an idiot of herself is drawing to a close, and if that horrible Mrs. Potters imagines that by helping my daughter to do what I abhor she is getting herself asked to my ball she will be woefully disappointed. . . . The Leytons, fortunately, are far too sensible and kindhearted to hold Minnie's follies for more than they are worth; still to set herself down like that in the pocket of such old friends of her people and do everything that bad taste can devise is, &c., &c." Mrs. Vivian goes on to ask if I have heard "that after all Charles's tirade against the muzzling order and the gross injustice of muzzling sheep dogs and letting hounds go free, that spiteful little Trixy of Minnie's bit the baby of the pet Socialist ploughman and the one 'mother' that Minnie had really reason to suppose she had torn from the Primrose League. The 'mother' sent to Lady Leyton—as everyone always does when in need—and Lady Leyton sent a groom in pursuit of the doctor, and the village is going solid, I hear, for George Baxter." (Charles will now sympathise with Jem's canine curse.) "The child was not really hurt, but that was not thanks to Trixy or Minnie. I have told her repeatedly he is not to be trusted. The horrid little wretch always growls at Azore, and if the dog were not a saint he would have killed him ages ago. Come to Marienbad, do, and take John off my hands."

In one respect I sincerely commiserate my married friends. Half of them seem to labour under the burden of fruitless Sisyphus-like endeavours to provide their husbands with congenial companionship. The braiding of St. Catherine's tresses must be a far less fatiguing task in the long run. "*Do*, my dear, go and see Mrs. ——, it would really be a charity." "Why can't you call upon ——? I am sure she would be delighted to see you, and it would give Rover a walk: I can't send Elise out with him to-day, as she must finish my gown." Mr. Vivian (with Azore, who requires regular exercise) calls upon us about every fifth Sunday, his whole demeanour telling that he has been driven to the door on the point of the sword by his wife. "Ralph hasn't a friend in the world," "Phil belongs to three clubs and goes to none," is what I constantly hear.

Here is the Camelry wandering into the room in search of another telegraph form. "Her ladyship, M'm, says as I'm to telegraph for the mincing machine. Her indigestion is getting that dreadful for the toughness of the meat, and she is coming in." (And through a gap in the privet-hedge I see, sure enough, the ferules of Laura's and Mrs. Le Marchant's ornate chiffon parasols approaching the house.) And here, too, is Cynthia saying, and saying truly, that the hour has struck for which we ordered the boat. Good-bye.

> " I'ya longtemps que je t'aime,
> Jamais je ne t'oublierai."

ELIZABETH.

P.S.—Out of this abundance I should like to send Margaret flowers, but the wild roses and bluebells—wise as well as lovely things—would not travel.

11 P.M. Thursday (my letter did not go to-day after all). I have opened the window. Listen, do you hear the splash and swirl of the water? Near

the stepping-stones there is a birch-tree—not a willow—"grows aslant the brook," and over the lower branches the river when in flood sweeps. Do you see the stars ? The loch looks like quicksilver while touched by the moonbeams. I would like to go out of doors. How pleasant it will be to be disembodied and to run no risk of hearing, "What in the world are you doing out at this hour ? Aren't you afraid of the damp ? You always say your throat——" I should like to be a ghost. Where should I go, I wonder ? To see you ? No, not first. I should go to look for someone who has not been mortal for seven long years, and with whom last I stood face to face not very far from here . . . I have been reading Emily Brontë's " Remembrance " to-night, and my fortitude rather goes to pieces after the reading of it. The light of many of the stars that we see is their light years ago, is it not, and that has taken time to reach us ? Is the light that I see in the sky to-night the light of that evening when we (I don't mean, dear, you and I) said good-bye, good-bye till to-morrow as we thought ? Richard, —— . . . Promise to befriend me always and be amiable when you write. (A knock at the door. "Please, M'm, her ladyship can't sleep nohow. This room's worse than any. The bed—— ") Good-night, Dickory.

XXVI.

From Sir Richard Etchingham, 83 Hans Place, S.W., to Miss Elizabeth Etchingham, Glenfearn, N.B.

My dear Elizabeth,

Margaret joined me here yesterday. She sends you her best love, and her regrets that she could not see you this time. "But," she adds, "the Protector of the Poor knows very well that I should not really have seen Aunt Elizabeth even if there had been room for me, what with the packing going on and other people coming in and out and never letting me alone." The other people mean one person, I need not tell you. Margaret could never abide Laura. Well, I suppose the time will come when we may really be together for a while at least. Meanwhile I console myself with the company of your books, and am beginning to make (or renew after years) pleasant acquaintances among your old friends in brown calf. Margaret has, of course, a fair shelf-knowledge of them already, and she seems to know something of the insides of a good many of them too. We find a curious pleasure in being alone in the middle of the London season ; I say "we," because Margaret does not seem at all anxious to plunge into general society. We shall see our own particular friends, and I shall look up old official superiors and colleagues—in some cases for duty, in others for pleasure ; otherwise we expect to be pretty domestic, and look forward to Arthur coming up for the Harrow match as our greatest dissipation. Margaret pleads for some concerts, and, though I have not her musical education or enthusiasm, I shall be well pleased to hear a good European orchestra. During my years of service I have at any rate endured a sufficient infinity of variations on *Táza ba táza* to feel that I deserve it.

Charles has been here once : he rushes off to Clayshott whenever he can steal half a day. He is running his head against a brick wall so far as I can see ; but it will give him a certain claim on his party for services rendered, which may be useful to him in his profession sooner or later. You will know more about the details than I do, as I have in self-defence kept myself ignorant of even the day of the election. If I have tried once to explain to Minnie that the only thing I can do, not at all sharing my brother's opinions, is to be strictly neutral, I have tried a dozen times ; while Harry has been working hard to make me see that it is my duty as head of the family to make a solemn public protest against Charles's lamentable defection from sound principles. The worst trial was when Minnie came here with an earnest Radical lady who must have bored Minnie nearly as much as she did us ; that was some comfort. Margaret put on the air of a very simple country girl, and chaffed

Minnie by asking innocent questions which the good lady took quite seriously. Finally, she said with extreme gravity that we found the affairs of Much Buckland so interesting and difficult that we could really spare no time for general English politics. As Minnie's friend could not deny the importance of local self-government, she rather lost her bearings, and tried to make a diversion by attacking me on the Indian National Congress. Now it was a little too much to be lectured on the government of India by a woman wholly ignorant of the subject whom I had never seen before. "Do you know," said I, "what are the really capable classes in India? Can you guess what the sort of Hindus and Mahometans I have lived among for the last dozen years would do with your National Congress if we let them?" "No, indeed." "Take the fluent English speech-making, English article-writing Babus—the oil-fed sons of the quill, as Lyall's old Pindári calls their kind—every man a couple, one in each hand, and chuck them into the Indian Ocean." Margaret intervened with an offer of more tea, which was declined. We don't think Minnie will bring that well-meaning lady here again.

Here comes a letter from Jem which puts Margaret in the seventh heaven. It appears that he and Shipley, months ago, got up a little party to go to the "Ring des Nibelungen" at Covent Garden, Mrs. Newton and one or two others besides themselves; I suspect it was in part a little conspiracy to take Mrs. Newton out of herself and her troubles if possible, for I know that Jem is an excellent fellow, and I don't know that he is a devoted Wagnerian, though his tastes are pretty catholic. However, it now turns out that Jem is wanted at Oxbridge to replace an examiner who has broken down ; he cannot well refuse the work, and it will keep him there all through July. So he writes to me to offer his place to Margaret—not as a gift, so you need not begin to spin a romance ; besides, he is sensible enough to know that we should not accept it in that way. You remember the elaborate plan we made last year for a meeting at Bayreuth, you two from the West and I from the East, by way of Brindisi or Trieste, and how disappointed Margaret was when it failed, like many other neatly contrived plans, chiefly for the commonplace reason that it turned out I could not get started for home anything like soon enough. There is no need to tell you how pleased the child is now. She says it is a pity I can't go too ; like most young people who are fond of their parents, she would like to educate me to all her tastes, and thinks it would be quite easy to do it. I tell her it is no matter, and that if she could take me she would only find me too old to learn. It is true I have charming recollections of Wagner's earlier operas heard long ago in Germany, before the British public knew anything about them, much less cared. But advanced Wagnerians, I understand, put these away as childish things. Stephen Leagrave talks in that way, not that I believe—or Margaret either —he really cares for music of any school. Never mind ; he did not hear " Lohengrin " at the old Dresden Theatre before it was burnt down. Such memories make one feel hugely old, but they are good all the same.

Leagrave, by the way, seems anxious to improve Margaret's knowledge of literature on his own correct and critical lines. No romance about that either, if you please ; it is pure intellectual benevolence for the good of his neighbour's mind, with a little touch of vanity and the natural hope that the young may be more teachable than the old. Not that it would be human nature for a preacher of æsthetic or any other principles to prefer his converts ugly—even when one has, like Stephen, about as little human nature as it is possible to go through the world with. Just now he is still dosing us with Maeterlinck. We took our revenge last night by concocting a Maeterlinckian scene—not to be shown to Stephen, I need not say, for he would be most solemnly and seriously aggrieved, and might feel bound to renounce our acquaintance. So I send it you—like various other things—to be out of harm's way.

I have to go to the Society of Arts to-morrow to support poor dear old Gritson. He has a theory of Indian currency which nobody can understand. You see that even in retirement one may still have to sacrifice oneself for the good of the service. When I come back from that function, if not before, I hope to be consoled by a letter from you telling me what sort of establishment you have made at Glenfearn—unless Laura has taken a fancy to stop at some other health resort by the way.

Your loving brother,
DICKORY.

Here follows the scene in question.

> LE ROI LYSAOR (*très vieux, immobile dans son fauteuil*).
> LE DUC YPNOCRATE.
> LA PRINCESSE DILBARINE.
> LE PRINCE HUGLIMUGH (*enfant*).
> LA DAME ELIANE, *gouvernante du prince.*

LYSAOR : Je ne digère pas bien. Je sens que quelque chose va certainement se casser.

ELIANE : Le roi croit que quelque chose va se casser.

HUGLIMUGH : Je ne comprends pas le sens de ces paroles. Les grands-pères disent toujours des choses qui n'ont pas de sens. Moi, je casse les choses quand l'envie m'en prend.

YPNOCRATE : O mon néant suprême ! n'es-tu pas bien heureuse ?

DILBARINE : Nous sommes bien heureux, effectivement.

YPNOCRATE : Mon âme voit pourtant que tu es inquiète. Dis-moi pourquoi tout de suite, cela sera plus simple pour l'auditoire.

DILBARINE : Je m'inquiète parceque la grand'mère est somnambule.

193   O

YPNOCRATE : D'abord nous le sommes tous. Puis tu l'as enfermée à clef dans sa chambre.

DILBARINE : Elle aura certainement trouvé l'autre clef.

YPNOCRATE : Comment sais-tu qu'il y en a une autre ?

DILBARINE : Parce que l'auteur en a besoin, ô mon abîme très précieux.

YPNOCRATE : Prends garde de dire ces choses-là, nous ne sommes pas seuls.

DILBARINE : Si fait, c'est à peu près la même chose.

YPNOCRATE : Comment ! tu trouves que c'est la même chose ? Le petit prince est tout oreilles.

DILBARINE : Comme tu manques de foi, mon obscurité chérie ! Pourquoi causons-nous amour dans la langue symbolique du maître, sinon pour que ni les personnages, ni le souffleur, ni le public n'y comprennent rien ?

YPNOCRATE : Et l'auteur ?

DILBARINE : Lui moins que personne.

YPNOCRATE : L'auteur n'y comprendrait rien ?

DILBARINE : Quand je te dis que non ! Cherche la raison toi-même.

YPNOCRATE : Je cherche donc . . . oui, j'y suis. C'est qu'il fait du symbolisme. Or ce n'est plus du symbolisme dès que quelqu'un commence à y comprendre quelque chose.

DILBARINE : Parfait. Continuons. Nous disons donc que je m'inquiète de ce que peut faire la grand'mère.

HUGLIMUGH (à la fenêtre) : Ah ! ah ! je vois quelque chose.

ELIANE : Le prince dit qu'il voit quelque chose.

LYSAOR : Une chose qui va se casser, j'en suis sûr.

HUGLIMUGH : Ah ! ah ! que c'est drôle ! Voilà la grand'-mère qui grimpe sur le pigeonnier.

ELIANE : La grand'mère est sur le pigeonnier.

DILBARINE : C'est bien cela, la grand'mère s'est évadée
pour grimper sur le pigeonnier.

HUGLIMUGH : Elle est au faîte ! Ah ! ah ! ah ! c'est
bien drôle . . . elle va sauter . . . elle saute . . .
elle tombe.

ELIANE : Il dit qu'elle tombe !

YPNOCRATE : On dit qu'elle tombe !

DILBARINE : Evidemment, il faut qu'elle tombe.

HUGLIMUGH : Elle s'est cassé le cou . . . hou, hou . . .
je n'aime pas à voir les gens qui se cassent le cou.

ELIANE : La grand'mère s'est cassé le cou !

YPNOCRATE : Elle s'est cassé le cou !

DILBARINE : Elle s'est bien cassé le cou !

HUGLIMUGH : Hou, hou, hou . . . j'ai bien peur . . .
c'est trop vilain . . . je veux qu'on interdise de
se casser le cou.

LYSAOR : Je disais bien que quelqu'un allait casser
quelque chose. Je ne digère pas bien.

XXVII.

*From Miss Elizabeth Etchingham, The Hotel, Glen-
fearn, N.B., to Sir Richard Etchingham,
83 Hans Place.*

MY DEAR TOLCARNE,

(One must do in Scotland as Scotland
does.) Our letters crossed—

> " When letters cross
> A double loss."

I meant to write the very day I heard from you, my pen set in motion by the impetus of what. I read, but impediments that Laura would speak of as "other claims" intervened, and then the semi-stupefaction that a very big dose of the open air produces laid the spirit of scribbling to rest; and here we are at Sunday and no letter has gone. I should certainly answer in the negative Renan's question, "*Peut-on travailler en province?*" In London, notwithstanding countless interruptions, I do as much in a day as here I do in a week.

Your Maeterlinck has converted me to Maeterlinck. I find it the missing link between Maeterlinck and life, and it has led me to a little discovery: Maeterlinck is not a symbolist but a satirist, and your satire satirises not only Maeterlinck but life. Read Maeterlinck as a satirist and see how finely he hits off the blunders, the blindness, the selfishness of human nature that pursues its own ends and clings to its own aims through thick and thin, light and darkness, virtue and sin. I find, too, a likeness between Maeterlinck and the Book of Job. Maeterlinck's characters play the part of Job's comforters one to another adroitly. "Your soul was never so beautiful as since I have broken your heart." "I am glad that my soul is so beautiful since you have broken my heart." In irony and humour surely Maeterlinck touches high water-mark? But if to read Maeterlinck as humorist and satirist contrasts too violently with your former attitude, read this pseudo-Maeterlinck as a satire on life not Maeter-linck, and see how well my theory works.

There is always a someone who announces "*Je ne digère pas bien*," when his wife or someone comes to grief. There is always a wiseacre, after the event, to declare " *Je disais bien que quelqu'un allait casser quelque chose*," be the "*quelque chose*" what it may, from a tea-cup to a bank. There is always an infant, young in intellect, if not in years, who finds the first act of a tragedy "*bien drôle*," and wishes that the last act of a tragedy had been forbidden ; and there is always another key to unlock the door that leads to destruction if Fate, the author, has need of it. As to repetition, the old "Oxford Spectator," whose wit I only made acquaintance with lately, may say that "the re-peated assertion of an insignificant fact tends to weaken and finally to destroy the mind : " but I don't know. Nature has vast recuperative power, and the repeated assertion of an insignificant and significant fact is going on all round, and has doubtless gone on since time began. Eve, probably never to the day of her death, fell into low spirits but that she asked Adam if the affair of the apple had not been very unfortunate, and Adam assuredly answered a thousand times, " Yes, Eve, it was very unfortunate."

By all means draw Alice Newton back into the world if you can. She probably feels more at ease and also less down-hearted with comparative strangers than with people who have looked into the four corners of her existence. In certain frames of mind it is a relief to be with the folk who know nothing and care less about one's worries. Not that Alice would find this indifference in you, but still you are not knit into her past, and your *rôle* in regard to her is not that of memorandum. You must make haste and get her out of her fastness and out of herself before Colonel Newton returns. Once he is at home again, an intangible something will come down and separate her from realities. Is it wicked to wish that Colonel Newton might be removed to another sphere? Yet I am sorry for him, for I believe he has still, in his unpleasant way, far more affection for her than she ever had for him, and the one who cares least, when it comes to extremities, has really the best of it. And then the poor man gets no pity. His affections may be blighted, but as he grows more hectoring, as well as fatter and redder, day by day, he does not win a scrap of sympathy. So, though he is what Harry calls an ill-conditioned brute (he is hated in the service, Harry says), I think the ill-conditioned brute has had his bad moments, poor wretch.

Is Margaret to be painted? And if so, by whom? Everybody has been painted already, I am inclined to say, and so why not let well alone? Everybody has been painted that is, but

the painting is not always, or often, in the possession of the original, or the original's family. If it
were so your portrait by Titian would not be in
the gallery at Florence, but in the cedar-room at
Tolcarne. Margaret's counterfeit presentment
hangs in the Louvre. After Leonardo, who need
trouble to paint her? Mrs. Vivian's picture is
labelled Mrs. Henslowe, and accredited to Corne-
lius Jansen, and I used to wish for no better
likeness of Alice Newton than Sir Joshua's Nelly
O'Brien. But she has gone away from her former
portrait and might sit for her own ghost. Sant
has set the full face of our worthy Laura upon
canvas, as I have already said, and for her profile
what do you think of the portrait of Simonetta
Vespucci at Florence, of which the guide books
rightly say, "*c'est une œuvre qui n'a pas un grand
charme.*"

Monday.—"*Tha na nedil a' dol an truimead,*"
which translated from the Gaelic into the vulgar
tongue means the clouds are becoming heavier.
. Which translated from the vulgar tongue into
Etchinghamese means that Laura has put on her
bonnet. Which idiom is closely related to the
phrase of the Mont Blanc guides, "*Il met son
bonnet,*" when they see the little cloud on the
mountain-top, the little cloud that foretells a storm.

Yes, Laura certainly has put on her metaphorical
bonnet. She has had it out of the bandbox since
the day of our arrival, and she clapped it on for

good and all, I fear, yesterday during dinner, when the waiter from Aber-r-r-r-deen entangled the cruet-stand in her hair, and a fellow-lodger of doubtless blameless character, but perhaps ún-polished manners, whose conversational overtures she had sternly rebuffed, joined with the waiter in his efforts to free that ram—the cruet-stand—from that thicket—Laura's tresses: "Let me redd it for y're Leddyship. He's just ravelin't mair." Poor Laura, it was indeed a sight to see her while the hands of the waiter from Aber-r-r-r-deen and Mr. Dugald McTavish, from Dundee, met in her nut-brown locks. The waiter, in his philanthropic anxiety to relieve Laura of the undesirable cruet, held the sauce-boat at an angle at which, unless the laws of gravity had been altered to save a gown, the melted butter could do nothing but form a cascade down Mrs. Le Marchant's neat silken back. "Damisht ye. Doe ye think a get butter for naething?" was Mr. McPhail's *sotto-voce* ejaculation from where he stood by the side-board; and no one was pleased but two rude bicycling boys, whose laughter was loud and long.

I wish you would write upon a postcard, "I trust Glenfearn is not too bracing for Laura," and I would let it lie about in noticeable places. With-out some such wile the unfortunate Camelry and myself will soon be in the thick of the transport business again, for Laura's present grievance is that this air is enervating.

Why is it my lot in life to be for ever thrown with persons whose need of bracing is insatiable? I, to whom no summer heat but that of a city proves enervating, no climate relaxing, find the thread of existence inextricably tangled with that of folk to whom, did one take them at their word, the proximity of icebergs is comforting, and who fail to distinguish between the summer temperature of the Highlands and that of the Black Hole of Calcutta. In Laura we have a perfect specimen of the ever-enervated type. She is parched when the sun shines. The sense of suffocation is hers continually. Her fate is it to feel "oppressed by the terrible heat," "overpowered by the sultriness," "unnerved by the airlessness," "unable to creep even as far as the post-office." She broils, she is in a vapour-bath, she burns, she pants, she likens Glenfearn to a furnace, she finds the weather stifling, "so airless that a thunderstorm must be imminent," "absolutely torrid," "perfectly tropical" —in fact, Cynthia and I pass a considerable portion of our time wondering why calcined or liquefied remains are not all that is left to a mourning world of her. It really is amazing, when you come to think of it, that unsinged and un-scalded she passed through the kilns and caldrons that await the unwary between King's Cross and Princes Street.

The climate of the West Highlands cannot, I allow, be characterised as bracing, but it is balmy, which I think better, and I feel disposed to beg the people with whom we come in contact not to speak in Laura's hearing disparagingly of the place from the atmospheric standpoint. " Tell her that she will be braced, if only she will have patience," is your sister's latest form of prayer, and most amiably it has been acceded to. Mr. Dugald McTavish, when a new-comer at the hotel, however, gave me a scare. Overhearing from the other side of the dinner-table Laura complain of enervation, he exclaimed emphatically " Braemar's the place for ye, Mum, if ye want to be set up." I seized the first occasion that offered to hint that the family generally did not want to be " set up ;" that "setting up" would kill Cynthia and me probably, and later he very cannily informed Laura that " there's sic a throng o' folk at Braemar that ye leddyship micht na get bed or meat." Picture Laura to yourself "na getting bed or meat." I have heard no more of a move to Braemar.

(On one point I have quite made up my mind. Before I travel with you I will have it in writing that your idea of a " thorough change " is not a sojourn in a refrigerator, and that in your vocabulary bracing air is not synonymous with the air of Paradise.)

To our landlord's delight, the inn garden, "a fine place for sitting in the Sabbath," still remains Laura's and Mrs. Le Marchant's favourite retreat.

Their extreme civility to one another is a matter of astonishment to me. They yesterday talked for an hour of "The Christian" and "Helbeck of Bannisdale," and so excessive was their politeness and so guarded the expression of their opinions that to the end it was never brought home to them that they were not discussing the self-same book.

Cynthia is melancholy, truly, but it is the pretty "white melancholy" from which she suffers, not the ugly black kind. It turns her to the reading of Shakespeare, and to sitting upon the floor with her head against my knee when she ought to be going to bed. She recognised, even sooner than I did, the handwriting of a letter, from Harry to me, that we found laid upon the "parlour" table when we came in from a long drive this afternoon.

So far Laura seems unable to get Sir Augustus out of her head. She tells me now that Mrs. Le Marchant, who she finds knows him, says his mother was of "very good family," and that, on the distaff side of the house, he has Plantagenet and Stuart blood in his veins. Cynthia has learnt this from her, also, apparently. Remember that we did not solve the problem of the family's future, though we did talk for about six hours daily while you were in Hans Place. Laura looks mysterious and Cynthia tearful when I speak of their setting up house together. I can't make out what Laura wants, or with whom she would ordain to live. Things may settle themselves, she says. To her huffs and misunderstandings are not as intolerable as they are to me. I think, if for any reason best known to themselves people can't live in peace and amity together, they had best live apart, but this opinion is by no means universally held. Yet in various ways Laura is not unamiable. If she married my father for the place—the " situation " —she nursed him with the greatest possible assiduity, and she is really good-natured, quite lavish in fact to Cynthia in the matters of frocks and fairings. Cynthia's drawing-room attire was ordered with a magnificent disregard of the bill, and did I develop consumption or *crétin*ism she would do her duty to the bitter end. But while I am neither bodily nor mentally afflicted to any unusual extent we shall never hit it off. We don't agree about one of the trivialities that go to make existence. In the matter of domestic economy, for instance, she fears big economies, and small economies fret me. To be carriageless I find a bearable privation, but to hear the cook's aptitude for consuming lard incessantly lamented is to me a bore. Laura could not metaphorically hold faster to the brougham were she a limpet and the carriage a rock, and she enjoys the lard lamenting —"the waking of the lard," as Harry, who once overheard her wails, termed the proceeding. Then our tastes are every bit as incalculable to her as are hers to us. I told you, did not I, that without *malice prepense*, with the air rather of a person conferring a favour, she suggested not long ago that we should have a permanent "Day," and deface our paste-board with "At home, Tuesdays, 3-7;" and I had accused myself of an indecent display of dislike for what Harry calls the violation of territory and bore raids to which we are subjected. (We have no "close time," he says.) Laura with benignant smile proposing the abhorred "Day" as a peace-offering reminds me for incongruity of the London young lady of eighteenth-century fame, who collected all the chicken bones upon her plate as a delicacy for her brother's horse.

I wish you could see the Glenfearn wild-flower and fern show. Great splendid foxgloves rise up from dim green shelters, and Pan does some of his most attractive meadow-gardening with pansies—

> " The little western flower,
> Before milk-white, now purple with love's wounds,
> And maidens call it love-in-idleness "

should be the little northern flower. In free blossoming and in intensity of colour the pansies of these northern meadows beat their cousins of the west hollow.

To-morrow's "Scotsman" will give Charles's fate, I suppose. "My ladies want the ' Scotchman,'" is the form in which Blake persists in asking for the paper. " Is the war any better ? " she inquired, when I was last reading the war news. Good Heavens! *What* a din! Really Mr. McPhail should be broken of beating his dinner gong with a violence that might be deemed excessive had he resolved to awaken the dead. But to him it is a " gran sound." " If it's owre muckle for ye, put tow in yer lugs," he said to a nervous old gentleman suffering from insomnia, who expostulated the other day. Lugs = ears.

Lover of strange tongues, I sign myself in the Gaelic.

EALASAID.

XXVIII.

From Sir Richard Etchingham, Hans Place, to Miss Elizabeth Etchingham, Glenfearn, N.B.

MY DEAR ELIZABETH (or whatever you make of it in the Gaelic),

Verily it must have been a spectacle worthy of kings and poets to see that Aberdonian waiter realising the Persian figure of speech for supreme ecstasy, "one hand on the cup"—read *cruet*—"and one hand in the locks of the Beloved." The genuineness of the back hair is, I believe, undisputed.

Charles is handsomely beaten, as you will have seen by this time, if indeed you take any note of

Southron by-elections. But he will not be inconsolable. He is the hero of paragraphs in the Opposition papers, which prove to the satisfaction of the writer, and I suppose his, that it was a moral victory; he has fought the election in a highly creditable and orthodox manner, if not with much wisdom of the serpent; in short, he has done everything a still rising political lawyer ought to do to establish a claim on the party, without going to such extremes as to be in anyone else's black books. Minnie goes about saying that the South of England is hopelessly stupid, and wants him to begin cultivating a northern constituency this very Long Vacation; which might be a judicious proceeding if he could go without her. I think he will leave it alone for the present.

The old Canadian boat-song is pleasing. I suppose the French colonists carried with them the tradition of the simple popular ballads which Molière immortalised by one specimen in "Le Misanthrope:"

> " Si le roi m'avoit donné
> Paris, sa grand'ville,
> Et qu'il me fallût quitter
> L'amour de ma mie :
> Je dirois au Roi Henri,
> Reprenez votre Paris :
> J'aime mieux ma mie, oh gay !
> J'aime mieux ma mie."

A simple thing enough, as Alceste says after his first recital of it :

> " La rime n'est pas riche, et le style en est vieux."

But what an exquisite turn of Molière's art to make him repeat it once more, and what a treat it was in the days now past to hear the double delivery of those lines by Bressant, rising at the end to a solemn triumphal dignity, the everlasting protest of a gentleman of the old school against ephemeral frivolity! Perhaps it was a little too impressive for dramatic probability. Bressant's Alceste would have swept the pedants and fribbles out of the room. Delaunay made more, I think, of the real humanity of Alceste; he was the man who would be sympathetic if any of those about him would show something deserving of his sympathy. Bressant was incomparable in the majesty of high comedy, unbending to generous humour or touched with tragedy as the action demands. One of the most tragic things I ever heard was his delivery of the last words in " Les Caprices de Marianne : " " Je ne vous aime pas, Marianne, c'était Cœlio qui vous aimait."

If there be poetic justice for good artists in Elysium, Bressant should be expounding the glories of French comedy—or rather *la* Comédie Française—to Charles Lamb, who had no chance of knowing them in this world, and Shakespeare and Musset should be in the front row. The Musset of " Comédies et Proverbes " I mean ; never mind the vexed question where his poetry ought to rank. Why don't I see Victor Hugo in that front row? Because I doubt whether the same row would hold him and Shakespeare. The old man was so cock-sure that he knew all about Shakespeare ; and then he would want Shakespeare's views on the universe and the wickedness of kings, and I don't think William would relish that sort of conversation between the acts.

M. Delaunay lives in honoured retirement, and, I believe, still imparts the traditions of the good school of acting to the younger generation. We old folk shall never believe the new-comers can be as good, for all that even a Delaunay can teach them : but we may be wrong, and anyhow we don't mean to despair of France while the Théâtre Français flourishes, or while the Collège de France can show scholars like James Darmesteter—the man who came out to India and got to know the Afghans as no Englishman knew them. I wrote to you about him when I met him on the frontier. Let us see what Shipley says, having studied for his own purposes in Paris (he has just called to settle the dining-out arrangements for the *Ring* week). "French degeneration?" answers he, as nearly snorting as an amiable man can. " I know nothing about French politics, but I shall begin to talk about France being degenerate when we have learnt at the Record Office half the things they can teach us at the Ecole des Chartes." Don't ask me, my dear Elizabeth, what the Ecole des Chartes is. First, because I do not clearly know, and next because you had better wait till you can ask

Shipley, who has been there. Something at the back of my head tells me that we may possibly come to see a good deal more of him. It would be with my good will. Not a word to anyone if you take my meaning, for it is only a dim surmise. I like the man much, especially when I can get him disengaged from our mixed visitors.

Mixed they are just now more than usual, being all full of grievances or projects of their own, and each with only half an ear for anything else. Minnie bemoans, as aforesaid, the darkness of the Clayshott division, while Leagrave congratulates himself—meaning a little to include the world, though he does not say so—upon that long-promised monograph on Drake being off his hands. Now he wants to turn to something literary, a lesser light of the seventeenth century for choice. It is rather embarrassing for Margaret to have to find an opinion whether Cowley or Henry More would be more suitable. It is useless in such a case to tell our excellent Stephen that you have read very little of the one author and not a word of the other. He only goes on as if he did not believe you. Harry, who is our usual resource on these occasions—having a military and official faculty of looking respectfully intelligent whenever re-quired—is himself engrossed in endeavouring to get sent to Egypt. He says he is afraid of becoming a mere pen-and-ink soldier if he does not go back to seeing the stuff his work is made of ; anyhow, he is pressing for something that will take him to the front, and, as his superiors are well pleased with him, I should think he is likely to get it. A fresh parting just when we are all (comparatively) together would be some disappointment—but we have always held in this family that we owe ourselves to the Queen and the country, and if the best work Harry can do for the Queen and country is up the Nile, we must not say a word that could make his going less cheerful.

Your pet minor English poets seem to be either at Tolcarne or (as I suspect) carried off by you to the parts of the North : I have not found them here. So I have nothing to say of them just now. The other day I spoke of Leconte de Lisle's handling of proper names ; one of his best performances that way is in " La Paix des Dieux," which still sleeps, I believe, in a *Revue des Deux Mondes* ten years old.* The spirit of man calls up before him all the gods he has ever worshipped :

> " Et l'Hôte intérieur qui parlait de la sorte
> Au gouffre ouvert des âmes et des temps révolus
> Evoqua lentement, dans leur majesté morte,
> Les apparitions des Dieux qui ne sont plus."

With submission to the judgment of native-born French ears, I know nothing in modern poetry to surpass the solemn cadence of these last two lines —but I was coming to the procession of the gods.

* [It is now (1899) reprinted in a volume entitled *Derniers Poëmes.*]

There is something Miltonic in the sequence of strange imposing names, with just enough adjective and explanation to colour them. Leconte de Lisle, being a pagan and a Hellenist, had no love for Semitic deities, and cannot be said to have treated them civilly ; this is how he marches them on:

> " Et tous les Baalim des nations farouches :
> Le Molok, du sang frais de l'enfance abreuvé,
> Halgâh, Gad, et Phégor, et le Seigneur des mouches,
> Et sur les Khéroubim le sinistre Iahvé."

He goes right back over the brilliant philosophy of the half-Greek Alexandrians and the expansive moral reform of the Prophets to the savage old thunder-god who came down from Sinai to war with Chemosh and Baal and overthrow Dagon, as they tell of him in the rugged fragments embedded in Judges and Genesis, so old that the pious post-exilic editors dared not smooth off their asperities; the Lord who captained his own battles, and would now chastise his unruly children, now argue with them and jest with them, like a modern frontier leader managing Afridis in about the same stage of tribal education. Modern respectability has forgotten him, and made unto itself a comfortable benevolent monarch, a sort of chairman of bank directors, author of the Economy of Nature and other valuable works—a *Iahvé-Pignouf* one might call him in Flaubertian language. What would the tellers of those wild stories of palace treasons and feud and murder in the Books of Kings have

thought of a peaceful rustic congregation sitting in
an English church to hear them droned out as
First Lessons, and taking them in a hypnotised
fashion as something which must somehow be
edifying to modern readers, since it is in the Bible?
But the Hebrews have not forgotten the old Lord
of Hosts, except maybe some who have become
too prosperous. Heine had not when he put those
lines into the mouth of an unsavoury Spanish rabbi
combating a no less unsavoury monk :

> " Unser Gott ist nicht die Liebe,
> Schäbeln ist nicht seine Sache,
> Denn er ist ein Donnergott
> Und er ist ein Gott der Rache.
>
> " Unser Gott, der ist lebendig
> Und in seiner Himmelshalle
> Existiret er drauf los
> Durch die Ewigkeiten alle."

Talk of German being an unmanageable
language! What writer in what language has
bettered the feat of achieving a grand poetical
effect with a dry abstract word like *existiren?*
But we are insular in prose only less than in poetry,
and in poetry only less than in theology. And in
the fine arts?—no, that is where our chance of
salvation seems to come in. But I begin to
ramble unconscionably: the letting out of waters
in the season of freedom long deferred. Old
Indians ramble about Service shop, my young
friends brutally tell me, when other topics fail them;
and probably I talk nonsense. Leagrave would

stick all this full of his critical pins in five minutes. Therefore I write not to Leagrave, but to a sister full of wisdom and toleration.

Talking of pictures, Margaret will be painted—when we are rich and you will catch me the ideal painter. What is that about a Leonardo in the Louvre? She does not set up to be like Mona Lisa, and I forget the looks of the other Leonardos there, if Leonardo's handiwork they be: there are not too many real ones in the world.

Your loving brother,
TOLCARNE.

XXVIII*a*.

(*Postcard.*)

Glad to hear you are well settled in the North, but don't presume on the climate. Neither you nor L. find it too bracing, I hope. Is it not liable to sudden changes? All well here.

R. E.

XXIX.

From Miss Elizabeth Etchingham, the Hotel, Glenfearn, N.B., to Sir Richard Etchingham, 83 Hans Place.

DEAREST DICKORY,

"Earthquakes as usual," or Laura-quakes, if you object to hyperbole.

What is the meaning of *Annosus?* A telegram came yesterday, addressed Etchingham, signed Leagrave, and consisting of one word—*Annosus.* We none of us knew what it meant. Laura, who, since Mr. McTavish's expressions of interest in her " setting up " and " getting bed and meat," has smiled more or less upon him (" not, of course, like ourselves, but a very worthy, well-meaning man "), passed the cryptic and, as we supposed, " Unicode " communication on to him as a last resort. Mr. McTavish laid down his fishing-tackle, the sound of the winding of the reel ceased, and he thought he had a copy of the " Unicode " " aboot " him. And so he had, and straightway went on to announce in matter of fact tones that *Annosus* signified, " Twins both dead, mother not expected to live."

Here was unlooked-for news upon a fine summer morning, and Laura, of course, was terribly un-nerved at once. The fact that for all our endeavour we could not place the disaster, of which the transmitter was, we supposed, Stephen, hardly served to compose her. Mr. McTavish's " It may be no true," our landlord's " Deed I've heard o' waur happenin'," and the " Na, Davy, that ye ne'er heard o' " of kind Mrs. McPhail (kind, save when the integrity of her drains is questioned), were intermingled with Laura's sighs, shivers, and awe-struck utterances expressive of the unex-pectedness of Fate—unexpected indeed in a case where, as I have already said, we did not even know upon whom to fasten the calamity. The arrival of the coaches and "shar-a-bangs" drove Laura from the inn door upstairs, and when her audience consisted of but Cynthia and myself we heard again the old story of the want of confidence with which she is treated by the family; the Cimmerian darkness to which she is consigned. "Anything might happen without my being prepared, and with an action of the heart like mine I do not consider it safe." After a little of this I sent the Camelry, who was weeping in premature sympathy, to the post office with a telegram telling Stephen to repeat the message. Hours of vague surmises, during which Laura dwelt upon the possibility of getting satisfactory mourning in Edinburgh and wondered if Charles were the bereaved husband and father; wondered if Colonel Leagrave had, unbeknown to us, taken to himself a second wife; wondered if Stephen himself had made a secret marriage and waited till now to inform us of the fact. "Sorrow, Elizabeth, though you may smile (and I think your smiles are very out of place), does soften people, and to whom should Stephen turn in the day of trouble, if not to me?" Mrs. Le Marchant also, sat with us and indulged in sepulchral recollections of the mothers and children she had known to be carried off at one fell swoop, and then at last the return telegram came: "*Annumero.*" I flew in search of Mr. McTavish. "*Annumero:*" "Book is not yet published."

"It's a peety folk doesna' say what they mean," was Mr. McPhail's comment.

All this has so shaken Laura that she feels "it is not fair to myself" to remain longer at Glenfearn; and consequently the head and shoulders of the Camelry have been buried in travelling trunks since breakfast time. A dentist and a shoemaker are our ostensible reasons for hurrying to Edinburgh. "Her ladyship says, M'm, that the filling is now gone from her tooth (perhaps it's the toughness of the meat has drawn it), and her heel's blistered that dreadful and painful that she don't know how to walk;" but as Mrs. Le Marchant (who has been spending odd days here between visits) leaves Glenfearn to-morrow, Laura anyway would have found this heathered place unendurable when deprived of her companionship. Mrs. Le Marchant has just proved the hair that prevented the sword of Damocles from falling and causing death from solitude. Laura has confided in her freely, and "grief is easy to carry when the burden is divided among friends" (I take this reflection from Reynard the Fox's uncle Martin). Your postcard too was wrongly read. "Don't presume upon the climate" Laura understood to mean that the enervation from which she now suffers is nothing to what she may expect.

With Mrs. Le Marchant as a warning, should

I ever have a house to call my own, nothing will induce me to let it and throw myself for months together upon the hospitality of my friends. The hospitality of our friends is delightful, so long as their hospitality is not our convenience, but to be fitting in visits, eking out one there, and squeezing in another here, I think it is detestable, almost depraving. And then there is a sort of atmosphere. unseverable from formal visits, that comes between oneself and the heart of the country. The very views from the windows become the property of host and hostess as much as do the pictures on the walls. I remember during a three days' visit to the Leytons hearing Laura praise the nightingale as if she were complimenting Lady Leyton on the musical performance of her niece; and she really spoke of a peculiarly brilliant sunset with a civility that led one to infer that she imputed the splendour of the evening sky to the admirable taste and feeling for colour of Lord Leyton himself.

I am sorry for Charles's disappointment. Minnie is not the first woman, and will not be the last, whose help has been a hindrance to her husband. ("When Job was afflicted, the loss of his wife was not included in his misfortunes," Mrs. Vivian once observed.) Charles has, however, as you say, established a claim upon his party, and to have established a claim in public, as in private life, is to gain possession of a potent weapon. Let us hope that, if he stands again, Minnie will be too deeply engrossed in "A Tribute of Tears," or some other work of imagination, to throw herself "heart and soul," as she calls it, into the campaign. Minnie is always posing as something or other. She has lately posed as the devoted "helpmate," the colleague as well as wife. (I don't mean that her affection for Charles is a pose, for of course it is not. I only mean she has consciously set herself to play the part.) If we could shift her pose and get her to take temporarily that of *femme incomprise*, or soulful woman linked to a soulless husband, whilst she was occupied in pouring the soul into a novel, Charles, uncompromised by his wife, might succeed in getting mind and body into St. Stephen's. Stephen Leagrave, by sympathy and approval, could possibly bring about this state of things. He has always treated Minnie's literary exploits with gratifying interest, and went the length of describing "Only a Woman's Heart" as a human document. And then, when Charles had taken his seat, Minnie might be gently pushed into another pose—the pose of the sensible young woman who played with her babies and minded her own business and was as kind and good-hearted as Minnie really is.

To be sure it *is* the *Mona Lisa* that I see as the portrait of your frank, unsophisticated, bicycle-riding Margaret. To revert to truth after this deviation from it, *La Belle Ferronnière* was in my mind when I wrote, and as soon as the letter was posted, I remembered, with staircase memory (staircase memory is allied to staircase wit), that *La Belle Ferronnière* is not, in these latter days, included in Leonardo's works. Have you a mind in which what you know lies dormant at times, and suddenly forces itself—mostly too late for use—upon your consciousness? Certainly not. The mind of Richard is better regulated doubtless. I should like your views of the *Mona Lisa.* Are you fascinated, as I am, or repelled? Had I to put a personality to her, I should choose, I think, that of another Margaret, that of a very far distant Margaret—Marguerite of Navarre. Pater's description of the picture does not please me, but then the beauty of Pater's writing is a beauty I fail to appreciate. I find something meretricious about it, and between that and honest beauty there is to me just the difference that lies between a field of cowslips or a bank of violets and a perfumer's shop.

And when do you accomplish your " Ring "? I hear from Mrs. Vivian that, on her way to choose a new brougham—"Our old one, as I have been telling John for years, looks as if poor Noah had used it when he drove up to the ark "—she saw Minnie and "that horrible Mrs. Potters (who only goes because she thinks it the right thing to do) tearing hot and hatless down Long Acre." Mrs. Vivian may be correct as to Mrs. Potters's reason for hearing Wagner, but I resent the general imputation that this or that in art or letters is liked because it is the Fashion. How are we to like that which we do not know? That mysterious influence, the Fashion, hawks ware, pedlar-wise, to and fro. Autolycus was a rogue, but as a distributor of "lawn" and "cyprus," "bugle-bracelet," "necklace-amber," he was of use. And as a distributor, too, that folly, the Fashion, has its use and brings before our notice much that otherwise would bloom unknown.

You excite my curiosity when you speak mysteriously of feeling at the back of your head that you will see more of Mr. Shipley. Is the subtle sensation at the back of your head engendered, Dickory, by anything very tangible that you see before your eyes? Tell me. Thoughts can fly far while one is braiding St. Catherine's tresses. I can see Margaret married and living happily ever after. I believe in William Shipley, for he is beloved by Alice, and if a brother is beloved by his sister he is not perhaps more wholly bad than you are yourself. And having excited my interest, don't, man-like, relapse into eternal silence on the subject, but tell me all about it, as is your bounden duty. Do not only tell me what you think, but tell me what reasons you have for thinking what you think, so that with my feminine skill in such affairs I may winnow the grain from the chaff of your premises. But, being a man, you are of course very much more communicative, a thousand times less discreet, when you talk than when you write. Being a man, you go in much greater fear of committing yourself upon paper than by word of mouth. And with me, as I am a woman, it is just the other way. And how, if you don't dispute them, do you account for these facts? Is it that the written word remains to rise up and testify, and the waves set in motion by the spoken word are not apparent to our senses, and so the discreet creature—man—speaks, and the indiscreet creature — woman — writes?

This old reason, new to me, for objecting to the hiding of foreheads by fringes of hair I send to Margaret: "John Rows of Warwick reproached the beaux of his time for suffering their long hair to cover their foreheads on which they had been marked with the Sign of the Cross at their baptism." The book which tells me this, tells me too that Henry V., when, as Prince of Wales, he "waited upon his father in order to make his peace, was dressed in a mantle or gown of blue satin full of small eyelet-holes, with a needle hanging by a silk thread at every hole." Very convenient this if the wearer or his friends wished to darn a rent.

Your observation on the thunder-god of the past and the Iahvé-Pignouf of the present reminds me of De Quincey, "As is the God of any nation such will be that nation;" and so the God of feudal times was "the great Suzerain to whom even kings pay homage." As the world grows more merciful, I suppose, it follows that a fuller and fuller measure of mercy will be ascribed to the Deity. The qualities that human nature admires are those with which it invests what it worships. Human nature does its best.

> " Nor is it possible to thought
> A greater than itself to know."

Poor little Cynthia is showing signs of distress. After hearing (from Laura, not from me) that Harry was keen to go to Egypt, she took refuge in her own room. I was afraid of worrying her, but yet, as she had not reappeared when the Aberdonian waiter (whose attitude the other evening so perfectly illustrates the Persian poem) banged down a great iron tea - tray upon the "parlour" table, I went in search of her. She was standing gazing forlornly out of the window, with a damp cobweb of a pocket-handkerchief in her hand. Then and there I determined to write to Harry, but half an hour after there came a belated letter that the witch-like old postmistress had till then ignored. The belated letter was from Harry. "The Rajah will have told you of my plans," he says. (You have not, atrocious Rajah, told me of his plans definitely.) " I'm off to-morrow," he goes on, " and hope it won't be a case of getting there the day after the fair." Then a postscript bids me tell Cynthia that Trelawney fattens and flourishes and deigns to accept Margaret as a slave. So now I incline to think I had best not write to Harry. If he is to go, or rather if he has gone, doubts as to the wisdom of his going will but unsettle him. What do you think? Write me a leader on the subject. How I wish he were safely home again. Till he is safely home again (I am touching wood as I write) I shall be for ever imagining ill. I do think for women who have leisure to sit and think, the lively fancy that pictures disaster with a vividness that outvies in vividness the actual is an engine of torture that the Inquisition need not have despised.

I hear from Enticknap that old Merlin has passed away. I wish it had not been in the absence of his family that the dear old dog breathed his last. Enticknap had a great opinion of the dog, as he has of everything that he counts ours, and was solicitous about him according to his lights. When once I inquired why in the world a large potato was pierced with a string and tied to Merlin's collar, Enticknap confessed that they did say a potato carried in the pocket would get the rheumatism out of the bones, and as the old dog had no pocket there was no saying but what the tying it to his collar might serve. (The potato cure for rheumatism is an old Devon superstition. It is supposed that, as the potato softens, the rheumatism lessens. The potato should by rights be placed in the patient's pocket by a member of the opposite sex and unobserved.) Poor old Merlin. The death of a faithful, affectionate, dumb thing hurts surprisingly. I like Carlyle upon the death of Nero: " Little dim white speck of Life, of Love, Fidelity and Feeling, girdled by the Darkness as of Night Eternal." And he could not have believed, he says, that his grief would have been the twentieth part of what it was. I was reading the other day, what Horace Walpole wrote on the death of Madame du Deffand's Tonton. A tenderness for animals was one of Horace Walpole's redeeming points. Enticknap tells me that he has laid old Merlin under the grass on the lawn near the filbert trees. I wish I could persuade you to write Merlin's epitaph. Almost the last verse that my father wrote was an epitaph in Latin on the first Merlin, this Merlin's father. Write something on this dear old dog. I wish I could have seen him again.

We are passing through such a lovely day. Why don't you conquer distance, span space, and come and take a walk ? Or if you are lazily inclined, you would find the knoll above the river where a knot of rugged old pines give shade, and grey rocks padded with wild thyme supply seats, a far and away pleasanter resting-place than a lifeless club. Carpets and curtains strike one as lifeless when contemplated from the site of reeds and trees. I should like to see the wind raising the carpets and tossing the curtains of the "East Indian," but then I suppose some old clubite would ring passionately for the waiter to close doors and windows. Crash! Here is that "gran" sound, the thunder of Mr. McPhail's dinner-gong again, and either there will be no walk for me or no dinner. The "gran" sound is too much for Blair and Atholl's nerves as it is too much for mine. Poor fellows, they flutter from side to side of their cage in wild alarm. Blair and Atholl are not a thousand miles away now from the place from which they take their names. Did you know that of old, Atholl was famous for witches? Two thousand and three hundred of these persons of greater skill than probity were, in the year of grace 1597, drawn up together upon an Atholl hill.

Farewell. I break off to consume mutton.

Your loving sister,
ELIZABETH.

P.S.—Is mutton bracing? Send your next letter to The Thistle Hotel, Princes Street.

(Enclosed in Letter XXIX. Posted at Stirling.)

After Ossian.

We went. In the hands of the Camelry was the immense dressing-bag of Laura. Filled with everything needless is the immense dressing-bag of Laura. In the thoughts of Laura was the awful fear of enervation. She waked her own sad tale at every step.

I met railway porters in fight. I took the tickets. I alone of all the Etchinghams took the tickets. I felt the strength of my soul.

Stately are Laura's steps in enervation. Stately is Laura on the platforms of railway stations. In her hands are no parcels. The Camelry is broken down with parcels. Many are the parcels of the Camelry. Many and immense.

O wonderful is the enervation of Laura. Wonderful are her fusses and fidgets. Often have I heard that no woman can fuss and fidget as Laura can.

The traveller shrinks in the midst of her journey. She shrinks from a fellow-traveller who eats jam sandwiches. Horror possesses her soul. Horror possesses the enervated soul of Laura.

Fat was the man from Glasgow who ate jam sandwiches. Fat and heated and red. Exulting in the strength of his appetite. O ye ghosts of heroes dead! behold Laura boxed up in a railway carriage with a fat man eating jam sandwiches. We looked, we wondered. Laura shrank.

XXX.

From Miss Margaret Etchingham, Hans Place, to Miss Elizabeth Etchingham, Edinburgh.

DEAREST AUNT ELIZABETH,

  I warn you that this letter is going to be about the Ring, and the Ring only. What else can I write about when the last week has been full of nothing else? So there. It is a most curious experience to have seen that wondrous work here. In Dresden, three years ago, it seemed quite a part of one's life there; but it is different here in the midst of London turmoil and traffic. One felt a little mad, starting off at four o'clock in one's evening clothes to be thrilled by Siegfried and Brünnhilde. And we were thrilled! I must allow that we were all a little damped the first day by "Das Rheingold." It depends so much less on dramatic interest than the other parts, that you want the orchestra and scenery to be perfect. Now this orchestra might be good enough for the common run of operas, though they would not think so at Dresden or Munich. But it seemed sadly rough and coarse for the magically delicate Rhine music. Then there were all sorts of little mishaps—and not all very little—in the stage arrangements. The singers were good, and struggled bravely not to be put out. It must have been even worse for them than for us, when a large agitated carpenter was seen crossing the stage instead of the expected Wotan. Poor old Wotan, he had enough to put up with besides having his entrance spoilt.

Two days later we set out undaunted for "Die Walküre," and we were much better pleased. It was something of a wrench when we bustled out after the first act, speechless and overwrought from the wonderful love-duet of Siegmund and Sieglinde—to get our dinner. Isn't it a wonderful thing?   You know the music in concerts.   But dining between the acts is a good plan ; it enables one to bear up under the emotion ever so much better.   It was quaint to see the lovely ladies in opera cloaks and diamonds tripping down Long Acre in the sunlight—but every one took it as a matter of course.   We found that the orchestra had pulled itself together and the staging was at least decent, and we could give ourselves up to the splendour of the music.

We were all in love with Fräulein Ternina ; she is a splendid, quite superhuman Bürnnhilde.   We couldn't make up our minds whether we were more impressed by the dignity of her warning to Siegmund in the second act, or the pathos of her appeal to Wotan at the end, which was quite unutterable and upsetting.   I don't mean that she couldn't utter it, because of course she did, but we couldn't speak of it.

Our third night—" Siegfried "—was the most delightful of all ; it is like a happy enchantment. One seems to feel the wind and the sunshine every time when Siegfried blows his horn.   We had a good young Siegfried, and he did not put on an aggressively childish manner, as some singers do. He was more than sufficient to cope with the Worm—for it was a very poor, lumbering reptile.

I have a difference with the rest of the party. They won't allow that Mime is a charming person. The cleverness of the way in which the music fits his odious character without being unmusical is to me particularly pleasing ; but I wonder why Siegfried did not kill him much sooner or set the bear at him. I know I should have done something to him. But what a glorious height of joy the last act rises to after Brünnhilde's awakening ! it is a thing to make one dizzy. Some people still say there are no tunes in Wagner. I suppose they do it merely to annoy—somebody always does. Did not people once complain that there was no tune in Beethoven ?

As for the "Götterdämmerung," it left us very weak and crushed, even the strongest of us. But the music is full of beauties, and Ternina and the De Reszkes were superb. It feels too flat and stale to go about ordering dinner when one's inner self is walking with those heroes in bearskins (though I must admit that Hagen's vassals are a poor stagy crowd in London), and Siegfried's horn still rings in one's ears.

Father got more and more excited about it and wanted to hear fuller accounts as it went on. I am sure he will take us to Bayreuth next year. He said we must all come here to supper to be restored after the "Götterdämmerung," and we had a very pleasant party, though we were all rather grave. I wish you could have been with us, and I wish you were here now to play over some of the music. Instead of which dinner has to be ordered. O dear, I wish it was all to come over again. Uncle Harry is somewhere in the Mediterranean by this time. I believe he is not

Those post-Shakespearian poets of yours (if Leagrave will allow any one but himself to claim any interest in them) seem curiously like our modern minor poets, of whom one or another is always going to dethrone Tennyson, or Browning, or Swinburne, and never does. It is the same story of the generation after the heroes; much deserving work, much excellence in detail, very fine things here and there, but the "pride and ample pinion" that make the difference between great poetry and good verse-writing nowhere. So far as workmanship goes, the workmanship of our moderns is, I think, better and more even. Whether their conceits are less violent than Crashaw's or Vaughan's will be for the twentieth century to judge.

But music reigns alone here for the present. Margaret has written to you about the Ring. Now I am free to wish I could have been there too. Did the company add to her enjoyment? Guess for yourself; you know as much as I do.

The only parting blessing I could think of to give Margaret on going to "Siegfried" was the clown's in "Antony and Cleopatra," "I wish you all joy of the worm." According to her report, the English stage worm is a very shallow monster, so a critic might well continue in the clown's language, "This is most fallible, the worm's an odd worm." Other things seem to have been odd too. "Spoiling the ship for a ha'p'orth of tar" is an English proverb, but when a work of art is in hand, nobody in this country seems to realise the importance of that ha'p'orth of tar.

After the last night's performance we had the whole party to supper here, including one Crewe of the Chancery Bar, one of the remnant who love learning for its own sake. Charles has mentioned him to me as an unpractical person with no public spirit—meaning thereby, I suspect, ambition. He quotes chapter and verse from seventeenth century books to show that a lawyer ought to be musical. Shipley has made friends with him on the ground of legal antiquities. While they were discussing the various possible meanings of the Ring, Crewe turned upon Shipley and said, "You are the only person here who will see that the true moral of this trilogy is professional." "How do you mean?" "Why, Loge was the first amateur lawyer, and the gods were punished for taking his bad advice." "We all know such wicked advice must be bad," said Mrs. Newton, taking it, as might be expected, seriously, though she seemed happier than usual. "He says it was bad law as well as wicked," explained Shipley : "Ancient Pistol, I do partly understand thy meaning. Let us hear." "Perpend then," said Crewe. "Loge tells Wotan it is safe stealing to steal from a thief, and Wotan believes him. But that is dead against the first principles of ancient German law, which have been preserved in our law. You may catch your thief red-handed if you can. If not, taking is keeping until the true owner comes to reclaim his goods, and Alberich had a better right to the treasure than Wotan, unless Wotan would retake it in the name of the Rhine-maidens." "But that was just what it did not suit him to do," I ventured to interpose. "Yes," continued Crewe, "but he ought to have known better, after giving an eye to purchase all the wisdom there was. Anyhow, putting his trust in Loge's thoroughly bad advice was his ruin." "Are you sure the point was settled so early?" said Shipley. Here Mrs. Newton called on him to take her away, and indeed it was pretty late.

An epitaph for Merlin, say you? Have not our masters, even Matthew Arnold and George Meredith, commemorated their dachshunds in verse? And who am I that I should botch where they have carved? One could wish that dogs lived longer, or that the long-lived animals were more interesting. A tortoise may be a good heirloom, but is not much of a companion. Even White of Selborne's interest in his old tortoise was more scientific than personal, I think.

What do I think of Mona Lisa? Mona Lisa was not easy to make acquaintance with, and was apt to be alarming during the period of slight acquaintance. She had not many friends, but to the few she had she was adorable, always knowing everything in a quiet way, never in a fuss, never out of temper ; one of the women who can be on terms of real friendship, no less, and nothing else, with a man. If she had been seriously angry with any one she would not have said much, but he would have found his plans crossed in some unexpected and particularly unpleasant way. I doubt whether she was often beloved (for the man had need of much daring and of the power to love heroically), or ever in love. If she had loved at all, it would have been so that the world must have heard of it. Other people, and Pater for all I know, may make her out quite different. I don't care if they do, and am not sure that I would take a contradiction from Leonardo himself.

Your loving brother,
RICHARD.

XXXII.

From Miss Elizabeth Etchingham, Edinburgh, to Sir Richard Etchingham, London.

Thistle Hotel, Princes Street, Edinburgh.

Many happy returns of the day, Sir Richard. A very fortunate day, this, for you. (It is not your own birthday to which I refer. Unlike most people, you are only allowed one a year.) I refer to my own.

I really do think, Dickory, it is rather horrid of you to have forgotten this universal festival. Not one word in your writing, not the ghost of a packet that looks like a present. My wrath is kindled against you. However, lest over severity drive you to despair, I will hint that I'm not implacable, and if you write me a long, long letter and promise me another Helleu etching, I may again like you almost as well as I like Sir Augustus Pampesford— The saints defend us! Richard! Speak of the deil—he—Sir Augustus, is in the room!

. . . .

With chastened spirit and the worst quill in the world, I return to my interrupted letter. *Eheu !* Sir Augustus is under this very roof—come to Edinburgh to interview Lyon King of Arms; come to look for a shooting; come to be civil to somebody (not to me). I never did see anything quite so solid and solemn as he looked projecting himself into the hotel drawing-room with a Royal Stuart plaid wound about his massive arm.

And the sight of him did not astound Laura as it did me. For once the shock and enervation and nerve prostration were mine. And what did I hear? I heard what led me to suppose that, while ministered to by the waiter from Aber-r-r-deen the other evening, we narrowly escaped the sight of Sir Augustus darkening the coffee-room window, shutting out the light of heaven, as his elephantine form descended by ladder from the roof of the station omnibus to the door-steps of the inn. But for some *contretemps* Sir Augustus would, it is plain, have joined us at Glenfearn the evening before last. He is in treaty for a shooting within easy distance of the inn. (Wait a minute, the post has come in.)

Thank you for your letter, dear. You will have heard what Mr. Shipley writes to tell me. Poor Colonel Newton. Frankfort railway station does not seem a suitable departure platform for another world. From what Mr. Shipley says, he died quite suddenly. His servant reports that during an altercation with the porters about the taking of small luggage into the carriage, he fell and never recovered consciousness. I shall be anxious for further news of Alice. I am rather glad that she had already gone back to Suffolk. Not that it can make any vital difference, but the influences of the country are soothing, and those of London are not. She asked Mr. Shipley to write to me and then, later, wrote a few lines herself. "Why could it not have been me?" she says. "I always thought Hubert could have been quite happy if he had married another sort of woman, and now there is an end to all that he might have had, and might have been."

There came, too, a characteristic, ghoulish letter from Mrs. Ware, Colonel Newton's sister, who has already started off on the tack of "I should have thought Alice would have wished the remains brought home for interment in the family vault; but this, from what I learn, is not, &c., &c. . . . . Alice herself seems wonderfully well. I have offered to be with her as long as she likes, regardless of serious personal inconvenience, but she is expecting Mr. Shipley on his return from Germany, it appears, and meanwhile does not feel the loneliness as one would have expected. For months after Mr. Ware's death I could not be left alone for an hour." Mr. Shipley's note differs wholly in purport. He fears that this shock will give yet another rude shake to Alice's shattered nerves, a far greater shock than news of the signing of her own death-warrant would have been. Charon must have the hunter's passion for pursuit. He despises willing prey.

Mrs. Vivian writes to tell me that as I am not available she is taking Ada Llanelly to Marienbad. " It is easier to take her than to shake her off, and now that Eddy Leyton's engagement to Wilfrida Home-Lennox is an accomplished fact, Ada does not give herself the airs that she did when imagining that she was to marry him herself. I heard from Lady Leyton this morning, who is thankful that it is not Ada. She likes the Home-Lennox girl. I certainly should be sorry for a son of mine to marry Ada. She is a regular Becky Sharp ; but she will do well enough at Marienbad, and John likes her, as she troubles herself to be civil to him. She would go and sit beside a scarecrow and be civil to it, if it wore a man's coat." Mrs. Vivian furthermore tells me that Mr. Biggleswade and Ada impressed each other very favourably when last he came to London " dressed, poor zany, to look as much like a guardsman as possible and making it plain that no one considered the Church a greater anachronism than he does himself."

Mrs. Vivian goes on to ask me, " How would it be if Mr. Biggleswade and Ada Llanelly made a match of it? They have each impressed the other with the sense of social ' smartness.' Ada wonders how Mr. Biggleswade ¦came to go into the Church " (a wonder after his own heart), " and he speaks of her as very ' good fun ' " (a verdict after hers). " She couldn't tolerate life in our vicarage, but she might tolerate it as the wife of a West or South-west London clergyman who remained in the Church because he thought it would be hard on the poor dowdy old Church if he threw her over, and who preached on secular subjects to a crowd of got-up women painted to their eyes." So says Mrs. Vivan.

Is it true that Stephen and Mr. Biggleswade are writing a play together? Since I received the " Unicode " telegram that my last inquiries concerning his book-making produced, I feel shy of putting questions on literary affairs to Stephen.

I did not tell you that while we were at Glenfearn I went over to Dalruogh. It was cowardly not to have gone before, but one side of me has been half crazed, I think, these years ; and I have had letters constantly ; and I have written constantly, as you know. (A letter had come from Dalruogh the morning of the day on which that foolish Sir Augustus first asked me to marry him.) And when I was at Glenfearn I felt as if I could not face the going there, though I felt too as if I should be sorry always afterwards if I did not. And then Mr. Fraser—Dalruogh, as he is in that country—rode across the moor to Glenfearn one afternoon when the others were out and seemed as if he wished me to come. We had met already at halfway places. He was growing old, he told me, and old folk had not overmuch time for getting their way, and he had a wish to see me there again and to give me one or two things I might care to have. So I went. I was deceitful, I am afraid, in concealing my intention from Laura. But I could not speak of it or have her, or even Cynthia, with me. Some things one can only do and endure alone.

Mr. Fraser still lives by himself. He and the collies—one of them the white collie I christened Fingal, now old and stiff—came out to meet me. The house looks just the same, and the gardens as peaceful and lovely as ever. I used to think how when you came home you would admire those hanging gardens overlooking the river, terrace divided from terrace by old iron gates, and the brilliant flowers thrown into relief by the background of dusky yew. I used to think of the library, too, how much you would like the books. And Mr. Fraser told me I was to tell you in detail of his treasures; they might perhaps tempt you to Dalruogh some day, and for this, he showed me a copy of the Montaigne in which Florio apologises for printers' and other errors by saying an engagement at Court had absorbed his time; and the first English New Testament printed at Geneva, and a folio Beaumont and Fletcher with the wreathed portrait and Hunnis's "Seven Psalms" and "Handful of Honeysuckle," and other rare books of old verse, and black-letter Bibles and wonderful missals, and then copies of about ten folio editions of Horace, and as many Virgils. They would all, he said, go to a ne'er-do-weel lad who would sell the lot to pay his racing debts. He had only one son.

We went to the churchyard. I had not seen the stone. The inscription just says, "Alastair Ian Fraser of Dalruogh. Born January 7th, 1852. Died August 12th, 1891"—from a gun accident. Suddenly—that was better perhaps than illness.

But why had it to be?

The stone looks quite grey and old, as if it had been there a long while now. Seven years is a long while, and yet it is nothing. A thousand years and but yesterday.

His life was very good while it lasted ; I like to think that. He was very successful in his profession and had interests all round. As keen a soldier as Harry, with a love for things bookish like you, and a love for the country like me. And his father and he were friends ; not only father and son ; and to his mother he was all the world. His dying sent the light out of her sky for ever, and it killed her, I think. I was tougher and young, and got acclimatised to living on in the dark.

I don't know why I am writing this to you, rending my heart but not my garments. Yes, I do know. I want to bring him back into your thoughts, if only for the moment, so that he may live in your memory; and I have never the fortitude to do it speaking, though I have often tried. For the dead *are* forgotten, Richard. We only pretend that they are not. To all my relations now it is as if he had never lived and died. Laura said to me the other day, " I think your nerves are getting out of order, Elizabeth; you wince when you hear a gun." It is true, I do. But I have not suddenly become what Harry would call gun-shy. I have been so ever since the day of a gun-accident on the moor above Dalruogh.

Mrs. Vivian would say I have had more in not marrying him than if we had been married. The half in such cases is greater, she declares, than the whole. The saints were mostly unmarried, or married to brutes or shrews, she is fond of announcing. I remember some one saying once, *à propos* of the engagement of a woman she knew, to a man who had been married before, " I should not be jealous of the woman he married, but of the woman he cared for and did not marry. It's the men and women that are beloved but not married that are canonised." But there are people in whom there is nothing that disillusions. Their trifling faults and failings are either lovable or seem to throw their virtues into higher relief. And even if there are graver faults, I don't think that would interfere ; unless they were base, ungenerous faults.   Pride, hot temper, self-will, obstinacy, arrogance, prejudice ; what am I that I could not forgive them all ?

It was even harder to pull myself from Dalruogh than the going there had been, and it was evening before I came away.   But I shall go back, I think. I think I shall go back soon ; I said I would. There, at least, he is not forgotten.   His guns and fishing-rods, all the inanimate things, are just as they used to be.   And when his father wished me good-bye he said, " God bless and keep you ; we have both the same sorrow in our hearts."

And then I drove the twelve miles over the hill to Glenfearn, and was met by Cynthia with many caresses, and by Blake with the tidings that " her ladyship was that alarmed, not knowing where you was, M'm, and them nasty tinkers about, that she's having tea instead of dinner."

For the rest that I had to say I cannot say it now.   Good-bye.

ELIZABETH.

XXXIII.

*From Sir Richard Etchingham, 83 Hans Place,
to Miss Elizabeth Etchingham, Ocean Hotel,
St. Kentigerns, N.B.*

DEAREST ELIZABETH,

How should I forget your birthday? It was the binder who was a few days late with his reverent mending of a little old eighteenth-century reprint of Sir John Davis's " Immortality of the Soul," which you should receive by this post or the next. I was sure you would not like it re-bound if the old binding could be saved. Sir John pleases me, I confess, better than your later English Platonists. His images are more noble and sustained, and he does not fly up like a sky-rocket to burst in a shower of crackling little conceits. I don't say he is free from affectations in his minor work. Only an Elizabethan lawyer-poet could have set down that " Every true wife bears an indented heart, wherein the covenants of love are writ." But I claim judgment for him, as every man ought to have it, on his best, the " Nosce Teipsum." What say you now to this?

" As a king's daughter, being in person sought
  Of divers princes, who do neighbour near,
On none of them can fix a constant thought,
  Though she to all do lend a gentle ear :

" Yet she can love a forrain Emperor,
  Whom of great worth and power she hears to be,
If she be woo'd but by Embassador,
  Or but his letters or his pictures see :

    " For well she knows that when she shall be brought
       Into the kingdom where her spouse doth reign,
    Her eyes shall see what she conceiv'd in thought,
       Himself, his state, his glory, and his train.

    " So while the virgin Soul on Earth doth stay,
       She woo'd and tempted is ten thousand ways,
    By these great powers, which on the Earth bear sway:
       The wisdom of the World, wealth, pleasure, praise:

    " With these sometimes she doth her time beguile,
       These do by fits her Fantasie possess ;
    But she distastes them all within a while,
       And in the sweetest finds a tediousness."

The conclusion of the simile is good, but not quite
so good. And some pages farther on :

    " Bodies are fed with things of mortal kind,
       And so are subject to mortality ;
    But Truth, which is eternal, feeds the mind,
       The Tree of life, which will not let her die.

      .   .   .   .   .   .

    " Heaven waxeth old, and all the spheres above
       Shall one day faint, and their swift motion stay ;
    And Time itself in time shall cease to move ;
       Only the Soul survives, and lives for aye.

      .   .   .   .   .   .

    " And when thou think'st of her eternity,
       Think not that Death against her nature is,
    Think it a birth ; and when thou goest to die,
       Sing like a swan, as if thou went'st to bliss."

Stanzas like these, when one considers the difficulty of handling a philosophical argument in
verse, appear to me to place the author's art very
high.

True it is that Sir John Davis has not convinced

the world that his aspirations amount to proof : nor has any one. For I take it that those who believe in personal immortality on direct conviction, not merely on authority, or as having convinced themselves that they ought to believe on authority, are no very large number. Indeed it is or has been an orthodox opinion that natural reason is not adequate for this purpose. But it is good to aspire. And for once I must disagree with you, though on things almost too sacred to discuss—I mean, when it comes to one's own personal application. Speculation is and ought to be absolutely free, but human weakness can preserve its freedom only by keeping it in general terms. But here is my difference. You say the dead are forgotten ; are you not unjust to the remembrance of the few—those who ought to remember—in confounding it with the large inert oblivion of the multitude ? No, our dead are not forgotten : least of all, perhaps, when least present to our conscious thought. None of us can really sound the depths of his own memory. They have entered into our lives and work with us, and all that we. do is their tribute. For the rest, I am content to be no wiser than the nameless sage whose wisdom was deemed worthy to borrow a name from Solomon. " Iustorum animae in manu Dei sunt."

The full solution is not for us now. But somehow, some time—or peradventure as much beyond our measures of time as beyond our limits of space

—the rules that keep our day-dreams in order—it is plain in the infinite thought of the One who wakes. If we may not pray with the saints, we can watch with the humble sinners. Which is the greater faith—to think that we have the secret of God's counsels, and can dispense it in daily rations, and earn doles of it by good conduct, or to trust God's knowledge far enough not to be afraid of confessing our ignorance?

> " Some draw the wine to drink thereof full deep,
> And some i' the mosque their night-long vigil keep—
> Unstedfast all, tossed on a shoreless flood ;
> For ONE doth wake ; fools in their folly sleep."

So says Omar Khayyám, the real and serious Omar, I conceive, when he rends the veil of his ambiguous conventional imagery and ceases from his antinomian flings against the formalism of both Mullahs and Súfis. How do I know, you may say, that this and not the other—or one of the others—is the real Omar? Well, I don't ; but this and like utterances—not fitting into the common forms even of unorthodoxy—seem far less likely to have been interpolated than the six hundred and one stanzas about wine and moonlight and the lips of the beloved by the lip of the field (the boundary between tilth and wilderness in a country living on irrigation), which scores of versifiers might have written at any time over several centuries. Not that the wine and moon, and so forth, need always have their literal meaning, or only that meaning. My own belief is that the reader is often wilfully left to take his choice as he may deserve : but that is yet another story.

As to more modern literature, it is quite true about Stephen Leagrave and Biggleswade. They are concocting an Elizabethan drama. Not much of it is written, so far as I can make out. Leagrave tells me of interminable discussions on the mint and anise and cummin of archaism. Biggleswade wants it to be written in Elizabethan spelling, with stage directions to impress on the reader at every turn that the action takes place under the conditions of the Elizabethan theatre, on a platform commanded by the audience all round, and with no costumes or scenery. You know—or don't know—that our incomparable Biggleswade is a professed enthusiast for the revival of the pure Elizabethan stage management. Apart from my general objection to Biggleswade and his works, that seems to me one of the queerest fads of an archaizing age—permissible, perhaps, as an occasional curious exercise. Not long ago, when Shipley was in Paris working with his friends at the Ecole des Chartes, he met one of the first living actors of France—one who has had to do with Shakespeare —and told him of these Elizabethan performances in London. The actor's comment was what a Frenchman would call "brutal" if an Englishman had said it. "C'est stupide!" What is more, I think Shakespeare would have called it stupid. If Shakespeare made "four or five most vile and ragged foils" and a few "chambers shot off" furnish forth the siege of Harfleur and the field of Agincourt, it was not because he liked it so, but because the stage and the property-room of the Globe could do no better for him. He tells us so himself. What is the inference to any one who has not drilled himself into the very lunacy of antiquarian pedantry? Surely that, if Shakespeare could be with us now, he would applaud Sir Henry Irving to the full, and work the resources of the modern theatre to their utmost capacity. Leagrave is dogmatic enough, but he is too much of a scholar to have broken with all the traditions of rational modern education, and he has not got to the point of despising everything done between 1590 and 1890. So I don't very well see how he and Biggleswade are going to hit it off. The play will no doubt find some one to praise it ; Biggleswade has at any rate not neglected the modern art of " ladling butter from alternate tubs." But it needs no great skill in fortune-telling to prophesy that it will have none to act it and very few to read.

Do you know the story of the minister at a Scottish funeral giving out the hymn?—" Let us sing hymn No. 297 : it was always a favourite hymn with the remains." Mrs. Ware may sing hymn No. 297 over Colonel Newton if she likes ; as indeed she is in duty bound. I shall not pretend to be sorry that poor Mrs. Newton, after apparently throwing away her life, has another chance of living. Margaret is sorry without much pretence, and it can hardly be for Colonel Newton.

Shipley took a hurried leave of us before going off to Frankfort to do what has to be done there; after which he will have to give an uncertain amount of time and trouble to putting things in order at home. I know nothing of Colonel Newton's affairs, except that he was the kind of man who is apt to leave most trouble to survivors—that is, he thought he was business-like, and was not. Mrs. Newton probably does not know the difference between a cheque and a bank-note, so Shipley will have to look to everything.

Arthur has come up for the Harrow match, and gone back disgusted with the usual inconclusive result (it seems that nowadays a drawn match is rather to be expected than not); but he is much pleased with his recent promotion to Sixth Form—to be captain of one's house and in Sixth Form is a great matter. Perhaps it is as near the position of a reigning Indian prince—with the house master for Resident and the head master for Viceroy—as anything this country can show. Meanwhile Shipley and I had spent a half-holiday afternoon and evening at Eton—the very day before Colonel Newton's death was announced. Arthur has most likely written to you since, as he is a pretty good correspondent. He is devoted to Shipley, as you are aware, and wanted very much to entertain him. I don't know which of us enjoyed it most. We rowed up to Boveney weir for a bathe, as all good Etonians ought when they get the chance ; and I am free to maintain that there is no better bathing-place in the world, and none so good, except perhaps in Rosia Bay near Europa Point at Gibraltar. And then tea with Lytewell in his garden—a real individual garden which he has made. Is that admirable type of scholar and gentleman—scholar all over, not merely in Latin verses and such like—threatened with extinction? Does it begin to seem antiquated to our young folk? Not to Arthur; I can answer for him : but he is only one. I hope not. Our public schools are not laid out for commercial seminaries, and will only be beaten at that game if they try. But the humanities have survived the great Useful Knowledge illusion of sixty years ago—an illusion not lasting enough to disturb the slumbers of Aklis with a Master of the Event—and they seem healthy enough for a while yet. "And what do you make at your public schools?" said a worthy *Privat-dozent*, still a little hazy about the idiomatic use of his English verbs, to a well-trained gunner going back to Indian service from his leave. The carefully self-informing German had already ascertained that his examinee had passed into Woolwich from Marlborough. "Men," said the gunner. And the *Privat-dozent*, having discovered his mistake by further questioning, made a careful note on the annoying refinements of the English verbs *make* and *do*. This was the last time I went out, somewhere off Crete.

Arthur was fuller of Shipley's praises than ever when he was at home, and Margaret seemed as if it got on her nerves somehow. What does that mean?

If there be anything in so-called Christian Science, Laura will surely be very ill one of these days—I suppose it works both ways.

Your loving brother,

RICHARD.

XXXIV.

From Lady Etchingham, Thistle Hotel, Edinburgh, to Sir Richard Etchingham, 83 Hans Place.

MY DEAR RICHARD,

Kindly send me Mr. Weekes's address *at once.* The Follits are away for their holidays—somewhere abroad, I fancy—so there might be delay in receiving an answer from them. I should be obliged if Margaret would have my bronchitis kettle (the largest of the three) got out of the cupboard in the Bath-room, where I hope it still is, *carefully packed,* and sent to me without losing a post to The Ocean Hotel, St. Kentigerns, N.B. (Grace must clean it thoroughly first.) I have not bronchitis at present, but my breathing since Sunday has not been quite free, and did I wait till an attack came on to write for the kettle it might reach me too late, and there is never any harm in being prepared.

We took some pretty drives at Glenfearn, but the air is terribly enervating, and it is scarcely a place to stay in. The food is very indifferent and the attendance thoroughly bad. Elizabeth did not, I think, notice the poorness of the accommodation. She seemed up in the clouds all the time. I was sorry that she should not have told us the day she went over to Dalruogh, but I positively had not the slightest idea of where she was going, and was more surprised than I can express when I heard from Blake, who asked the driver, where she had been. Neither I nor Cynthia know Dalruogh, and we should have enjoyed the drive. As it was, we wasted the day, which was one of the finest we have had. An old invalid gentleman from Bournemouth, with a very objectionable pushing young nurse, took the other landau, and I had to do without my daily drive.

It must have seemed odd to Mr. Fraser that, when we were all in the neighbourhood, Elizabeth should be the only one of the party to call. As that pleasant Mrs. Le Marchant said, it might look as if we were not on good terms for Elizabeth to go off like that by herself. It is much better for people to keep together, and it makes less gossip.

This hotel is very well managed and the beds are good. We go on to St. Kentigerns to-morrow (Mrs. Le Marchant assured me that I might depend upon the east coast of Scotland being most bracing and invigorating), and we expect to be at home on Saturday. Elizabeth will let Mrs.

Baker know about dinner when she has looked out the trains. She has now gone off again to St. Giles's. If it can be managed, I shall take Cynthia to Holyrood before we leave. I suppose one ought to see it.

Colonel Newton's sudden death from heat apoplexy is very shocking. Perhaps Mrs. Newton now will be sorry that they did not get on better together. Here, too, it is excessively warm, but the weather may change.

I hope Margaret will see that the *spout* of the kettle is properly packed, and that the parcel is labelled "*Fragile*," "*With great care*," as well as "*Immediate*."

With kindest love,
Affectionately yours,
LAURA F. ETCHINGHAM.

P.S.—Tell Margaret *without the spout* the kettle is *useless*, and Grace is so terribly heedless that she had better make sure herself that it is all sent and *registered*.

XXXV.

From Sir Richard Etchingham, 83 Hans Place, S.W., to the Dowager Lady Etchingham, Ocean Hotel, St. Kentigerns, N.B.

MY DEAR LAURA,

I am sorry I cannot help you to Mr. Weekes's address, as I have not seen or heard anything of him since he left Much Buckland. Neither do I know Mr. Follett's present address. If you ascertain it and have occasion to write to him, please observe that he spells his name with an *e* and two *t*'s. He is an old-fashioned scholar and particular about such things.

Should Mrs. Le Marchant, with whom I have not the honour to be acquainted, or any other person, trouble you with any more conjectures as to Elizabeth's visit to Dalruogh, you have my authority to tell him or her that I am fully informed of Elizabeth's reasons, and that they are perfectly good.

We can find no bronchitis kettle here at all answering your description, but only an old kettle and a spout which do not fit one another. I should guess that your large kettle went with the rest of your luggage to Glenfearn and has been accidentally left there. If not, I should presume that " whitesmith " is good Scots for a man who makes, or will make, bronchitis kettles, and that he and they are to be met with in Edinburgh.

London is particularly pleasant and healthy this summer, and cool for the time of year.

Yours affectionately,

RICHARD ETCHINGHAM.

XXXVI.

*From Miss Elizabeth Etchingham, Ocean Hotel,
St. Kentigerns, to Sir Richard Etchingham,
83 Hans Place.*

DEAREST DICKORY,

You don't know how grateful I am to
you for your letter. "They that are whole need
not a physician, but they that are sick," and virtue
went out of you when you wrote. I wanted you
to contradict what I said about the forgetting of
those who are gone. When I feel as I felt when
my letter was written, I am unjust, I know.

I have been all out of gear lately, unjustly
resenting that people did not realise what I do
my best to conceal. It is unfair to blame Laura,
or blame any one, for hurting, when my object is
to pretend to pretty-well every one that I am
callous. You know what is amiss by instinct, and,
as far as I go, it is only those who do know what
is amiss by instinct, who understand, whether we
will or not, whose handling of the ill is bearable.

It is stupid to mind the things that I often have
minded. If we are to live with our fellow creatures,
we must take our chance and rough it. But the
merest trifles can give the feeling of a great un-
bridgeable gulf fixed between what we really are,
and all around us. When Charles, the evening
before I left London, looked surprised, and asked,
in astonished accents, across the table at dinner,

how in the world I came to any knowledge of the "honours" on the Black Watch colours, it made me feel—I don't know what it made me feel, unless it was that I and the present were, by everything that exists, divided. And that time when Laura found that I had been to Dalruogh, she not only regretted that Cynthia and she had missed the drive, but said that Blake might have sat upon the box. Richard, is it a fortunate or unfortunate accomplishment to be able at the same time, as I am, to laugh with one's mind, and cry with one's heart?

People are handicapped, I think, for sensible rational behaviour who have the gift of seeing with their thoughts as vividly as with their eyes. Sometimes, halfway through a dinner party, or when I have taken Cynthia to a ball, I could see suddenly, just as if it was let down before my eyes, what happened that day on Dalruogh moor. I could see it all, I could even hear the ripple of the burn from which they must have brought water, and the—— But I *will* not let myself think of it now.

After the first it was never jarringly desolate at Tolcarne, as it was during the time in London. We had been together at Tolcarne, and there were associations and a background not alien from all I felt. But in that Hans Place house, where he has never been, and where there is nothing of which the look was to him familiar, I have gone through all the agonies. (You are to make over a hovel to me at Tolcarne in my old age—you really must.)

There, now I have told you, and I wish I had told you before ; for of you one does not ask bread and get a stone, nor does one get what is worse than a stone—that obtrusive, publicly shown after-sympathy with which the tactless molest the harassed.

Since your letter came I have wanted an analogy for the present and the past—the present which is the outcome of the past. It is not, for all of us, the flower of the past ; but do you think that it is the seemingly withered seed, not beautiful to look at and not fragrant, but still as much part of the flower that has gone as of the flower that will come ?

You must have known beforehand that I would like the verses from the " Immortality of the Soul." I wish the book would appear. I really did think that you had forgotten my birthday, but then I was all to wrongs and in a mood to fear the worst.

As to the battles of the creeds, it is, I think, easier to believe that we ourselves can go out like a candle than can those for whom we care. It is not as if we had seen life while we know life exists. It is not as if we have seen the motive power as well as the machinery, what propels as well as what is propelled. The manifestations of life, not life itself, are apparent—the outward and visible sign, not the inward and spiritual grace. What it is that makes personality—what inspires what we do and are—is no more visible in what we call life than if the change that we call Death had come. There is something in us that enables us to realise what is too fine for our senses to grasp; and the sceptics, as far as I know, do not prove that Death can touch that.

Margaret's letter must be answered now. It deserved a quicker response; and I have a letter from Arthur to answer as well. (Both the creatures are fashioning their handwriting upon yours.) Arthur's letter is in the key of Mr. Shipley, and indignation prompts his pen. Here was I, Elizabeth Etchingham, honoured by acquaintance with this phœnix, and I had bottled up the important fact during a period of many lengthy years. Arthur had not the ghost of a notion that I knew the man. Had he known it, he would have raised my pedestal sky high. That he makes plain. Black deceit, double-dealing indeed, never to have let out that I was acquainted with this prodigy— this athlete, this wit, this everything valiant and valuable rolled into one.

Margaret's raptures are for the "Ring." Mr. Shipley does not come into her letter, which does not, of course, prove that he does not come into her thoughts. When I try, however, I find I can't put Margaret's possible emotions under the microscope. But from what Alice Newton wrote to me a little while ago I gather that he is very much occupied with her—"I hope Sir Richard won't think that Will is giving the family too much of his company; he seems unable to tear himself away from Hans Place." I heard this more than once. Can Mr. Shipley be back from Frankfort before you and Margaret leave London? Your instinct would be to take her away, I believe, even though you think he is everything that he can be. For does any man seem quite good enough to another man when looked upon as the lover of his daughter? I once heard Mrs. Vivian wish that people came into the world and went out of it in congenial pairs. "It would be deadly dull and would leave nothing to write books or invent falsehoods about," she said, "but it would save endless trouble and unpleasantness." (Her last "mot" on Mr. Vivian's taciturnity is that she wishes, to break the silence, "he could be fitted up with a spring, as Hugo Ennismore says was that colossal statue of Memnon at Thebes which struck a musical note at sunrise." The Army and Navy Co-operative Society might do the work, she believes.)

Your letter to Laura did not miss fire. It was just the very letter to huff her most, and she had it out of her dressing-bag to read three times between Edinburgh and St. Kentigerns, and seemed after each perusal more and more enervated. She does not like to be addressed as the Dowager Lady Etchingham—"Laura, Lady Etchingham looks more like me." And that allusion to the temperate climate of London was a cruel sting in the epistle's tail. You are certainly formidable as an antagonist, and never turn, please, from my friend to my foe. Laura only read out selections from the letter to me, but what I heard of the odd kettle and spout and the London temperature was quite enough to account for the Christian-martyr air with which she travelled, and the many restoratives that she required on the way.

The red rocks of this shore remind me of the rocks of the West, and between the sea and the Lammermoors there should be romance. And there are other sights more humanly impressive than the sights of the sea and the hills. Under lowering grey clouds, and to the playing of the "Dead March," a soldier's funeral passed to-day up the very wide grass-grown street of this quietest of quiet towns. Then there is contrast here as well as harmony. Cynthia and I made use this morning of the St. Kentigerns Grange garden keys, lent to us by the absent owner. A clear trout-stream, a lake on which swans float, a rose-garden, rose-full, and a sun-dial bound about with honey-suckle, delighted us. And to pass through a little door in the high sea-wall, over which China roses blow profusely, was to find ourselves upon the beach with salt-water for fresh, seaweed for roses, and seagulls for swans. Is your Paradise provided with salt-water or fresh, seaweed or roses, seagulls or swans, green lawns bordered with lilies or yellow shell-strewn sands? Do you prefer the sound of the river or the sound of the sea? The "many waters" of my dreams are the waters of many rivers.

We saw enough and to spare of Sir Augustus in Edinburgh. I believe, I believe, I believe— (Enter the waiter, "Any more letters, M'm?" "Yes.") Good-bye.

ELIZABETH.

XXXVII.

From Lady Etchingham, Ocean Hotel, St. Kentigerns, to Sir Richard Etchingham, 83 Hans Place.

MY DEAR RICHARD,

You being the representative of your father, whose first object was my happiness, I write to tell you that I have promised to become the wife of Sir Augustus Pampesford. I feel sure I shall have your good wishes for my future. I have always tried to perform the duties of a delicate position, and I have the satisfaction of feeling that no effort of mine has been wanting to promote your happiness and that of your sister and brothers.

In justice to Sir Augustus and myself I cannot refrain from saying that evidently a very erroneous view of his former sentiments was entertained. He once fancied, it is true, that an alliance with a woman he could trust and respect would satisfy the needs of his heart and mind; but I believe he pretended to no intense affection for Elizabeth—

in fact, he has informed me that it is only comparatively recently that he realised the extent of the devotion that a woman could inspire. I explain this because I should not like Elizabeth or you, who have sometimes seemed jealous for her, to suppose that I have supplanted her, or even taken what she rejected. I am accepting what was never hers.

The living and chaplaincy of Pampesford-Royal being vacant, we propose to appoint Mr. Weekes.

Trusting that you and Margaret are well, and with kind love to both,

Ever affectionately yours,
LAURA F. ETCHINGHAM.

XXXVIII.

Miss Elizabeth Etchingham, Ocean Hotel, St. Kentigerns, to Sir Richard Etchingham.

Laura, with the Great Mogul at her elbow, if not with his hand on her pen, is writing, Richard, to tell you of her engagement to him. (Self-importance is but a weak word with which to describe the inflated grandiloquence of their bearing.) Is it not a most merciful dispensation of Providence? I am sure, as Mrs. Vivian said to her of Christian Science, that she will like it (like being Lady Pampesford) very much. Double-barrelled pomposity is far less subject to discomfiture than is the one-barrelled species, and Sir Augustus and Lady Pampesford may imagine their dual existence to be the pivot on which the world turns, and run no risk of a rude awakening.

The more I reflect, the happier I think are the auguries. He can and will give her all that she asks. And he will never puzzle, and by puzzling disconcert and disturb her, as you have done. You know your comments, that she only suspects are sarcastic by seeing some one else try not to laugh, have always bewildered and displeased her ; and then she had no confidante in the family. She would have liked us better if we had liked each other less. To carry out the divide-and-govern advice has been, where her step-children were concerned, impossible. If felicity is bad for our morals, it is mostly good for our manners, and she will be far and away pleasanter with an admiring Sir Augustus at her elbow than she has been with people much more taken up with each other than with her. Laura, in certain narrow grooves, is genuinely amiable, and to imagine herself of importance always puts her into a good humour. For grievances we shall now, I feel sure, have graciousness.

And Mr. Weekes is to go to Pampesford-Royal. The meek little man will devolop an obsequiousness equal to, if not surpassing, that which bowed down Mr. Collins before Lady Catherine De Bourgh. No clergyman with a backbone would stand the blend of interference and condescension that his patrons will dispense, and I think they have shown a masterly choice of tools.

Write as amiably as you can to Laura. She
has suffered many things at my hands, if not at
yours, and I am really delighted that she has
got at last what she likes. The bronchitis kettle
is forgotten and the air here is found most invigorating.

"Trustie and wel-beloved," are you taking care
of yourself? If not you are selfish and bad.

ELIZABETH.

P.S.—I am writing to Harry.

XXXIX.

*From Sir Richard Etchingham, 83 Hans Place,
S.W., to Miss Elizabeth Etchingham, Ocean
Hotel, St. Kentigerns.*

MY DEAR ELIZABETH,

Your second letter, and a solemn announcement from Laura which confirms the same,
have come together just as I was going to answer
the first. Their contents are really too good.
Erring and purblind creatures that we were not to
perceive for what an appropriate use in the world
the great Sir Augustus was reserved! Gladly let
us dine with them once a year—even twice if need
be—for the rest of our joint lives. We, dear sister,
because the hovel called Tolcarne, though it is not
a great house, is wide enough to hold us both.
If we find harmony too dull we can always quarrel
over the binding of a book. Talking of bindings,

Jem has been very mysterious about my Tod's "Rajasthan" ever since he carried it off: he would not tell me exactly where he meant to take it, and insisted on having unlimited discretion. And now Jem has appeared in his proper person, on a flying visit in a respite of his examination work, bearing the book in its new garment. It is bound in a rich deep russet, not so far from the dark brown you wanted; only it is Eastern morocco, not calf, and relieved with dull gold ornaments of Eastern design. One could almost believe it the work of a native craftsman. It is not by Jem's man at Oxbridge. While Jem had it out in his rooms at Silvertoe, there came round one day the Professor of Romance Languages, who naturally finds few students of Provençal or Catalan, but knows everything else from Iceland to Japan, and is ready to tell it in every way except officially. He pounced on the book, which he had never seen before, became deeply interested in it, firmly vetoed Jem's and my plans about the binding, and took it out of Jem's hands to an art school, of which he will not reveal the exact location. Jem has been wondering all these weeks whether I should ever see my Tod again; without cause, as it now appears. I am interrupted; a mysterious visitor, it seems. . . . Truly Sir Augustus is our benefactor, but he has not delivered us for nothing. What should I find in the drawing-room but two ladies I had never seen before, rather tall, angular, very correct in bearing, very antique in dress (it seemed to my inexpert eyes) very—well, let us say rather—antique in person ; armoured and glistening in many beads and bugles ; one of them black, or nearly black, the other dark purple. I could not think who they were, and they did not look as if they expected me or knew who I was. "I beg your pardon," I began feebly. No response, only puzzled and timid glances exchanged between the two personages. They must be sisters ; were they two spinsters, or widow and spinster ? What could they want ? Perhaps it was a begging dodge for some doubtful or worse than doubtful would-be charitable enterprise. I bethought me of the sage cautions of the C.O.S. (Charles had been telling me a lot about it ; he is a zealous committee-man in his district, whereby he does more good than by politics), and tried that tack. "If you have called on behalf of any—institution —would you kindly leave the prospectus with me and give me time to consider it?" Expression of pained surprise and polite but firm deprecation ; their feelings apparently too bad for words. So that was a failure, anyhow. Then I remembered that Margaret had entered into relations with our district committee. No beggars these, then, but more likely stewards of charity, stern but efficient dragons, and wisely benevolent under their scales, though the scales were many and wondrously shiny. "A thousand pardons," I resumed. "I think it must be quite the other way. Perhaps you came to see my daughter on Committee business? I am sorry she is out." The visages relaxed slightly, and the necks (I believe dragons' necks are wrinkled) bridled with a certain complacence as if to acknowledge the apology. But still I was off the mark. All signs of a hit were wanting. Another pause, in which I felt all sorts of colours.

At last the blacker dame seemed to be labouring at a spring somewhere in her vocal chords, as one struggles with that stout back-spring of a Spanish knife.—"For the love of God, Señor, lend me a dollar to ease the spring of my knife," says your sturdy Spanish tramp; and the wayfarer, if not armed and ready with his arms, finds it well to produce the dollar, and not be urgent for its return. —Well, the spring gave, and out came a high dry voice with a quaver in it. "We have the pleasure to speak with Sir Richard Etchingham?"—"That is my name."—"The present head of the family?" Thus joined in the voice of the purple one, a fat, blurting voice, with an occasional uncontrollable falsetto in wrong places, which rather spoilt the intention of dignified ease.—"At your service."— "Teresa!" resumed the first with a monitory aside. "It is true, Sir Richard, that we intended in the first instance to pay our compliments to Miss Margaret Etchingham, but I am sure you will readily, quite readily, admit our claim on your acquaintance." I felt blanker and blanker. Could Jem have sent me two mad undergraduates in masquerade? Had something gone wrong in the

Zodiac and made it a Gilbert and Sullivan world?
"Because," plumped out the second, "dear Lady
Laura being so soon to be our sister makes Miss
Margaret a kind of niece to us, and we thought it
would be so nice to know you all, and indeed
a want of duty, with an example to set in our
neighbourhood, too, if we delayed." "*Teresa!*
Familiarity will perhaps be more in place when
Sir Richard Etchingham has received the full
statement of the circumstances and reasons to
which he is entitled. And, to be sure, we should
not complain of Sir Richard for being properly
cautious, though I should have thought the
name——." "Excuse me," I cried in despair,
"but I have heard no name at all!" Here enter
Grace—who is so careless, as Laura says; she
really is a good soul, with fits of wool-gathering—
bearing an abashed countenance and a salver.
"Please, Sir Richard, I forgot the ladies' cards."
I took; I read:

> *Miss Pampesford,*
> *Miss Teresa Pampesford.*

101, *Palace Gardens.*

So they were the sisters of Him, the *semper Augustus.*
They worship him; they have shrivelled in watching his growth, as in an old cookery-book I saw
long ago two cutlets are "victimised" for a third,
which is cooked between them and absorbs all
their goodness. For twenty-five minutes did those
much-absorbed spinsters descant in treble and alto

on the nobility of their brother and the virtues of Laura. My agreement that it was an eminently proper match, and entirely satisfactory to me, so far as I had any right to an opinion, was genuine so far as it went, though I could scarcely abound in their sense. We had a very polite leave-taking. Five minutes later Margaret came in. I suppose she will have to call on them.

Meanwhile the Elizabethan drama runs to alarms and excursions. It will soon be "Enter *Biggleswade and Leagrave*, fighting." Biggleswade's epistles on the points of spelling and stage directions have been exacting, peremptory, rude, violent. He has worked himself up to threatening Leagrave with an action to compel him to carry out the plan —according to Biggleswade's interpretation; and having written his solemn threat, he has taken advice on its legal value. Charles, who does permit himself to be amused by professional jokes, came in at breakfast-time this morning chuckling over an opinion which Crewe had shown him before he sent it out. Biggleswade's solicitor, finding his client intractable, laid a case before Crewe, with a hint that nothing short of a full and learned opinion would give satisfaction; and he got one, it seems. Crewe has proved with many authorities that no court of law or conscience, in the time of Queen Elizabeth or at any time since till this year 1898 inclusive, would undertake to compel a man to write a play. My somewhat vague and distant recollections of the Indian

Specific Relief Act confirm the soundness of his conclusion ; this somewhat to Charles's surprise, for Charles is under the impression that all Indian judges and magistrates exercise a despotic and patriarchal jurisdiction with the most arbitrary discretion, and I have never been able to remove it. Not that I do not personally wish one could frame some literary frontier regulations of a summary pattern, and apply them to Biggleswade and one or two others. Frontier regulations ought to be good for bounders.

Charles and Minnie are perhaps coming to the neighbourhood of Tolcarne when the courts rise on August 12. They have heard of one or two houses which might possibly do. I fear this means that he is still hankering after the Clayshott Division ; but he must go his own way in that respect. Meanwhile, he can help Mrs. Tallis and me to settle that little boundary question in the simplest manner which the wonderful land laws of this part of the British Empire will allow. But he maintains through thick and thin, whenever I mention the subject, that the system here is the only one suited to English habits, and that my praise of Indian land transfer at the expense of the English family solicitor (for whose only benefit the whole business seems to me to exist) is just another piece of official prejudice. This is not exactly what, by the light of nature, one would expect from an enlightened and advanced Radical. But I have met with few Radicals who are not intensely conservative about something, generally belonging to their own profession.

We must clear out of this, I suppose, a day before you come back. The house won't hold us all, and Laura will, of course, expect to find everything, down to the old unserviceable kettle, well swept and garnished.

Ever your loving
RICHARD.

XL.

From Sir Richard Etchingham, Hans Place, to the Dowager Lady Etchingham, Ocean Hotel, St. Kentigerns.

MY DEAR LAURA,

Accept my best congratulations on your engagement to Sir Augustus Pampesford, in which Margaret begs to be joined.

It seems in every way an excellent and most suitable match, and Elizabeth will no doubt confirm me in saying that I express her opinion as well as mine.

Wishing you all prosperity and happiness,
I am yours affectionately,
RICHARD ETCHINGHAM.

XLI.

*From Miss Elizabeth Etchingham, St. Kentigerns,
to Sir Richard Etchingham, London.*

Is there imbecility, dear, in the family (the Pampesford family), or was it only imbecility's counterfeit, nervousness, that made her put Laura into the peerage and twist Margaret—Laura's step grand-daughter—into her own "kind of niece"? Find out, do, if they are *all* feeble-minded, and leave a note to say "Yes" or "No" upon the chimney-piece in my room. And what was Grace doing straying about the drawing-room with cards on a salver? Heaven help her if Laura hears of her proceedings. Laura would inquire in severe and shocked accents "Where, pray, was Turnbull?"

I will write from Hans Place. At this moment salt water is running from the hem of my garments and making pools upon the floor big enough to accommodate salmon. Such magnificently towering waves are breaking to-day over the sea-wall, and I was childish—or imbecile—enough to wish that one would break over me. One obligingly did.

Yours ever and always,

ELIZABETH.

XLII.

*From Sir Richard Etchingham to Miss Elizabeth
Etchingham, 83 Hans Place, S.W., to await
arrival.*

No, my dear wave-salted sister, it was not
natural imbecility, but anxiety to talk with polite
ease and show that they knew the world. They
ought to have married auctioneers in a small
borough, and devoted their ambitions to qualifying
a daughter to marry the town clerk. Plenty of
nerves, certainly, and not too much brains.

Biggleswade has sent Leagrave another furious
letter, declaring that everybody, including his own
solicitors and counsel, is in a conspiracy against
him. Stephen's troubles are not likely to be at
an end. He is advised that Biggleswade will probably fall into the hands of some shady solicitor,
who will carry hopeless proceedings just far
enough to run up a nice little bill of costs; after
which there remains the lowest depth of being
a plaintiff in person. Biggleswade is capable of
that. He thinks he knows as much as Shakespeare; we are told that Shakespeare was a
lawyer; argal, Biggleswade must be a lawyer;
and, with the proverbial fool for his client, he may
plague honest men for a season.

Thine, R. E.

275

XLIII.

From Miss Elizabeth Etchingham, 83 Hans Place,
to Sir Richard Etchingham, Tolcarne.

Renseignements Mondains.

Arrivés à Londres et descendus à l'hôtel Etchingham—

Your stepmother.

Your stepfather-in-law (Milord Auguste Pampesford-Royal, Bart.).

Your sister.

Your stepmother's niece.

La Camelrie.

Les singing-birds.

(I was once at Dieppe for an hour, and, like a
better known personage, without wholly acquiring
the French tongue, lost the complete knowledge
of my own, and have spoken broken English ever
since.)

It was grievous to find only your note, and not
you. But St. Kentigerns, when enjoyed in the
company of Sir Augustus, proved so enchantingly
bracing that Laura would not cut down her stay
there by an hour. I was sorry for some reasons to
cross the Border. But it shall not be " Lochaber
no more."

You tell me that, when confronted with the Miss
Pampesfords, you asked in your bewilderment if
they had called on behalf of any institution. Well,

I really do think they did call on behalf of an institution. I, who have now travelled with him, assure you that Sir Augustus is nearer to an institution than to a man. And a prospectus would befit him better than a character. Surely he is the personification of an Institution, or a Corporation, or a City Company, or a Board. His solemnity is appalling, and perfectly illustrates the Gallic definition of gravity: " Gravity is a mysterious carriage of the body invented to cover the defects of the mind." And Laura enjoys and finds safety in the "mysterious carriage;" she approves of the seriousness with which he takes himself and takes her, instead of being bored to death by it. Solemnity is to me suffocating; and as to love-making, I agree with—

> " He had been a fool,
> An unfit man for any one to love,
> Had he not laugh'd thus at me."

A bantering epistle has reached me from Harry, who had just received my note telling him of Laura's engagement when he wrote. He is in high spirits, and in answer to my enquiries says the hourly bulletins will be discontinued, as his usual rude health shows no sign of breaking. He is kept fully employed, and has, he informs me, no quarrel worth mentioning with Fate at present.

Poor Stephen came in to see us last night. He has suffered acutely at the hands of Mr. Biggleswade. And as Mr. Biggleswade carries his seventeenth-century madness to the point of allowing no words to pass till not only he, but his friend Mr. Ledache, is satisfied that it is used in its strict Elizabethan sense, and as Mr. Biggleswade and Mr. Ledache, are not always in accord, Stephen's tortures, legal proceedings apart, are likely to be long drawn out. Then his collaborator writes an almost illegible hand and uses lead-pencil that effaces itself in transit, so the wretched Stephen, while knowing that he is rated and reviled, can only guess at the exact drift of the ratings and revilings: a pleasant part in truth. Mr. Biggleswade began by insisting on a masque and anti-masque, and when Stephen objected, as anachronistic stage directions, to "enter Cupid in a yellow hair," and "the Masquers are discovered seated in their several sieges," Mr. Biggleswade dealt with the demur as if it were an affair of pistols for two, coffee for one. Has not Shakespeare in the "Midsummer Night's Dream" himself parodied the Elizabethan Society's theories? The Elizabethan Society seems, at last, to have reached Paris, and "Measure for Measure" is to be put upon the stage after its primitive methods. But it is the older Parisian attempts to give Shakespeare that are amusing. To carry King Lear on to the stage upon a bed of roses, to enable him to see the sunrise, was a charming notion.

A letter from Mrs. Vivian was waiting for me. Her charity is to be found, not in her words, but in her deeds, and she writes from Marienbad to say that she wishes she could believe that "semper Augustus" and Laura would irritate each other as much as they irritate her. "And I congratulate you on losing your place of *Bonne à tout faire.* Lady Etchingham will now indulge in paid servants, I trust. But the poor in intellect being always with us, some other silly woman will most likely tack herself on to you now." Mrs. Vivian wishes to know what is to become of "that lovely child." That lovely child's father, Colonel Leagrave, is most opportunely coming home for good this autumn, and Stephen talks of going as far East as time will allow to meet him. The Vivians speak of India for the winter too. " Why does not Sir Richard take a jungle ? Would it not amuse him ? " Mrs. Vivian asks. When you know that the omnipotent " Hugo Ennismore " and " Jock Home-Lennox " are taking jungles, you will, she thinks, be disposed to follow suit. The P. and O. that takes out the Vivians, including Blanche, will be the boat, I think, in which Stephen will engage a berth. He talks to Minnie but he looks at Blanche, and Blanche won't sit by silent and hear him pulled to pieces by her mother. But the Stephen and Blanche romance, if it exists, is the other side of our border, and there will be little of Stephen left for romantic or other purposes if Mr. Biggleswade does not soon tame down.

"People must be beginning to fight shy of Ada Llanelly, your brother Harry's old flame," Mrs.

Vivian also tells me. "She has become so abnormally civil to every respectable old female bore in the place. This is quite a new thing. She toadies Lady Clementine Mure, to whom she used to be frightfully off-hand and rude, and Lady Clementine is made very nervous by the unprovoked attentions, as she does not give balls or anything. She thinks Ada would never take so much trouble unless she meant to marry her boy —the conceited clever one who has just got a decent appointment in Egypt."

Azore is now with us. Azore with his bangles, his silver-backed brushes, his blue silk wadded dressing-gown, for wearing should the nights be chilly when he is recently clipped, his gilded basket, and his crystal water-trough, on which "Azore," in gold letters, is engraved. Mrs. Vivian refused to leave him in Minnie's charge whilst she was abroad. "Minnie has no sense of justice, and she would let the dog see that she preferred that abominable little Trixy to him. And if she found a bite upon the small boys she would be certain to accuse Azore." So Azore is here, bounding and bouncing as poodles can. He nearly flung "semper Augustus" just now. The only personality he respects is Trelawney's. Trelawney has but to meet his eye and he retires, saddened and solemnised.

It is very good to me to hear what you say of "the hovel called Tolcarne"—"that it is wide enough to hold us both." Of course, that would be, as you know quite well, what I would like best. But while you have Margaret I will not come permanently. Though Margaret would not admit it even to herself, I think that things as they are suit her best. They would have suited me best, far, if I were in her place. (I would not wish aunt Jane brought in were I keeping house for my father.) The child was in the state of pupilage when she and I were together at Tolcarne. I might not always seem to remember that it is more her house and garden now than mine, and creatures of her age are jealous of prerogative. Nature did not make me a "peace at any price" soul; but close proximity to Laura has affected me with nervousness, I suppose, and I have come to fear the very ghosts and shadows of jars and misunderstandings with those for whom I care as I care for your children.

When you are bereaved of Margaret, I will come like a shot, and be thankful to come, and will quarrel with you over bindings as often as you like, for binding quarrels are not the misunderstandings that I dread, and my courage remains high for such encounters. (Not that I did quarrel with you over Colonel Tod's uniform, for I gave in then, and am still ready to admit that mine was a poor khaki suggestion compared to the Durbar finery in which the gallant gentleman is now clad.) And Margaret will marry. She will marry all too soon for your wishes, probably, and then I will pack up Trelawney and les singing birds, label myself and the baggage "Tolcarne," and inflict myself upon you for life. "Port after stormie seas."

Your loving sister,

ELIZABETH.

P.S.—Send me some rosemary. You took the temperate climate, of which you boasted to Laura, away in your portmanteau seemingly, and London is oppressive and not rosemary-scented.

XLIV.

From Sir Richard Etchingham, Tolcarne, to Miss Elizabeth Etchingham, 83 Hans Place, S.W.

MY DEAR ELIZABETH,

It was a pity to miss you, but it could not have been much of a meeting. I wonder whether our devious course (Margaret's, Jem's, and mine) has been made at all clear to you by a hasty telegram and three or four sleepy post-cards. Jem turned up to dinner on our last evening, having got free of tormenting his young men at Oxbridge, and with no plans for the next week or so, but wanting a great deal of fresh air; and I asked him if Tolcarne air would not serve as well as any other; and he liked the notion, but begged to be left to come in his own fashion; and then it occurred to us that it might be good sport if we all made a wheeling tour together part of the way, leaving Jem to complete the rest at fifteen miles an hour if he chose. Thereupon Jem sketched out, straight off, three or four alternative plans to suit various winds and weathers. Laura's feelings might be shocked at hearing of such a departure, but we considered that her happiness would make her comparatively tolerant, and bound her to be dignified. Indeed, she may not realise the facts at all.

And so the morning, being fine with a light north-easterly breeze, found us at Slough. We caught Arthur and Lytewell for a passing saluta-tion, and had a lovely ride through Windsor Park, up Queen Anne's ride and across the head of the Long Walk, and out through wood and warren across the western end of Virginia Water. They say foreigners envy us our parks and turf: I know I envied them in India. But how should Conti-nentals not envy a country which—but for mere flea-bites of civil broils, and those fading into historic distance—has had centuries of peace within its own borders? Not the least wise of Maine's wise sayings was when he pointed out this wonderful good fortune of England, and told us— or rather left us, as his way was, to read the counsel between the lines—not to be puffed up with any folly about our merits or our fathers' having deserved it. But the Muse of the historic present tells of a wheatsheaf which, notwithstanding its vegetable name, hath fleshpots ; of that wheatsheaf as a tempter ; and of Jem the strenuous—whether as leading the party into temptation, or hardening their hearts to push on in the direct line to some humbler entertainment, it boots not to mention. Enough that we sped on through the land of Bagshot, skirting the odorous fir-woods of the Wellington College country. Jem is indignant with those who say cyclists observe nothing, and maintains that the noiseless approach of the pneumatic wheel gives them special advantages. A yaffle, sitting just inside the bank of a fir-plantation, got up within a few feet of us to justify him.

We cunningly avoided Aldershot (the cunning, of course, was Jem's) to earn our rest in Farnham. There my lord bishop has a park almost as fine as the Queen's, and a castle of all dates from the Dark Ages to the Restoration, but scant leisure for enjoying either: for they tell me he bustles about like a mediæval king of England, and is seldom more than three days together in one place. Lazy bishops, I take it, are about as common in England now as hookah-smoking nabobs in India, and the fabulous wealth of both is equally extinct. I should not have said fabulous, though, for the colleges founded by Wykeham and Fox are no fables. Have not we moderns lost something of the noble use of wealth?

Talking of India, Harry is hard at work in Cairo at something which I suspect to be experiments with high explosive shells; I know he was making a speciality of such things before he went to the Intelligence Department. (There was another experiment he offered to try a month or two ago, but the chance never came. We met some American ladies who were rather nervous about the chances of a Spanish fleet bombarding their country house on the coast somewhere near Salem. Harry tried to reassure them by undertaking to eat the bursting charge of every Spanish shell that fell on New England or any other American ground. They ought to feel safe by this time.) Well, Harry observes a proper discretion as to his doings and probable movements : only he gives me to understand that he is not likely to go to the front. A man can't well complain of being put to confidential work which he is particularly fit for, and which will not be forgotten in the proper quarter, though the public know nothing of it. But I guess he is a little disappointed. I cannot be sorry for the chance of seeing him back sooner in an honourable way. We have all earned our peace, I think.

From Farnham to Winchester is a well-beaten highway, and in part rather dull when judged by the high standard of Surrey and Hampshire picturesqueness. Yet it is a good road and a good ride, and we paid our respects to Jane Austen's house at Chawton, which is on one of the prettiest bits. From puzzling remarks made to us about our country we gathered that we were taken for Americans. Almost every visitor who inquires for Miss Austen's house is an American, it seems, and we were classed according to the presumption founded on experience. Perhaps English callers will increase now, since Miss Austen is decidedly in fashion, to judge by the number of recent editions and the figure they make in the book-shops. The length of the villages or small towns along this road is curious ; it looks as if everybody had insisted on having a frontage to the turnpike —all highway and no byway. On the whole, the effect is pleasing and sociable, even if it verges on fraud for a place like Alton to be nearly a mile long.

You should know Winchester better than I do. There is a special reverence due to the school from Eton men, for if Henry VI. was our father, William of Wykeham was our grandfather ; not only was his foundation our pious founder's model, but Eton was actually started with a colony of Winchester boys. Apart from that, it is one of the most famous and also one of the most delectable places in Eng-land. A small thing that greatly took my fancy was the clear trout stream that runs along between the main street and the public garden, where the fish—and sizeable fish, too—well knowing that they may not be caught by tickling, angling, or otherwise, lie out on the gravel in full view, and do not trouble themselves to move even if you drop in pebbles over them. I should like to believe King Alfred put them there.

Finally, we took the train to Salisbury—Margaret and I, that is—reserving the New Forest for some other time. Jem, as route-finder and guide, took charge of sending forward all the impediments, so that we had next to no weight to carry, and enjoyed the riding thoroughly. Jem's own things are now being carted up from Buckland Road station, and we expect him at some uncertain time this evening.

The Folletts have been back some few days: they have been strolling among French castles and churches, and winding up their tour at a very modest Norman watering-place not far from William the Conqueror's reputed port of embarkation. A friendly and cheerful country, Mr. Follett says, where all the villages have double names, grand in proportion to the smallness of the village. Who would not be proud of having to walk a mile or two to buy his stamps at Sassetot-le-Mauconduit? And at Angerville-le-Martel Mr. Follett bought a fabulously cheap pair of slippers, which he declares are the best he ever had. Bréauté-Beuzeville is a name of noble and historic sound; the place is in fact a small railway junction. Perhaps, the Vicar thinks, it was the place of origin of the wicked Fawkes de Bréauté, who at last for his sins died suddenly by poison, and was found, as the chronicler relates, "dead, black, stinking, *and intestate*"—this last, it seems, a terrible combination of spiritual and temporal opprobrium.

Much pleased was Mr. Follett at being able to revive his old pastime of swimming to his heart's content under civilised conditions, and without anybody thinking it the least odd for a reverend gentleman of his age. Sea-bathing is certainly one of the matters they order better in France. We have never grasped the possibility of fitting it into social life, or the ease of making it a decorous and even graceful form of social amusement. In America they wisely do as the French do, I understand—yes, in Puritan New England; while we continue to flatter ourselves that there is some occult virtue, some fetish that ensures British success, in our stupid neglect to study human amenity. Such are our joint reflections, the Vicar's and mine, in our afternoon stroll—which somehow gets much entangled in our respective gardens. Enticknap is muttering about things being cruel dry, and we are rather anxious for the late summer.

The story of Biggleswade and Leagrave caused Mr. Follett to smile a rather grim smile. I have a notion that he knows Biggleswade's Bishop fairly well. One day or another I hope the creature may be choked off, before he reaches the plaintiff-in-person stage; not that I care the least about his making a fool of himself, but Leagrave has already had quite as much annoyance as he deserves.

Margaret and I are both all the better for our expedition, I assure you, and still have increased appetites. Jem was most ingenious and considerate in laying out the stages so that we were never hurried. When he wanted to let off his own superfluous energy he did it by pushing ahead to order lunch or see that our quarters were all right. Behold, as I close this, he rides up like a catherine-wheel device of white dust, overhauling the messenger with the letter-bag.

Your loving

DICKORY.

XLV.

From Miss Elizabeth Etchingham, 83 Hans Place, to Sir Richard Etchingham, Tolcarne.

"DEAR AND RESPECTABLE SIR,"

Thank you very much for the letter, the copy of Sir John Davis's poems, and the stack of rosemary just received—

("Up and down and everywhere
I strew the herbs to purge the air").

Your binder, Richard, has mended Sir John Davis's back perfectly. I will appoint him spinal instrument maker-in-ordinary to my old authors. I like my present and I like the verse you wrote on the flyleaf. To whose garden of poetry did you go to gather it? (Don't forget to answer this.) And my birthday has brought me other desirable possessions. Mrs. Vivian, whom we should all think as kind as she really is, did she not tell us to the contrary, sent me by the hand of Minnie an old Psalm Book—the white silk cover embroidered in silver and coloured threads by the

Nuns of Little Gidding. And Charles presented me with an efficacious umbrella, which confirms my opinion that character shows itself in gifts. (Charles brought his son when he last visited us, and little Harry clamoured to be taken home on the *ceiling* of the omnibus.) Mrs. Vivian journeys homeward from Marienbad almost immediately. She tells me that Ada Llanelly is now "glueing herself to that horrible Mrs. Potters, who has turned up here and means to winter in Egypt, and Lady Clementine's dread that Ada intends to marry her boy, who will be at Cairo too, has increased to panic point. But she surely would find your brother Harry less tiresome. George Mure may be clever, but for choice I prefer the cleverness that doesn't make everyone brought in contact with it feel qualified for Earlswood." Lady Clementine has given up Christian Science. Her son-in-law, according to Mrs. Vivian, informed her in harsh positive tones that it was "all rubbish," and the poor woman's state is again —"to what God shall we now offer up our sacrifice ? "

That Harry does not go to the front is, to a craven like myself, most excellent news. He wrote to Cynthia after receiving the tidings of the Pampesford engagement. He wrote, and wrote in that mystic diction that expresses less than is by it understood. It amused me to find that Harry—guileless Harry—knew in advance of "semper Augustus's " invasion of Scotland,

and kept his own counsel, which is yet another instance of the secretive effect of falling in love. Cynthia showed me his letter not very long after she received it. And she answered it, and I do not believe that there were as many words in the epistle as it took minutes to write them. Then she went on posting errand herself. I wish second sight could have enabled Harry to see his postwoman escorting her letter the first stage of the way. When all of a sudden no member of a household, no proven friend, well-loved relation, faithful servant, is to be trusted to post a letter, the letter-writer is perhaps rather far gone through the faëry land of Romance.

The confession of Harry's devotion took Cynthia by surprise, but as soon as the shock of the surprise had passed she realised, I think, how much he was to her. She accepted us all, you see, as relations; and had this been otherwise, Harry's demeanour has misled less unsophisticated beings. That half-chaffing, half-solicitous, and wholly courteous manner of his may mean everything or nothing. If she was slow to know her own mind, I myself am disposed to sympathise with the mind slow in such recognition. She is a dear, good child, and I think we may feel quite happy and content about her and about Harry, for, soon or syne, Ada Llanelly at Cairo or not at Cairo, all I believe will be well.

Did I tell you that Mrs. Carstairs has lent Laura her house at Wimbledon, and it is to be our headquarters till the day that transforms our step-mother to a Pampesford? (Laura Lawn, Wimbledon, is the address.) Mr. Weekes has been found —at Worthing. Worthing somehow seems to befit Mr. Weekes as environment. Sir Augustus is most attentive. Laura beams and bridles. It is all quite delightful and studded with diamonds and ushered in on massive gold plate.

We dined with the Pampesford family last night. The house, as Harry said of Mrs. Potters' house, reeks of money. And though the contents, taken separately, are really above reproach, yet the whole effect is not beautiful in the least, but boastful and nothing more. I was then and there convinced that even Corots and Millets can be vulgarised by the machinations of frame-makers and paper-hangers, and that old Italian cabinets and old Persian prayer-rugs can be over-done up and over-done till they speak of nothing but bank-notes. The very flowers — poor dears, what a shame—looked purse-proud. I came home, determined that when my room next needs decorating, it shall be decorated *à la* cell. There is no "moss" in that Palace Gardens house, and no refining touch of utility. I would give its plenishings from roof to basement for the contents of my mother's sitting-room at Tolcarne. (I hope Mrs. Enticknap attended to instructions and re-arranged everything after we came away as it was before Laura's reign.) Dreams have a trick of reverting to the past for their background, and I dream of that room sometimes now, and think I see the David Cox water-colours, the delft china, the old lacquer cabinet, in which the mother-of-pearl fish counter lived with which we used to play at commerce, the tortoise-shell workbox, the oval hand-screens upon the chimney-piece with their faint embroidery of faded flowers—but I need not write an inventory of that upper chamber in your very own house. Don't you like an upstairs country sitting-room where the windows are on a level with the heart of a tree? Especially when the tree is a cedar-tree, and the windows give upon the west, and the· sunset is to be seen framed by the great level cedar-boughs? And when the windows of a room are on a level with the heart of a tree, the birds come so delightfully near. I trust that the jays have not been improved away from the Wellington College fir-woods? The flash of blue wings used to spangle those shades as with gleams of blue fire.

Back to our Pampesford dinner after this country excursion I go. The company was just what we might have expected. Apathetic or restlessly ill-at-ease women " stuck o'er," not " with yew " but, diamonds. Men who looked—what did they look? I don't know. What I do know is that, from these persons, Cynthia and Stephen in appearance and manner seemed as far removed as do the etchings of M. Helleu from Gustave Doré's oil paintings, or as the " Voyage autour de ma Chambre " does from the " Dampshire Times's " full report of the wedding gifts to a local bride and bridegroom. The heat was asphyxiating. I sat nerving myself to see the scarlet, choleric-looking gentlemen on either side of me fall insensible into their priceless china plates. The dinner was abnormally long. There was far too much dinner—there was far too much of everything that money brings.

But never you trouble, dear, to describe feminine attire to me again. You said that the Miss Pampesfords' apparel, even to your eyes, looked antique. Antique? No, Dickory. They go clad in the ·latest fashion. The colouring sombre certainly, as becomes the wearers' age, but you will be calling Mrs. Vivian *démodée* next. My old black rags and Cynthia's new white frock were nowhere beside our hostesses' splendour, and even the gown that Blake terms "her ladyship's best ruby" was cowed by the splendid trappings of Laura's future sisters-in-law. The Miss Pampesfords' minds may be dowdy, but their raiment, believe me, is not.

It must be fear of mankind, I think, that frightens the old ladies into the paroxysms of perturbed silence that you described. They talked quite freely the other evening ; not during dinner certainly, nor did it seem to occur to the various editions of Dives present that their hostesses were there to be spoken to. Stephen made valiant attempts to storm the citadel of Miss Teresa's dumb embarrassment, but sank back in his chair with a look of profoundest depression and mental exhaustion about the period of the fish. After dinner, however, there was a buzz of talk. Laura told everybody what she could digest, or rather what she could not. ("Je ne digère pas bien" is nowadays a well-worn theme.) And Miss Pampesford recommended digestive biscuits, and Miss Teresa recommended digestive—I forget what. It was eleven o'clock before poor Stephen and the rest of the company "joined us," and as Laura wished to go on somewhere we had not to wait long for the order of release.

Elsenham Market Hall, Suffolk : Sunday.

Alice needed an excuse for the warding off of Mrs. Ware, and so sent for me, and I kept my letter back to give you news of her. Mrs. Ware is one of those gruesomely disposed persons who insist upon the etiquette and pomp of woe. Do you remember Harry's story of the resentment of his servant's widow, because the poor man's funeral paraphernalia did not include "plumes"?—"I did, Sir, count upon plumes." Mrs. Ware counts upon plumes, and comes periodically to see if Alice is mourning in orthodox fashion and if the crape is deep as can be upon both her skirt and her soul. I prefer "soldiers' sadness" to plumes :—

> "What his funerals lacked
> In images and pomp they had supplied
> With honourable sorrow, soldiers' sadness,
> A kind of silent mourning, such as men
> Who know no tears, but from their captives', use
> To shew in so great losses."

You will be glad to hear that Alice is in rather

better case than I had gathered from former reports, and Mr. Shipley, who, by the way, says his work will take him to Winchester next week—thinks, too, that she has turned the corner. She does not seem quite as restless or look quite as over-driven as she did. This is peaceful, pleasant enough country —the country that Constable painted—and the Stour threads the meadows through which this morning we walked to church. I would give the languid Stour from start to finish for a span of the least Highland burn that splashes the heather, but Alice likes this country, and the country cottage people like her.

I hope and believe that her life will fill itself with wholesome interests, and that she may recover as much tranquillity, if not happiness, as has to serve for many a one. She is unselfish, and so, when not harassed and fretted almost beyond endurance, she will find pleasure in the well-being of others. I don't say that she will not pauperise the village, but there are infirm aged folk and ailing babies whose moral fibre will not be permanently injured by a rather over-lavish distribution of supplies. Poor Colonel Newton was for ever denouncing "useless vagabonds" and "able-bodied beggars who would not work." Very likely there was some truth in his indictment; but we may perhaps hope that we are not doing much harm by smoothing the last stretch of the way for the old and feeble, and trying to make pain less for a sick or crippled child.

Alice is full of dreamy fancies, always. She would not be Alice if she were not. But her fancies bring hope and comfort to her, and why they should excite Mrs. Ware's disapproval and suspicion I don't know. "Have you ever noticed," she said to me just now, "that when the birds spread their wings to fly they make the sign of the cross?"

The post goes early to-day, so good-bye.

ELIZABETH.

N.B.—" I'ya longtemps que je t'aime,
Jamais je ne t'oublierai."

XLVI.

From Sir Richard Etchingham, Tolcarne, to Miss Elizabeth Etchingham, Laurel Lawn, Wimbledon.

MY DEAR ELIZABETH,

Our only postive news is that Arthur is home for the holidays (having missed you in London by your excursion into Suffolk); and the Folletts expect Shipley for a short visit. Those charters, or whatever they are, at Thursborough seem not to be exhausted. Mrs. Ware and her kind, who love the pomp of woe, have an ancestry so respectable and so widely spread that one almost thinks their frame of mind must be the real primitive human nature. It flourishes in the West country, as witness the dialogue between a groom and his uncle, overheard in a Devonshire stable, and recorded among the sayings of Mr. Hicks of Bodmin :

"Well, Jem, you didn't come to Betsey's burying ?"

"No, Uncle, I couldn't get away."

"Ah, you'd 've enjied yourzelf. We had dree quarts of gin, one quart of brandy, and one quart of rum, roast beef, and viggy pudden."

Then a sighing eulogium on the "poor, dear, patient creature," followed after a pause by the matter-of-fact information that "her lied screeching vower hours afore her died." Such dialogues need Sir Thomas Browne for a commentator, to show us that there is no real break between the humours and the solemnity of life. Heine would have done even better perhaps, if he had not been disqualified by invincible ignorance of English character. Why is it that even the cleverest and most pains-taking continental writers are apt to make at least one grotesque blunder when they write about England ? Of course, our half-educated public make quite as absurd ones about French, German, and American, not to mention Anglo - Indian matters ; but not our best people, I think. Taine, I have been told, was really accurate, and the younger Frenchmen of his school are following suit ; for Darmesteter—a scholar of quite original genius—I think I can answer. But Jem won't admit that any foreigner has ever touched English Universities with impunity.

The name of Darmesteter reminds me—you will

see why directly—of the verses I copied on Sir John Davis's fly-leaf. I thought you would hardly guess whose they were.

> " For in my Soul a temple have I made,
>   Set on a height, divine, and steep and far ;
>   Nor often may I hope those floors to tread,
>   Or reach the gates that glimmer like a star."

There is an old-world flavour about them, but they are very modern indeed—Madame James Darmesteter's. Her verse has to me more of the real singing quality in it than can be found in almost any of our living poets junior to Mr. Swinburne, save one—and that one is a woman, too, so there is another guess for you. The thought exactly marks the difference of the nineteenth from the seventeenth century. Our speculation has travelled wider, and learnt not despair, as some impatient folk would have it, but patience and modesty, and the renunciation of expecting precise and formal agreement even from our dearest friends.

Margaret and I have been watching the education of Songstress's puppies with deep interest and occasional controversy. Margaret believes that puppies and kittens are very clever and remember all sorts of things, which I don't. But we agree that there is nothing more fascinating to see than a young creature, dog or cat, playing with an older one. Those who have observed this know that there is nothing new in the modern tyranny of children over their parents. It is curious, too, to see how, with plentiful display of teeth and claws, they manage never to hurt one another. Enticknap has three kittens at his cottage, of whom we call one Joab, as being "him that first getteth up to the gutter"—he did it at quite an early age by judicious use of a creeper ; the gutter of the tool-house in the garden I mean. So he is "the agile Joab," as Margaret finds it written in a silly book of Scripture history that Laura gave her once with a view of doing her good. The other two are Sampson and Filipina ("the connection of which with the plot one sees"). Filipina seems of a lively disposition enough, but Sampson is at present very proud and shy. People used to talk as if character depended merely on education ; and yet, if they had kept their eyes open, they could have seen the most marked differences in character between puppies and kittens of the same litter at a few weeks old. Which is also rather bad for astrology, as they must have pretty much the same horoscope ; but no doubt an astrologer would be ready, like all professors of pseudo-sciences, to patch the breach of his fictitious rule by finding an equally fictitious exception. When you have once begun the business of com-plicated fallacy, "cycle on epicycle," one fiction more costs nothing. Joab has climbed in at the study window and is trying to eat the feather end of my pen while I am writing. I don't think he is laid out for a house cat. No, Joab, I am not the Philistines or the children of Ammon that you

should scratch me, and your manners have not
that repose which elderly persons desire in a
domestic companion. I love cats, but a restless
cat gets on one's nerves. I shall go to the stable
and talk to the snub-nosed puppies ; they are
rather soothing. Cats have more roving and
miscellaneous curiosity than dogs ; a dog begins
to get a working notion of what concerns him and
what not almost as soon as he finds out anything ;
and then he proceeds to leave a lot of things alone.
A cat is not satisfied till he has accounted for
everything in the room. In other words, the cat
might say, you mean that the dog is a business
man, a tradesman, a pursuer of the main chance,
and I am a philosopher ? That is so.—But the cat
would be a sophist, or else (as he is likely to be)
incapable of seeing the point that the dog has
attained the state of a sociable animal, which very
few cats do, though I have known it in some. It
is harder to appreciate cats than dogs, because you
want so much more detachment ; in fact, you have
all the way to go to the cat, while the dog comes
half-way to meet man. But it does not follow that
the cat is the nobler animal. More interesting
as a study in some ways, perhaps. Arthur calls
me to the puppies. He is at the age that dis-
tinctly prefers dogs.

——I have been turning over Cobbett's " Rural
Rides," a book I had not looked at for many years
—indeed I had all but forgotten its existence. Cobbett is delightful, not only for his racy downright

English and love of the country (as country, not
as a collection of subjects for pictures), but for
the perpetual paradox of his being what he is.   He
was a Tory by nature, if ever there was one, hating
cities, standing armies, foreign trees, free trade,
paper money, and Dissenters, especially Unitarians.
And yet he became famous as a Radical.   If he
had come a generation or two later he would have
been a pioneer, or at least a pillar, of the new
Toryism.   The wretched Unitarians get the
choicest vials of his wrath, like this outpouring
when he rides past the Devil's Jumps on the way
from Selborne to Thursley: " The Unitarians will
not believe in the Trinity because they cannot
account for it.   Will they come here to Churt, go
and look at these Devil's Jumps, and account to
me for the placing of those three hills, in the shape
of three rather squat sugar-loaves, along in a line
upon this heath, or the placing of a rock-stone
upon the top of one of them as big as a church
tower ? "   And again, where he says—after mentioning the conversion or perversion of his old friend,
Baron Maseres, to Unitarianism—" I do most
heartily despise this priggish set for their conceit
and impudence "—and proceeds to pose them with
a series of questions in natural history, most of
them absurd and founded on vulgar errors, though
Cobbett boldly says that the facts are all notoriously
true.   The middle one of the seven questions—
" What causes horse-hair to become living things ? "
—is a fair specimen.

Next to Unitarians, Cobbett hated Scotch fir and barren common lands. Hind Head, which is now frequented for its wild beauty, is for Cobbett "certainly the most villanous spot that God ever made." It is another question whether the increase of building, villas, boarding-houses, convalescent homes, and what not, will not soon cause Hind Head and several other formerly secluded places to vie with one another for being the most villanous blot on fair country that man ever made. But this would be nothing to Cobbett. Perhaps he was the last of the writers on rustic matters who frankly made no pretence to an eye for the picturesque. He could admire a smiling landscape, but a soil where crops would not grow was in his vocabulary ugly, nasty, "spewy," or blackguard.

And so no more at present from your loving brother,

RICHARD.

XLVII.

From Miss Elizabeth Etchingham, Laurel Lawn, Wimbledon, to Sir Richard Etchingham, Tolcarne.

DEAREST DICKORY,

Some folk prove incorrigible. I *will* not be told by post to guess. How irritating you are.

How weak-minded I am. Had I any real strength of character, I should sweep your provoking conundrums out of my mind and have done with them ; but as, demon, I weakly desire to know your opinion about everything, I let your guessing orders disturb me. I went out to buy a Tennyson to enable me to come to a conclusion when you last bade me guess, but I am not at this hour going out to buy the works of all the modern women poets. Their name is legion. I can't gather

> " into quires
> The scattered nightingales."

It would need every van with Carter Paterson's name upon it to bring the quires here, and I should be taken up by the police for obstruction, doubtless, did I attempt the task.

The women poets with whom I am intimate are the women who lived on the other and more romantic side of the border ; and they are long dead and gone. (I rather think I like my verse, as I like my china, old.) Jane Elliot, Lady Anne Lindsay, Lady Wardlaw, Lady Nairne. I don't know that women now can write as they did, but then I know little about it. I have, however, an acquaintance among the latter-day Philomels, and she wrote this :

> " Time brought me many another friend
>   That loved me longer,
> New love was kind, but in the end
>   Old love was stronger.

> Years come and go. No New Year yet
>   Hath slain December,
> And all that should have cried, Forget !
>   Cries but—Remember !"

I like the song. I like the sentiment. But it was not my intention to quote verse to-day or to look through that cypress and rosemary bordered avenue backward :

> " Tis not the air I wished to play,
>   The strain I wished to sing ;
> My wilful spirit slipped away
>   And struck another string."

I meant to reprove you for ruffling a temper, smooth, till you touched it, as an angel's wing, and then to pass on to Pampesford and present affairs. You would have scoffed to see the folding of your sister to the heart of Miss Pampesford and Miss Teresa Pampesford yesterday. This is how the folding to the heart befel. While Laura was undergoing the process known as "being fitted " (she really must be as strong as a horse, as she goes to London and back nearly every day through this overwhelming heat) I thought I would do a politeness and call upon the Miss Pampesfords, who had repeatedly begged me to "come in and have tea informally." I found them alone and apparently unoccupied, the nearest approach to occupation being the " Times," " Morning Post," and " Illustrated London News " neatly folded and lying upon a console—I suppose you would call the marble-and-gilt splendour. I tried them with various subjects and strove to discover what really is their "shop," that I might get them to talk it. Their brother is their "shop." I sympathise with the people who have a long-standing craze for another human creature, particularly if the other human creature is not of the same sex as the crazed—(don't betray this sentiment to Laura or Mrs. Carstairs)—and there is something pathetic in their idolisation of "Augustus." After a while I began to think that I quite admired him too.

"I don't know if we ought to say it to you," Miss Pampesford said at last, growing more and more confidential ; "but you seem to feel kindly, and you have brothers yourself, and so perhaps we should not be misunderstood if we tell you that our thankfulness in the prospect of Augustus' happiness is intensified by the fact that for many years we feared that happiness would never be his again." "Yes," poor old Miss Teresa said, wiping her eyes with a magnificently laced handkerchief, "we feared that happiness would never be his again." "In the prime of youth," Miss Pampesford went on, "he became attached to and married a very sweet young thing. She had no fortune and no high-born connections (she was a governess, my dear Miss Etchingham), she had just the fortune of a sweet, grateful, lovable nature, and a most lovely face." "Yes," Miss Teresa repeated, "a sweet, grateful, lovable nature, and a most lovely face." "She died, my dear Miss Etchingham, she and the dear little baby, on the first anniversary of her wedding day." Poor Miss

Pampesford tried to speak on, but her voice for a moment or two left her. "Our brother," she continued after what seemed a long pause, "was a changed man. He would sit by the hour silent and abstracted, scarcely answering when addressed. It is very hard, my dear Miss Etchingham, to be able to do nothing to lessen the suffering of those one loves." (It is. Do you know anything very much harder? I don't.)

They have hearts, Richard, and when grim old dragons, even, have hearts, I like them. I hope Laura won't trample them to death.

I conveyed Azore yesterday to Prince's Gardens that he might there be re-united to Mrs. Vivian as she passed through London on her way from Marienbad to Vivian-End. ("My saint looks well," she admitted.) She has been advising Lady Clementine Mure, "who travelled home with us, looking, Elizabeth, as we crossed, for all the world like *un mouton qui rêve*, either to marry Admiral Tidenham or go round the world: Admiral Tidenham, being deaf as a post, is cut out to have a silly wife who talks incessantly about nothing, as he won't hear a word she says. You," she told me, "are still too young for marriage, or globe-trotting, as the fashion now is. Wait till you are fifty." But a third alternative presents itself to Lady Clementine. On board the Channel boat she was the thankful witness of Ada Llanelly's and Mr. Biggleswade's cordial relations. (He was on his way back from Paris. "London," he says,

" is too suburban for me, I admit." You know, I suppose, that he has come into a big fortune ?) " Ada," Mrs. Vivian tells me, " forsook all others, including George Mure, and cleaved to Mr. Biggleswade from Calais to Charing Cross." Furthermore, the next morning's post brought a letter from him announcing his intention of leaving the Church, "as literary engagements and the duties of a landed proprietor," &c., &c. Vivian-End living is in Mr. Vivian's gift, and there is a very excellent " High Church " Alick Mure (Lady Clementine's youngest son) now half killing himself and destroying his delicate lungs with curate's overwork in the South London parish to which Mrs. Vivian plays Lady Bountiful. Alick Mure will go to that delightful rose-and-jasmine embowered Vivian-End vicarage, and poor rudderless Lady Clementine can make her home with him. He is the only one of her family who has never bullied or been rude to her. She will of course become "High Church" too, and embroider stoles and altar-hangings in peaceful precincts for the rest of her natural life. So that is all right.

Commend me to your dogs and cats, your kittens and puppies. (You have not said a word lately of Tracy.) Dogs I consider the most lovable, cats the most fascinating, of animals. To fall beneath the fascination of a cat, especially of a Persian cat, endowed both with the languor and the fire of the East, is to be under a spell. Friendship with a dog means the finding of a dear, perfect, sympathetic, faithful friend. I don't know that a cat's fidelity is to be trusted. When Azore ailed slightly the other day (he had taken to himself a ham from the sideboard), I sent for his doctor, who gave me various instances of the gratitude of dogs as patients. I then inquired about horses as patients. " Horses have no way to demonstrate," he said. " And cats ?" I asked. The expression of Azore's medical attendant changed from mild philanthropy to long-pent-up indignation. " Cats !" he exclaimed with heat— " I don't get any gratitude from cats." But this perhaps is an exceptional experience.

Treat kindly the little knot of white heather that I enclose. Some heather and bog-myrtle came just now from Dalruogh. A day or two ago dear Mr. Fraser sent us grouse, and then the story of my erratic conduct in going off to Dalruogh alone was related to Sir Augustus. " Augustus asked me if it is not unusual for ladies to pay afternoon visits at houses where there is no hostess," Laura told me afterwards. Oh dear, oh dear, the imbecility, and worse than imbecility, of this sort of thing. Should men and women be buried in the same churchyard, do you think? Mrs. Le Marchant and Mrs. Carstairs would say No. Mrs. Carstairs, if I may be forgiven for thinking so while living, though not as her guest, under her roof, is the type of woman that I trust evolution will rid us of shortly. She is an adept in sinister insinuation and in unpleasant interpretation of innocent acts. The world, according to her, is made up of jealous wives and hoodwinked husbands, or the other way round. The folly or falsehood of insisting that such cases are the rule, not the exception, surprises me anew whenever I am confronted by the point of view. But it is not worth being angry with, though it does sometimes anger me. And then I think that the women whose thoughts run in such grooves are mostly objects for compassion. Unloved and unlovable, they wither for want of the sunshine of wholesome human affection. Mrs. Vivian's tirades are of a wholly different nature. Her tongue may be sharp, and she may indulge over-freely in feline amenities, but adder's poison is not under her lips, and her nature has no trace of the ugly twist that makes Mrs. Carstairs my *bête noire*. Why cannot we in nine hundred and ninety-nine cases out of a thousand think of and treat human beings as our fellow creatures, not in that stupid uncomfortable way of —I am a woman and you are a man? I never had any patience with it.

Farewell, Dickory, I have known worse folk than you.

ELIZABETH.

XLVIII.

From Sir Richard Etchingham, Tolcarne, to Miss Elizabeth Etchingham, Laurel Lawn, Wimbledon.

MY DEAR ELIZABETH,

There is news for you this time. You are to keep your Christmas at Tolcarne and not go away again. No refusal this time. For if Elizabeth will not come and reign with Richard at Tolcarne, there will be nothing left for Richard but to get up a lawsuit with Mrs. Tallis to occupy his declining years, and steal her housekeeper as an episode. Marry, how? Shipley is at the vicarage, and we went there to afternoon tea ; and Mr. Follett was full of Anglo-Saxon antiquities, and in great indignation with somebody who had been vamping up some of the old nonsense about King Alfred—the fable of his hanging forty odd unjust judges, I think it was ; and Shipley was too busy to go out with Arthur, and yet he did not stay with us to talk of King Alfred ; and Mrs. Follett was engaged with her gardener over the fowls. Her game-fowls are a fine breed. They want a great deal of attention when certain visitors are seen approaching—and at other times. And so, when the Vicar and I went out into his quercus walk, and he was showing me how the trees had come on this summer, who should meet us but

Margaret and Shipley hand in hand, and she was looking—well, not as she looked after a certain interview with Mr. Weekes, of Worthing that is and of Pampesford Royal that is to be. They had settled something that was more to him than Alfred and Edward and all their charters. And the Vicar beamed, and I—never mind exactly what I did.

But this morning I took out the two seals you know, which for years I had looked at only once a year, those that my dear old Munshi got engraved after the writing of a cunning scribe at Agra. Mine—the one that reads " I said *Alif* "— is to be Shipley's, and Maggie's, inscribed " My soul said, *Say no more*," is for Margaret. They are to have them on the wedding-day. You remember the interpretation of the lines those words come from ?

I said *Alif:* my soul said, *Say no more:* If One is in the house, one letter is enough.

Margaret will tell you more.

Yours in joy,
RICHARD.

P.S.—The poet whose name you will not guess is Mrs. Margaret Woods.

XLIX.

From Miss Elizabeth Etchingham, Laurel Lawn, Wimbledon, to Sir Richard Etchingham, Tolcarne.

DEAREST DICKORY,

You are the most unselfish creature in the world (I may have mentioned this before, as it is a conclusion I came to as soon as I could come to conclusions). I have a very happy note from dear Margaret, but she thinks much more of you than you do of yourself, and "leaving father" is already a cloud on her horizon. You have won her affections, as I knew you would, during the short time you have been together. I am thinking of Maggie now, and thinking that she would be glad (she and I always agreed about people). She would have liked and believed in "Will" Shipley; and she would have wished Margaret to marry. She was far too happy with you not to consider marriage the happiest destiny for a woman. And I think he is a good man, upright and "trustie"; and then he is quick-witted on the surface and will not, for want of intuition, hurt his wife. I have often admired the tact and self-control with which he handled the many entanglements of the Newton household. To succeed in being everything to Alice, while for her sake remaining on good terms with Colonel Newton, was a great diplomatic achievement. The marriage will delight Alice ; and Arthur will not withhold his consent.

No refusal from me this time, you say. No. Don't flatter yourself that you could keep me at a distance if you tried. I am coming, and coming to stay.

I remember about the seals, and what you tell me now made me go rather blind for a minute. In a way I want the child and her "man" to have them, but I want you to keep them too, and I think I want you to keep them most. Have others made. Do not give up those till you are where you will not need seals, dear. But perhaps I am wrong. As I have no children, perhaps I cannot realise that what a parent gives to a child a parent keeps.

Laura's reception of the news would have amused you. Being Laura, she does not quite like honours to be divided, and would have preferred one engagement at a time in the family. Still she is benevolently inclined to Margaret, and "enters into Margaret's feelings as only those can who know what it is." "You, Elizabeth," she told me, "as I have often heard people say, live in books; which, perhaps, is fortunate, as you don't seem to attract. But I have always found my happiness in my affections, and Margaret is, I think, like me." One of Margaret's most valuable presents will be "from Sir Augustus and Lady Pampesford," and Laura's feelings for her are sisterly and emotional to the verge of tears, and not step-grandmotherly at all. I shall see you and my dear Margaret soon, if bulwarks of wedding presents and wedding garments allow me to see anyone. Don't indulge in "a recurrence of your old attacks," and so escape the ceremony. You must witness the turning of Laura into a Pampesford. "It is expected of you." We go back to Hans Place next week.

Your loving sister,
ELIZABETH.

P.S.—Keep the seals. I can't bear you not to have them. I can't bear it for you or for Maggie. I think, if she knew, she would rather they were yours, only, still. I know she would. Keep them, please.

L.

From Sir Richard Etchingham, Tolcarne, to Miss Elizabeth Etchingham, 83 Hans Place.

To my most excellent sister, Elizabeth, by the hands of our well-beloved daughter, these :

A touch of that old malaria, with a measurable temperature, a touch to swear by. Margaret says I must not think of going to Laura's wedding, and I dutifully think of not going. There is much to be thought of here, and it would never do for me to be disabled. A medical certificate will be furnished if desired. Our old enemies do sometimes befriend us. A modern Amritsar rug, not bad, but gaudy enough to please Laura, must help to make my excuses go down.

We are childishly happy and given up to ourselves. Tracy is the only exception ; he is rather sulky at the exuberant youth of Songstress's puppies, whom Margaret insists on calling John and Edward (*i.e.* De Reszke) in defiance of all sporting traditions. Likewise he despises the cats, though he would not commit himself to anything so vulgar as active hostility. John and Edward, on the other hand, have passed through a stage of diplomatic but cold relations to fraternising, which leads to admired disorder from the human point of view. Mr. and Mrs. Square came to pay us a state visit on Wednesday, charged with solemn congratulation (the engagement is known, of course). They found us entirely occupied with watching John and Edward laying siege to Sampson, who had entrenched himself under the sofa ; the puppies whining with excitement, Sampson uttering an occasional mew defiant, Arthur crying " Fetch en out !", Mr. Follett aiding and abetting with most un-padre-like laughter. The young people had just been telling him they would have nobody else to marry them. The whole party rather wanted to let off steam in some direction, and the puppies and the kitten obligingly supplied an object. The Squares must have thought us quite mad, but I believe they thought so before.

Mrs. Tallis, who was beginning to think it time for either a marriage or a murder to happen in the neighbourhood, is as brisk as may be, and regrets that there is no more dancing at weddings. She has won Arthur's heart by surrendering to Shipley at the first encounter; it so fell out that he knew more of a local genealogy than she did, having lately found a missing piece of decisive evidence among the witnesses to one of the Thursborough deeds. But Mrs. Tallis has one trouble. A sailor nephew has sent her, with infinite precaution, a charming little Italian owl, and the housekeeper is in mortal fear of bad luck following it. I find these edifying and sound remarks in a paper by an educated Parsi gentleman on superstitions common to Europe and India, in the Bombay Anthropological Society's journal. "The ugly owl is everywhere considered a bird full of bad omen. I remember the peace of mind of even an English schoolmaster of a high school being disturbed at the sight of an owl on the roof of his school. He did not rest till he made it leave his premises by means of stones." Mrs. Tallis's housekeeper must be taught not to attempt any counter-charm by means of stones or such like. Perhaps we can persuade her that the Italian owl is quite different from the common owl. Why does anybody think an owl ugly? Or a toad, for the matter of that? I do not even share the supposed inborn aversion to snakes. Vipers have, no doubt, to be treated as enemies of man because they are accustomed to bite hounds, not to speak of common dogs. But I maintain that in themselves they are pretty creatures enough. Indian poison-snakes are a graver matter—though you know that more people die officially of snake-bite than ever felt a serpent's tooth. Another maligned bird is the puckeridge, *vulgo*, night-jar, without whose soothing monotone I consider no fine summer evening complete. Was it the noiseless flight that seemed uncanny to our ancestors?

Mr. Follett is a naughtier and more secular clerk than I knew. He and Mrs. Follett were captured by an American family at their Norman village, and the Americans taught them euchre, which they have proceeded to teach us. I am not converted to holding the four-handed game, where the partners are constant, anything like an adequate substitute for whist, though it may do for the young and giddy. But with Shipley we make up five, and then it is a bewildering but fascinating system of shifting triple and dual alliances, with occasional tacit coalitions against a player who is dangerously near the winning score. Towards the end of the game there is need for high political judgment in bidding or not bidding for the lead, as you have to weigh the advantage of gaining points for yourself against the risk of advancing temporary partners who are also rivals. Altogether it is very like a picture in little of the so-called concert of the Great Powers in Europe. I leave to wiser heads the question who has been most cuchred in that game.

I all but forgot to tell you that Harry is on his way home with confidential despatches, and may be in time to represent me at the great function; I have sent a request to that effect to catch him at the War Office. But I expect he has written or telegraphed to you himself.

As to the seals, what I felt was that in the young folks' hands they would be alive for me too. But Margaret and Shipley had something like your thought; they begged to consult before deciding, and they say they will gladly have copies, but I must keep the originals for my own time. So now I hope you will approve without reserve.

Tell me all about the most august wedding.

Your loving brother,

DICKORY.

LI.

From Miss Elizabeth Etchingham, 83 Hans Place, to Sir Richard Etchingham, Tolcarne.

Oh, Richard, Richard, 'tis a shocking thing to be wholly depraved. What am I to do with a creature who, when he should be hasting to the wedding in Sloane Street, remains in Devonshire, and sits down calmly at home to comment upon toads and snakes and vipers and Mrs. Tallises and owls and night-jars? Is this a time to turn to wondering why night-flying " foules " are birds of ill omen, and to quote learned Parsees and Bombay anthropological journals ? If refusing to haste to the wedding, surely good feeling would have prompted the throwing off of a prothalamion sort of note, a song of " swans of goodly hue," " fair plumes " and " silken feathers," and a dismissal till more opportune moments of your evil-boding, fatal owl? I am grieved to the core. And your truancy cost us Arthur too.

As to the recurrence of your old attacks, I tell you plainly, my dear, I don't believe in it. When I said to Margaret, " Is your father really ill ? " Margaret smiled ; and though Laura, whose invariable interest in diseases was aroused, had already reached the point of suggesting " packing " for the lowering of your temperature, " Will " (I still speak his name between inverted commas), with the crass simplicity of a man, casually let out that you had seen your family off from Buckland Road station and intended to take the parsonage on your way home. Was there ever such an abandoned wretch ? (Phantom) toads, snakes, vipers, Mrs. Tallises, owls, night-jars are subjects on which the delirious wax eloquent, but I know you too well to think that your mind, when you wrote, wandered, and no doctor of medicine, but rather a doctor of divinity, would suit the needs of your case, Dickory. However, no more of this for now. I am soon to take charge of you for life, and shall feel it my duty to re-mould your character from the roots. There's one thing, however, I may mention : if Mrs. Tallis is to keep her owl, I must keep my falcon—my merlin to be correct—"To a king belonged the gerfalcon, to a prince the falcon gentle ; to an earl the peregrine, *to a lady the merlin*, to a young squire the hobby, while a yeoman carried a goshawk, a priest a sparrow-hawk, and a knave or servant a kestrel." (I think my first request to Enticknap will be that he should carry a kestrel.) Mr. Follett's copy of Pliny will explain why Mrs. Tallis's owl requires my falcon—"The falcon, by a secret instinct and societie of nature, seeing the poor howlet thus distressed" (beset by a multitude of antagonistic birds), "cometh to succour and taketh equal part with him, and so endeth the fray." Good heavens, what am I doing? Evil communications do corrupt good manners, and I am writing of "howlets" and leaving every hymeneal task undone.

Presents are pouring in and furniture is pouring out to make room for the wedding-guests that to-morrow will bring. (Trelawney followed his favourite velvet chair to the box-room and, having been searched for high and low, was found there with paws neatly folded under his heavily furred person.) Laura's trunks block every passage ; Laura prophesies imminent faints ; Blake runs constantly to inform me that her "ladyship feels she may go off any moment." There is Margaret to talk to and Cynthia to fortify—dear little

Cynthia, who has looked tremulous since she heard that Harry may appear at any moment. There is Minnie in the offing very full of "A Tribute of Tears," and Charles equally full of the homicidal system of drainage that converts the Rectory, of which he has temporary possession, into a "death-trap," "a disseminator of typhoid," a booking-office for Styx. (I don't believe it is ever safe to trust a clergyman's word on his own drains.) There are flowers to arrange and a thousand marjoram-wreath, saffron-robe, pine-tree torch deeds to do and to prevent being done, so I will wait till to-morrow, till Laura is Lady Pampesford, for my epistle's end.

Wednesday.—The August wedding day. "Hail, Hymen, Hymenæus hail!"

Richard, as I was coming out of the church after *the* ceremony, I felt my arm gripped and I heard a voice say, "Any orders to-day, M'm?" and there was my beloved Harry, safe, sound, and sunburnt. Then he greeted Cynthia, and she could not find her voice to answer, and I thought for a moment she would have answered by fainting, for she was as white as her frock. But she did not faint, and Harry saw what I did and was equal to the occasion. In another moment he had put her into a hansom, had followed her into a hansom, and had shouted directions to the driver. Is there time driving from Holy Trinity Church, Sloane Street, to 83 Hans Place, to speak words that alter the hereafter of two lives? Apparently there is. When I caught sight of Harry and Cynthia again, Cynthia was smiling shyly—and Harry? Harry had the desire of his heart, and knew that there are other triumphs than those of an Egyptian campaign. He succeeded in pushing his way presently through the wedding-guest throng that filled to overflowing the drawing-room and found an opportunity to say, "Is not she a darling?" Yes, she is a darling, and he is something good and delightful also, and they are to be married before he goes out again in November. And they will be happy. They *must* be happy. Why am I so violently anxious that the people I care for should have what they want, when I am always telling myself, and trying to make myself believe, that happiness is but a paltry thing, a thing of small moment after all?

Well, now, again for the wedding. Experts tell me that the wedding went off very well. Consciousness of her gown's merits and regard for what Blake calls its "set," wound Laura up to the semblance of stoical fortitude. (The Camelry has already determined to follow Cynthia's fortunes and not to be tempted by the flesh-pots of Pampesford-Royal.) "Augustus" showed honest emotion, and I quite liked him, when wishing me good-bye he said, with real feeling if pompous diction, that it was his "earnest hope that the most cordial relations would be preserved between the families." (In marrying Laura he imagines himself to be depriving us of something that our unselfishness alone enables us to part with will- ingly.) The Miss Pampesfords (who have taken the lease of this house off our hands) furtively wiped tears from their eyes, and embraced Margaret and Cynthia and Minnie as well as me. I hoped they were going to press Charles to their hearts, but Mrs. Vivian dispatched him upon one of her many errands before this caress was brought off. How should you like to find yourself in the clasp of your black and purple dragons?

The time and the place considered, the family and the family's friends and acquaintances made rather a brave show. You were, of course, sorely missed, but yours was about the only vacant place on the daïs. The services were well to the fore, as a tottering Admiral uncle was produced by Laura to give her away, and Sir Augustus was "supported" by a Major Sampson Pampesford, who is evidently looked upon as the Lothario of the house of Pampesford. (Miss Teresa, with kind care for my peace of mind, murmured that "the Major, though excessively pleasing, is not a man of domestic tastes, and fitted for conjugal happiness, like our brother, my dear Miss Etchingham.") Mrs. Vivian killed two birds with one stone— bringing Azore to see his doctor, and herself and Mr. Vivian to see Laura married. (She asked if I had noticed that the form of Solemnisation of Matrimony was followed in the Prayer Book by the order for the Visitation of the Sick—"the compilers of the Prayer Book, my good Elizabeth, took in the likelihood that in every marriage one or other would quickly be tormented and worried to death.")   Margaret and her Will, I regret to tell you, did their duty by no one but each other. Charles, arms folded and back to wall, sustained the bridegroom with his theories on drainage. Minnie sought fervid copy among Laura's conventionalities.   Lady Clementine Mure devoted herself to the wedding's most genial Colonial Bishop.   Stephen found Blanche Vivian, and Blanche seemed well content to be found.   Mr. Weekes, glancing nervously round the room the while, made timid efforts to talk down Admiral Tidenham's ear-trumpet.   Aunt Jane broke out of a bath-chair upon the astounded world, crowned with a bonnet from which sprang a gorgeous orange crest and from which waved an equally gorgeous and striking orange plume.   (Laura has hinted that my place for the future is at Aunt Jane's side, but Aunt Jane does not feel herself in need of a caretaker, and prefers, like many other invalids, liberty, as far as she can get it in a bath-chair, to supervision.)   Jem kept Mr. Vivian's taciturnity in countenance, and flew before the orange crest and plume of Aunt Jane, whose passionate desire to learn from his own lips if he found the climate of Oxbridge healthy was thus frustrated.   Our cousin, Canon Etchingham, joked ecclesiastically with the self-satisfaction of a portly Church dignitary used to an audience of minor clergy and holy women.

The Canoness (very gaudily, not very prettily, attired) was crushed, without realising the crushing, by Mrs. Vivian. Mrs. Carstairs and Mrs. Le Marchant lacerated their neighbours' reputations and arranged for a continuance of an acquaintance thus promisingly begun. Minnie's Mrs. Potters attached herself to the absent-minded Lord Leyton, who failed to discover that he was politely returning the attentions of a woman who for years has lived within a stone's throw of one of his lodges and has been persistently ignored by Lady Leyton and himself. Lady Leyton meanwhile was too deep in conversation with Mrs. Vivian, and too closely hemmed in by Mrs. Vivian's retinue, to notice the irrevocable catastrophe and recall Lord Leyton to her side and his senses. "If," said Aunt Jane, "that Miss Llanelly" (who asked herself) "and Mr. Biggleswade" (whom Laura would ask) "are *not* engaged to be married, I really, really do not know what sort of behaviour we may expect to see next. I really, really do not." For the rest you must wait till we meet.

We shall meet very soon now, and the play of which the scene is London is very nearly done. (Trelawney and les singing birds travel back to their native land with your child to-morrow. She and Will found many books to turn over in the back drawing-room this evening, and Harry and Cynthia did equally well without books on the balcony.) Three days with Alice Newton, two at

Vivian-End, and then peaceful Tolcarne for always.
. . . . I have been saying "Bless you my children"
all round, and I feel to-night as if I wanted to
hear some one say, as my father used, and as Mr.
Fraser still does, "God bless you" to me.

Good-bye, Dickory.

Your loving sister,
ELIZABETH.

LII.

*From Sir Richard Etchingham, Tolcarne, to Miss
Elizabeth Etchingham, 83 Hans Place.*

Ai zabar-dast u zar-dast dzár !

Most imperious and sceptical of sisters, I
never said I was ill. I said I had monitory
symptoms. If I had very much wanted to go to
Laura's wedding, and be taken to the hearts of
sentimental dragons, I should have gone in defiance
of the doctor. Instead of which, Arthur showed
a most filial anxiety that I should take care of
myself, and, moreover, was willing to renounce
the ceremony (Margaret having the best of escort)
in order to stay at home too and take care of me.
Why should I disappoint his piety ? Well, you
have done your duty and mine. *Sab tamásha
hogyá.* There is something brutal in women's way
of abusing their power, and driving poor men to
lay bare the weakness of their skill in excuse.
We have not your subtilty ; which being confessed,
you might leave it there. As the ingenious author
of "Cupid's Whirligig" remarked in 1630, "Man

was made when Nature was but an apprentice ;
but woman when shee was a skilfull Mistress of
her Arte."

And you are really to be here in a week, and
this is, I hope, my last letter to you for ever so
long. In witness whereof you will note that I
seal this with the seal inscribed, " Say no more."

Leagrave has sent Biggleswade a polite and
solemn renunciation of all his interest in the pro-
jected play. Biggleswade, being mollified with
his late good fortune, has been pleased to accept
it ; so Mr. Follett will not have to set the bishop
on him, and the dead season will be the poorer
by a curious plaintiff-in-person suit that will not
come into court; and the play will be all the
work of the egregious Biggleswade and a very
precious piece of Wardour Street antiquity.

Now let us indeed say no more, and abide in
the beatitude of the other verse : " If one is in the
house, one letter is enough." It is a fine quality
of mystic aphorisms that they will carry many
meanings, as the sunlight is one, and yet breaks
up into infinite sparkles and colours.

" Guftam ki alif: guft digar Hích ma-gú :
dar khánah agar kas ast yak ḥarf bas ast."

Your loving brother,
RICHARD.

THE END.

PRINTED BY WILLIAM CLOWES AND SONS, LIMITED, LONDON AND BECCLES.

CATALOGUE

OF

MACMILLAN'S COLONIAL LIBRARY

OF COPYRIGHT BOOKS

FOR

CIRCULATION ONLY IN INDIA

AND

THE COLONIES

All the volumes are issued in paper covers and in cloth.

391. **Via Crucis.** By F. MARION CRAWFORD.
390. **A Bitter Vintage.** By K. D. KING.
389. **She Walks in Beauty.** By Mrs. HINKSON (Katharine Tynan).
388. **Richard Carvel.** By WINSTON CHURCHILL.
387. **Little Novels of Italy.** By M. HEWLETT.
386. **Stalky and Co.** By RUDYARD KIPLING.
385. **Miranda of the Balcony.** By A. E. W. MASON.
384. **War to the Knife.** By ROLF BOLDREWOOD.
383. **The Log of a Sea-Waif.** By F. T. BULLEN.
382. **The Enchanter.** By Miss U. L. SILBERRAD.
381. **The Cardinal's Page.** By JAMES BAKER.
380. **A Drama in Sunshine.** By H. A. VACHELL.
379. **Rupert, by the Grace of God—** By DORA MCCHESNEY.
378. **Black Douglas.** By S. R. CROCKETT.
377. **The Etchingham Letters.** By Mrs. FULLER MAITLAND and Sir
        F. POLLOCK, Bart.
376. **A Modern Mercenary.** By K. and H. PRICHARD.
375. **Cruise of the "Cachalot."** By F. T. BULLEN.
374. **On many Seas.** By H. E. HAMBLEN.
373. **The Pride of Life.** By Sir W. MAGNAY, Bart.
372. **Off the High Road.** By ELEANOR C. PRICE.
371. **Young April.** By EGERTON CASTLE.
370. **The Pride of Jennico.** By EGERTON CASTLE.
369. **The Game and the Candle.** By RHODA BROUGHTON.
368. **One of the Grenvilles.** By S. R. LYSAGHT.
367. **Selah Harrison.** By S. MACNAUGHTAN.
366. **The Adventures of François.** By S. WEIR MITCHELL.
365. **For the Term of his Natural Life.** By MARCUS CLARKE.
364. **The Gospel Writ in Steel.** By ARTHUR PATERSON.
363. **Bismillah.** By A. J. DAWSON.
362. **A Treasury Officer's Wooing.** By C. LOWIS.
361. **The Ashes of Empire.** By R. W. CHAMBERS.
360. **That Little Cutty.** By Mrs. OLIPHANT.
359. **Her Memory.** By MAARTEN MAARTENS.
358. **A Romance of Canvas Town.** By ROLF BOLDREWOOD.
357. **The Red Axe.** By S. R. CROCKETT.
356. **The Castle Inn.** By STANLEY J. WEYMAN.
355. **Roden's Corner.** By H. SETON MERRIMAN.
354. **The Day's Work.** By RUDYARD KIPLING.
353. **The Changeling.** By Sir WALTER BESANT.
352. **Helbeck of Bannisdale.** By Mrs. HUMPHRY WARD.
350. **The Forest Lovers.** By MAURICE HEWLETT.
349. **The Concert-Director.** By Miss NELLIE K. BLISSETT.
348. **The Philosopher's Romance.** By JOHN BERWICK.
347. **The Man of the Family.** By F. EMILY PHILLIPS.
345. **Plain Living.** By ROLF BOLDREWOOD.
344. **Rupert of Hentzau.** By ANTHONY HOPE.
342. **The Choir Invisible.** By J. LANE ALLEN.
341. **A Chapter of Accidents.** By Mrs. HUGH FRASER.
340. **For Prince and People.** By E. K. SANDERS.
339. **Corleone.** By F. MARION CRAWFORD.
338. **The Lion of Janina.** By MAURUS JOKAI.
337. **Unkist Unkind.** By VIOLET HUNT.
336. **The Well Beloved.** By THOMAS HARDY.

277. **Thirty Years of Paris.** By A. DAUDET.
276. **Recollections of a Literary Man.** By A. DAUDET
275. **Kings in Exile.** By A. DAUDET.
274. **Tartarin of the Alps.** By A. DAUDET.
273. **Tartarin of Tarascon.** By A. DAUDET.
272. **Disturbing Elements.** By M. C. BIRCHENOUGH.
271. **The Sowers.** By H. S. MERRIMAN.
270. **Cleg Kelly.** By S. R. CROCKETT.
269. **The Judge of the Four Corners.** By G. B. BURGIN.
268. **The Release.** By CHARLOTTE M. YONGE.
267. **The Atheist's Mass, etc.** By H. DE BALZAC.
266. **Old Goriot.** By H. DE BALZAC.
265. **Mr. Witt's Widow.** By ANTHONY HOPE.
264. **The Courtship of Morrice Buckler.** By A. E. W. MASON.
263. **Where Highways Cross.** By J. S. FLETCHER.
262. **A Ringby Lass.** By MARY BEAUMONT.
261. **A Modern Man.** By ELLA MACMAHON.
260. **Maureen's Fairing.** By JANE BARLOW.
259. **A Lost Endeavour.** By GUY BOOTHBY.
258. **Tryphena in Love.** By W. RAYMOND.
257. **The Old Pastures.** By Mrs. LEITH-ADAMS.
256. **Lindsay's Girl.** By Mrs. HERBERT MARTIN.
255. **Ursule Mirouët.** By H. DE BALZAC.
254. **The Quest of the Absolute.** By H. DE BALZAC.
253. **Wee Willie Winkie, etc.** By RUDYARD KIPLING.
252. **Soldiers Three, etc.** By RUDYARD KIPLING.
251. **Many Inventions, etc.** By RUDYARD KIPLING.
250. **Life's Handicap, etc.** By RUDYARD KIPLING.
249. **The Light that Failed.** By RUDYARD KIPLING.
248. **Plain Tales from the Hills.** By RUDYARD KIPLING.
247. **The Country Doctor.** By H. DE BALZAC.
246. **The Chouans.** By H. DE BALZAC.
245. **Eugenie Grandet.** By H. DE BALZAC.
244. **At the sign of the Cat and Racket.** By H. DE BALZAC.
243. **The Wild Ass's Skin.** By H. DE BALZAC.
242. **The Story of a Marriage.** By Mrs. A. BALDWIN.
241. **The Wonderful Visit.** By H. G. WELLS.
240. **A Youth of Parnassus.** By L. PEARSALL SMITH.
239. **A Sweet Disorder.** By NORMA LORIMER.
238. **The Education of Antonio.** By F. E. PHILLIPS.
237. **For Love of Prue.** By LESLIE KEITH.
236. **The Wooing of Doris.** By Mrs. J. K. SPENDER.
235. **Captain Flick.** By FERGUS HUME.
234. **Not Exactly.** By E. M. STOOKE.
233. **A Set of Rogues.** By FRANK BARRETT.
232. **Minor Dialogues.** By W. PETT RIDGE.
231. **My Honey.** By the Author of "Tipcat."
230. **The Shoulder of Shasta.** By BRAM STOKER.
229. **Casa Braccio.** By F. MARION CRAWFORD.
228. **The Salt of the Earth.** By P. LAFARGUE.
227. **The Horseman's Word.** By NEIL ROY.
226. **Comrades in Arms.** By ARTHUR AMYAND.
225 **The Wild Rose.** By FRANCIS FRANCIS.
224. **The Crooked Stick.** By ROLF BOLDREWOOD.

112. **Wheat and Tares.** By Sir HENRY CUNNINGHAM.
111. **A Cigarette-Maker's Romance.** By F. MARION CRAWFORD.
110. **A South Sea Lover.** By ALFRED ST. JOHNSTON.
109. **The Tragic Muse.** By HENRY JAMES.
108. **The Ring of Amasis.** By Lord LYTTON.
107. **The Miner's Right.** By ROLF BOLDREWOOD.
106. **The Heriots.** By Sir HENRY CUNNINGHAM.
105. **A Lover of the Beautiful.** By the Marchioness of CARMARTHEN.
104. **John Vale's Guardian.** By D. CHRISTIE MURRAY.
103. **The New Continent.** By Mrs. WORTHEY.
101. **English Traits.** By RALPH WALDO EMERSON.
100. **The Heritage of Dedlow Marsh, etc.** By BRET HARTE.
99. **Sant' Ilario.** By F. MARION CRAWFORD.
98. **Marooned.** By W. CLARK RUSSELL.
97. **A Reputed Changeling.** By CHARLOTTE M. YONGE.
96. **The Intellectual Life.** By PHILIP GILBERT HAMERTON.
95. **The Gospel of the Resurrection.** By Bishop WESTCOTT.
94. **Robbery under Arms.** By ROLF BOLDREWOOD.
93. **An Author's Love.**
92. **French and English : A Comparison.** By P. G. HAMERTON.
91. **Schwartz.** By D. CHRISTIE MURRAY.
90. **Neighbours on the Green.** By Mrs. OLIPHANT.
89. **Greifenstein.** By F. MARION CRAWFORD.
88. **Essays in Criticism.** Second Series. By MATTHEW ARNOLD.
87. **Reuben Sachs.** By AMY LEVY.
86. **The Journal Intime of Henri-Frédéric Amiel.** Translated.
85. **Kophetua the Thirteenth.** By JULIAN CORBETT.
84. **Miss Bretherton.** By Mrs. HUMPHRY WARD.
83. **Beechcroft at Rockstone.** By CHARLOTTE M. YONGE.
82. **The Countess Eve.** By J. H. SHORTHOUSE.
81. **The Weaker Vessel.** By D. CHRISTIE MURRAY.
80. **The Mediation of Ralph Hardelot.** By WM. MINTO.
79. **Cressy.** By BRET HARTE.
78. **Fraternity : A Romance.**
76. **With the Immortals.** By F. MARION CRAWFORD.
75. **The Lasses of Leverhouse : A Story.** By JESSIE FOTHERGILL.
74. **Wessex Tales.** By THOMAS HARDY.
73. **For God and Gold.** By JULIAN CORBETT.
72. **The Argonauts of North Liberty.** By BRET HARTE.
71. **Joyce.** By Mrs. OLIPHANT.
70. **Chris.** By W. E. NORRIS.
69. **A Teacher of the Violin, and other Tales.** By J. H. SHORTHOUSE.
68. **The New Judgment of Paris : A Novel.** By PHILIP LAFARGUE.
67. **Realmah.** By the Author of " Friends in Council."
66. **Biographical Sketches.** By HARRIET MARTINEAU.
65. **Paul Patoff.** By F. MARION CRAWFORD.
64. **Marzio's Crucifix.** By F. MARION CRAWFORD.
63. **The Second Son.** By Mrs. OLIPHANT.
61, 62. **Harmonia.** By the Author of " Estelle Russell." 2 vols.
60. **Hithersea Mere.** By Lady AUGUSTA NOEL.
59. **Zoroaster.** By F. MARION CRAWFORD.
57, 58. **Ismay's Children.** By the Author of " Hogan, M.P." 2 vols.
56. **The Cœruleans : A Vacation Idyll.** By Sir H. S. CUNNINGHAM.

55. The Crusade of "The Excelsior." By BRET HARTE.
53, 54. The New Antigone: A Romance. 2 vols.
52. Frederick Hazzleden. By HUGH WESTBURY.
51. Jill and Jack. By E. A. DILLWYN.
50. Jill. By E. A. DILLWYN.
49. The Woodlanders. By THOMAS HARDY.
47. A Garden of Memories, etc. By MARGARET VELEY.
46. Saracinesca. By F. MARION CRAWFORD.
45. A Millionaire of Rough-and-Ready: Devil's Ford. By BRET HARTE.
44. Critical Miscellanies. By JOHN MORLEY.
43. A Beleaguered City. By Mrs. OLIPHANT.
42. The Dove in the Eagle's Nest. By CHARLOTTE M. YONGE.
41. Tom Brown's School Days. By an Old Boy.
40. Essays in Criticism. By MATTHEW ARNOLD.
38. About Money. By the Author of "John Halifax, Gentleman."
37. A House Divided against Itself. By Mrs. OLIPHANT.
36. Sir Percival. By J. H. SHORTHOUSE.
35. A Modern Telemachus. By CHARLOTTE M. YONGE.
34. Margaret Jermine. By FAYR MADOC.
33. Neæra: A Tale of Ancient Rome. By J. W. GRAHAM.
32. The Mayor of Casterbridge. By THOMAS HARDY.
31. King Arthur. By the Author of "John Halifax, Gentleman."
30. Hurrish: A Study. By the Hon. EMILY LAWLESS.
29. My Friend Jim. By W. E. NORRIS, Author of "Matrimony."
28. A Northern Lily. By JOANNA HARRISON.
27. Effie Ogilvie. By Mrs. OLIPHANT.
26. Living or Dead. By HUGH CONWAY, Author of "Called Back," etc.
25. Mrs. Lorimer: A Sketch in Black and White. By LUCAS MALET.
24. Miss Tommy. By the Author of "John Halifax, Gentleman."
22. Chantry House. By CHARLOTTE M. YONGE.
21. Aunt Rachel. By D. CHRISTIE MURRAY.
20. Camping among Cannibals. By ALFRED ST. JOHNSTON.
17, 18, 19. The Literary History of England. 3 vols. By Mrs. OLIPHANT.
16. A Country Gentleman. By Mrs. OLIPHANT.
15. Tales of Old Japan. By A. B. MITFORD. With Illustrations.
14. Tales of Three Cities. By HENRY JAMES.
13. Oldbury. By ANNIE KEARY.
12. Human Intercourse. By P. G. HAMERTON.
11. Souvenirs of some Continents. By ARCHIBALD FORBES, LL.D.
10. Seekers after God. By the Venerable F. W. FARRAR, D.D.
9. The Conduct of Life. By RALPH WALDO EMERSON.
8. A Tale of a Lonely Parish. By F. MARION CRAWFORD.
7. A Roman Singer. By F. MARION CRAWFORD.
6. Dr. Claudius: A True Story. By F. MARION CRAWFORD.
5. Mr. Isaacs: A Tale of Modern India. By F. MARION CRAWFORD.
4. A Family Affair. By HUGH CONWAY, Author of "Called Back."
2. A Year's House-keeping in South Africa. By Lady BARKER.
1. Station Life in New Zealand. By Lady BARKER.

. *Complete Catalogues sent post free on application.*

MACMILLAN AND CO., LTD., LONDON.